The Reluctant Terrorist

The Reluctant Terrorist

Tony Lockwood

Writer's Showcase presented by *Writer's Digest*
San Jose New York Lincoln Shanghai

The Reluctant Terrorist

Published by Writer's Showcase presented by *Writer's Digest*
an imprint of iUniverse.com, Inc.

For information address:
iUniverse.com, Inc.
620 North 48th Street
Suite 201
Lincoln, NE 68504-3467
www.iuniverse.com

ISBN: 0-595-09684-0

Printed in the United States of America

For my wife, Sue.

Forward

A secret late night visit to the White House by the Ambassador and Private Secretary to the President of Bakaar, a near bankrupt, little known, former British colony, could alter the balance of world power…

Acknowledgements

My sincere thanks to Joan Noble Pinkham, my mentor, editor and agent, without whom I would not be writing today. And special thanks to Bill Thurber and my friends and family who commented and critiqued.

Chapter 1

The bedside phone rang and rang again. The President stirred, turned over in the darkened room and lifted the phone. He was expecting the call but had fallen asleep. The dim red glow from the clock showed 3.20 a.m.

He listened intently for a moment then replied, "I'm on my way, show them into the study. I'll be there in ten minutes…Have you called Secretary Palmer? Good. And I want you in the room after I arrive…yes, in the room."

He dressed hurriedly in a sweater and pants, searching for his glasses, which he now needed more often. He did not hide the fact that he needed help reading, but still avoided wearing glasses for public appearances.

In less than the promised ten minutes he was in the elevator on his way to the private study, set off to one side of the Oval Office. As he approached in the almost deserted West Wing two Secret Service Agents stood guard in the dimly lit hallway outside the study door. The Agent who had called him from his bed opened the door and yellow light flooded into the hallway from the lamp on the study desk. The President entered the room. One of the Agents followed him as instructed, closed the door, and stood in front of it blocking the exit. The desk lamp lit up the faces of the two men seated in the chairs at the desk throwing long dramatic shadows across the carpet.

The two men were black Africans from Bakaar, a small East African state. Both were around forty-five years of age. They were dressed in dark business suits the color of which was hard to determine in the harsh glow of the single light. One wore a tie the other an open necked dress shirt. The one wearing the tie seemed nervous, almost jumpy. Pat Palmer, the Secretary for Defense, was already in the room leaning on the bookcase absorbed in an examination of his nails. As the President entered both men at the desk stood up and turned towards him their shadows extending dramatically across the entire rear wall of the office. Their faces were tense. The smaller of the two, wearing the tie, had beads of perspiration trickling down his temple. As the President walked past Pat Palmer he looked up from his visual manicure. The two men exchanged glances but did not speak. They both knew why the Africans were there. There was nothing to say. The Africans had attended a preliminary meeting with Louise Henderson, Deputy Assistant to the President, earlier in the day. It was at that meeting that they dropped their bombshell. The public meeting with the President, scheduled that afternoon, had been immediately cancelled and this secret meeting was hurriedly arranged.

"Good evening…well, good morning, gentlemen," the President greeted them coldly, as he sat down. Both of the Africans nodded but said nothing.

"Please, sit down."

The man with the tie cleared his throat, "We gave it to the Agent at the gate…"

"Yes, I know," the President responded quickly. "How long?" he asked of the Agent by the door.

"As I said on the phone, sir, it went straight to the lab." The Agent looked at his watch. "We should have confirmation in about twenty minutes."

"Good. We don't have long to wait." The President replied.

This was a meeting of the utmost secrecy. The Bakaarans, the Ambassador to the United Kingdom and the Private Secretary to President Berruda had been brought into the White House at night, in a service van, to avoid the eyes of the media and to prevent any publicity. If there were even a whisper of the reason for their visit a media, hungry to scoop the stirrings of World War III, would besiege the White House. Their cameras, lights and satellite trucks the modern equivalent of the ballistas and siege engines of the middle ages.

"Can we rustle up a cup of coffee without waking the kitchen?" the President asked the Agent.

"My colleague could organize that, sir. If we can do without him for a few minutes?"

The President looked at Pat Palmer, "I'm sure we're safe in here. I don't think I have anything to fear personally from these gentlemen." He nodded toward the two Africans and then addressed them directly, "Would you like some coffee?"

The Ambassador, the man with the tie, looked quickly between the President, the Secretary of Defense and his colleague. As if he feared for his own life he did not answer the President's question, "No sir, you have nothing to fear from us."

The President ignored the comment and requested the Secret Service Agent to organize the much needed coffee.

The President glanced across at Pat Palmer now sitting in a chair drawn up to the side of the desk, who on feeling his gaze, looked up from the papers he was now studying. The two men, without saying a word and without the knowledge of the Bakaarans, exchanged looks of disbelief that this could be happening.

Following the revelations from Louise Henderson's meeting with the Bakaarans, the President's crisis team had met to discuss tactics well into the previous night. It had been agreed by all, including Pat Palmer, that if Iraq, Iran or even Libya became aware that the U.S. might have to face this threat, it would harden anti-U.S. feelings. The international temperature could again rise to boiling point. This meeting and the reason for it had to remain secret.

The President looked at the Bakaarans and almost smiled. The two men sitting nervously across the desk could, depending on the outcome of the awaited tests change the balance of world power. Twenty years ago, that would have taken the might of the USSR, thousands of troops, sophisticated military hardware and an array of nuclear tipped missiles. But not now! A small package, a desperate and determined country and world order was at stake.

The past year had been a tough one and it had taken its toll on the President. He was mentally exhausted and feared that another period of intense pressure could result in flawed decisions. He knew the results from the lab were going to be positive but desperately hoped they would not be. He needed a break. A long weekend would help. The knock on the door awakened him from his musings. Just let it be the coffee. The Agent opened the door and reached to take something from the unseen caller. The door closed and the Agent, receiving unspoken confirmation that he should bring the envelope to the President, walked towards the desk.

Chapter 2

"Mr. Barnard, I have President Berruda on the phone!" Rose Brown, George Barnard's long time secretary, announced. She had ceased to be impressed by the calls from the rich and famous. President Berruda rolled off her tongue as easily as Tony Blair, or any of the multitude of politicians who called upon her boss for advice and favors.

"Mr. President, Good morning, how are you?" George greeted his old friend.

"As well as can be expected," Berruda responded in perfect, public school English, acquired during his education at Eton.

"How goes the battle?" George inquired.

"Not well! Back in the seventies, when we were young, independence was a wonderful thing. But it comes at a price. We've had to survive on our own. We've become one of the world's beggar nations. It's not easy. But that's the reason for the call."

Bakaar had been the final bastion of British colonialism in Africa. It had hung on as a colony until it had become an embarrassment to the British Government. It was the last to be persuaded that it had to stand on its own feet. The trouble was it had no industry, no oil, no crops and no way to earn its living. It was a tiny State with only one reason for being. It had a deep-water harbor. In the days of Empire it had permitted the gunboats and battleships of the British Navy to be refueled and provisioned on their way to put down insurrection and show the flag in the far flung eastern corners.

Without the harbor and its British garrison, Bakaar would not have existed. While the British needed it they provided a source of income, education, medical care and of course plumbing. The capital, Rapanda was blessed with piped water and flushing toilets.

But that was the past. For twenty-five years Bakaar had survived on handouts and charity and now at the end of the nineties it was fast approaching bankruptcy and bloodshed.

"How can I help?" George inquired.

"I don't want to discuss it on the telephone...can I ask you to come out to Bakaar and meet with me?"

George's construction company had built several projects in the years following independence, including the airport at Rapanda. At that time there had still been British money in the Bakaaran coffers and optimism that the country could survive. George and Berruda had first met during construction of the airport when they were both in their late twenties. Berruda was a brilliant, but very young, Minister of the Interior in his newly independent country and George had just inherited one of the biggest privately held construction companies in Britian. Since then a great deal had changed. Berruda had become the President and virtual, albeit benign, dictator of Bakaar. George had ruthlessly built his company into one of the biggest construction conglomerates in the world.

"How quickly do you want to meet?" George asked.

"As soon as possible! We're in a desperate state." Berruda paused uncertain whether to say more, but then decided to continue, "Iraq has provided an example for my people, I can see a way for us to survive but we have to act now. We have no money, George. I have one awful opportunity and if I can pull it off I hope to avert bloodshed and save millions from starvation, but I have to act quickly. I only have a few weeks, or months at best."

George could hear the desperation in his old friends voice, "I'll be on the next plane out of here. How often is there a flight into Rapanda?"

"You have to come in through Nairobi. There's one flight a day. Our 737 is still flying. You won't need me to get you a seat, few people come here anymore."

"I'll send you the times of my flights as soon as I've made reservations. Will you get me picked up at the airport?"

"Yes, of course…many thanks George."

"I haven't done anything yet!" George cut off the call and flashed Rose, "Rose, I need a ticket to Bakaar…tomorrow!"

Chapter 3

Forty-eight hours after the phone call from Robert Berruda, George was walking down the jet way from a British Airways 747 at Nairobi Airport. He hopefully had only four hours to wait for the scheduled, once daily, Air Bakaar flight into Rapanda. But the travel agent had warned Rose that the flights were far from reliable. Air Bakaar was down to one Boeing 737 and if it needed maintenance, the delay could be days rather than hours. But there was no choice; Air Bakaar was the only flight into Rapanda.

Bakaar lies some six hundred miles to the south of Nairobi, a thin strip of land extending nearly five hundred miles inland between Mozambique and Tanzania. Its western border running along the center of Lake Malawi. Its eastern boundary is just fifty miles of coastline on the Indian Ocean. Rapanda is the capital and harbor once used by the British to replenish their gunboats. Twenty years ago George was familiar with the city. Back in the days when he had first met Robert Berruda, the Barnard Company was constructing the airport into which he would now fly.

Robert Berruda was in and out of London a few times each year and he and George met now and again over dinner or at some political function. There had never been a need and George had not been back to Bakaar since the airport was completed. He now had mixed feelings. He was interested to see the place again, but from what he had heard, feared that he would be shocked by the deterioration. There had been a piece in the Times, which he had read on the flight into Nairobi.

> '*Starvation and disease is widespread and old tribal tensions are surfacing. There is talk of civil unrest, not directed at Robert Berruda, but between the tribes. Berruda still seems to be seen by both sides as their potential savior.*'

George headed for the British Airways Executive Club to spend his four hours in relative comfort. Three hours, two pots of coffee and a plate of cookies later, his Air Bakaar flight gained a surprising, 'on-time' notation on the departures screen.

Air Bakaar's account for ground services at Nairobi had not been paid for months. All services were now on an up-front in cash basis, and cash meant U.S. Dollars not Bakaaran currency. After landing, the captain, clutching an envelope full of dollars drawn on the Bank of Bakaar the previous day, had to go to the office of the fuel contractor to ensure that he could take on sufficient for the flight back to Rapanda and tomorrow's return to Nairobi. Although fuel was the immediate concern, maintenance posed another. If anything ceased to function on the flight to Nairobi, unless it physically stopped the aircraft flying, it was ignored until the aircraft was back in Bakaar.

George boarded the 737 twenty minutes before flight time, one of only eleven passengers. He was the sole occupant of the eight comfortable, worn leather first class seats in the front cabin. The door was closed and the flight attendants busied themselves performing their departure ritual. Each time they came within earshot of each other, they continued an anxious dialogue in their native language. The senior attendant made frequent trips to the flight deck and each time she returned she appeared to be passing on information and updating the other members of the cabin crew. There was a sense of anxiety.

The aircraft left on time, nothing which would prevent it flying malfunctioned and the flight was uneventful. The sun had already set as the aircraft turned onto final approach at Rapanda in the all enveloping African darkness. The wheels had hardly touched the ground when George was thrown forward against his inadequate seat belt as the captain selected reverse thrust to slow the shuddering jet down to braking speed. The brakes were applied violently and the aircraft came to a stop. A complete stop about three-quarters of the way down the runway. George remembered, it was a single runway, with a taxiway at both ends. There was no need for the aircraft to turn round and backtrack the runway to get to the terminal. Why had it stopped?

Out of the window George could see the runway lights, but from his position could see little else. They sat quietly for nearly two minutes without comment or explanation from the flight deck, then the engines spooled up. Immediately it began to move forward, the flight attendants were out of their seats. One looked anxiously through the small window in the cabin door on the opposite side from George and another was kneeling on an empty first class seat, her nose pressed against the window.

"Is there a problem?" George ventured to ask the attendant glued to the window.

"No, no there's nothing to worry about," she replied without conviction.

Most people endure rather than enjoy flying. Cooped up in a metal cylinder with no control over anything is far from the top of the list of most enjoyable experiences. With six or seven miles of nothing between the aircraft and the ground it is so alien to our biological being that it forces suspension of our primal sense of self preservation for the duration of the flight. However, when the wheels touch the ground confidence returns and once again we try to take command. After landing, the cabin bustles with reluctant flyers pushing and shoving to escape the claustrophobia and return to their own world as quickly as possible. With only eleven passengers on the Air Bakaar 737 there was no desperation, but what was missing from the passengers was more than made up for by the cabin crew.

The aircraft made the turn on to the taxiway but George was still on the wrong side to see the terminal out of his window. Five minutes later the jet was parked on the ramp and the engines were silent. There were no jet ways at Rapanda. The term 'gate' retained its original meaning–a door through which passengers entered the terminal after leaving the aircraft down airstairs carried on the back of a truck looking like a crustacean with its shell. As with many African airports, Rapanda, even in its heyday, was not busy at night. These airports usually had the feeling of a lonely, rural railroad station. But not tonight.

While the passengers waited for their means of escape, George could see activity around the terminal. Off to one side of the single story building, out of the light, he thought he caught a glimpse of a tank, or armored personnel carrier. These vehicles could well have been the reason for the delay in taxiing to the terminal. Now, as he looked more carefully he could see soldiers stationed all around the terminal.

"What's going on?" George asked the flight attendant who was still looking out through the little window in the cabin door. She shouted something to her colleague in whatever language and then as if in response to George's question, translated, "The airstairs are coming!"

The cabin door was opened and George was the first to feel the heat still rising from the black tarmac of the ramp. There was activity everywhere. There were military vehicles on both sides of the chain link fence which formed a protective perimeter for the airport. There were jeeps, trucks and several of the personnel carriers he had spotted from the aircraft, one of which was out by the runway and he assumed must have been the reason for the abrupt stop. Soldiers in scruffy uniforms, carrying Chinese AK47's, stood guard along the fence and on the ramp watching the Boeing. George descended the stairs and walked towards the terminal, the only white man in the small group of arriving passengers. The door opened as he approached. A man dressed in a khaki shirt and pants stepped out accompanied by two guards. The guards were dressed not in the green uniforms of the troops around the airport, but in dark blue similar to an American SWAT team. One of them carried a sub-machine gun swinging from a shoulder strap.

George was unsure whether to feel welcome or threatened.

"Good evening, Mr. Barnard," the man said in excellent English, a smile spreading across his face, his hand extended. "I'm Hassan Maalin, President Berruda's private secretary. Welcome to Bakaar."

"Good evening," George responded cautiously shaking the extended hand.

"We will take you to your hotel. I am sure you are tired. Just follow me."

Hassan Maalin turned on his heel and George followed him into the terminal. They walked straight through immigration and customs avoiding the rubber stamp and paper nightmare of entering any small African nation.

Outside the terminal, the driver of the parked black Mercedes held the door open and George and Hassan climbed into the rear seats. The car swung out of the airport and George turned to Hassan, "I appreciate the welcome and lack of formality, but what's going on. The airport's so busy?"

"As you know, we are not without our problems and the President felt that your arrival tonight should not be the focus of any unwanted attention."

"Seems to me there was plenty of attention!" George replied.

Hassan smiled, "Oh no! No. The troops were not there for your benefit. I am afraid they are at the airport all the time now. The President did not want you to register your arrival or tell anyone who you are."

George felt far from relaxed but had little choice other than to trust his host. The car was headed into the center of the city. It was a rough ride, the surface of the road had all but broken up and the heavy, bullet proof Mercedes lurched and rocked as the driver turned and braked to avoid the worst of the potholes.

Thirty minutes after leaving the airport, the car turned into the entrance of the Presidential Hotel, a twenty-five year old, ten story building, overlooking what George remembered as a park alongside the river which ran down into the harbor.

George was ushered into the building. It was depressing to say the least. What had been a grand and imposing reception area, the walls covered in stirring murals depicting the independence ceremonies, was now dimly lit and run-down. Bulbs were missing from the light fixtures, the walls were stained and cracked. The murals had faded into almost colorless outlines of the promise, pomp and ceremony of independence. Hassan Maalin was handed a room key by the clerk and beckoned George to the elevator. The two guards followed close behind.

"What about my baggage?" George said as they ascended towards the Presidential Suite on the tenth floor.

"No problem," Hassan replied, "it will be here in a few minutes. It will be delivered to your room."

George thanked him. Hassan opened the door of the suite and stood to one side allowing George to enter. When it was new it would have been impressive, but like the reception area, the furnishings had faded and the drawn curtain running the entire width of the window wall was gaping loose, several of its hooks long gone.

"Please make yourself at home. I am leaving one of my colleagues with you. He will remain at the door and tomorrow will escort you to the President".

Hassan departed. George took a much needed shower and climbed into bed.

• • •

George awoke with a start, his heart beating loudly, and his forehead clammy with perspiration. His eyes searched around the still dark room. Yes, there it was again. The staccato chatter, of what he thought was a machine gun. He got out of bed and walked through the sitting room to the window. He drew back the drooping curtain with difficulty and opened the sliding glass door to the balcony. Any remaining doubts disappeared. Gunfire was coming from the other side of the park. A pack of frightened dogs ran along the street outside the hotel, barking and yelping as they passed. Suddenly a sharp crack and a whine from above his head as a bullet crashed into the wall of the hotel and ricocheted into the night, warned him that he might be safer back in his bedroom. He shut the door and retreated to his bed.

The shooting continued for a couple of hours. The sound gradually drifted away, until, by daybreak all was quiet. George's bags had still not arrived and he dressed in his traveling clothes to go in search of breakfast and explanations. He opened his door and was surprised by the guard sitting on a bench across the hallway who jumped up and gave a half-hearted salute. It was one of the soldiers who had accompanied him from the airport. George had forgotten about him.

"Morning, I'd forgotten you were here. You been on duty all night?" George asked.

"Yes, sir." The guard replied, "I have your luggage, sir." The guard stretched around George and placed the bag inside the door to George's room.

"Thank you. I'm going to have breakfast. Are you going to join me?" George guessed his companion had eaten nothing since the previous night and George wanted information.

"I have to stay with you, sir. Orders!" The guard replied smiling.

"Yes, I know. Let's have some breakfast."

The guard followed and they selected a table in the deserted dining room. A waiter appeared, placed a couple of bread rolls on the table and poured some coffee.

"Did you hear the gunfire last night?" George asked.

"Yes. It came from the other side of the park."

The guard did not seem the least bit surprised at George's question. He answered in a matter of fact manner which suggested it was as normal as if George had asked if he had heard dogs barking.

"What was the shooting about?" George asked.

"Gangs of kids from rival tribes," the guard answered. "Started a few weeks ago…with machetes, but last week they broke into an armory and now they got automatic weapons. They say they're fighting over territory, but it's food. The families are starving. There's a risk it will blow up into civil war."

"Where did you learn your English?" George asked complimenting him.

"At school here in Rapanda. We all have to speak English."

George ordered more rolls and coffee and learned a little more about the plight of Bakaar from his companion.

At nine thirty, Hassan called to say that the meeting with Berruda had been delayed. At the insistence of his guard George did not venture outside the hotel and returned to his room to wait. Finally, at one thirty, Hassan knocked on the door.

"Mr. Barnard, I am very sorry, but we've had to make some changes to our plans. The President cannot see you today…he will not be able to meet with you here in Rapanda."

"Is the President alright?" George asked concerned as to the welfare of his friend.

"Yes, he's O.K. but the fighting last night caused some problems and we have to deal with them quickly. He apologizes for any inconvenience. For your own safety, I am taking you back to the airport and you will go back to Nairobi today. I will wait for you downstairs."

"Just a minute," George called out to Hassan as he turned and left. "I've come a long way. I'm happy to sit it out. If he can't see me today, I'll wait until tomorrow."

Hassan seemed determined. "My instructions are to take you back to the airport. We cannot guarantee your safety. It would be wise, sir."

"Yeah, that may be but it's..."

"I am sure that the President will make contact with you. He knows we are going back to the airport."

George was annoyed, but knew Robert Berruda well enough to know that he must have good reasons for canceling the meeting. In any event George was a firm believer that there was no merit catching a bullet in a battle that was not of his own making.

He resigned himself to leaving and quickly packed and headed down to the ground floor. Hassan stood up as he approached and without delay, he, George and the guard, climbed aboard the now familiar armor plated black Mercedes, in which they had arrived. However, this time a jeep with a machine gun mounted on a tripod where the front passenger seat should have been, stood guard behind it. George was certain he was doing the right thing. It was time to go.

As they arrived at the airport, they were waved through several military checkpoints, which had not been evident the day before. The Mercedes drove directly onto the ramp and stopped at the bottom of the air stairs of the waiting Boeing. George bade farewell to Hassan, who did not get out of the car. His bags were carried on board by his guard and companion of the past twenty-four hours, and George made himself comfortable in the same seat he had occupied on the way in. There were no other passengers.

Half an hour passed, it was now an hour beyond the normal departure time. The flight deck door was open and the captain and first officer were in their seats chatting. They showed no signs of preparing to depart and offered George no explanation.

Another half-hour passed and George noticed activity on the ramp. The gate alongside the terminal through which he had entered a little over an hour and a half before, opened and a truck full of troops drove out towards the aircraft. George was becoming concerned as the soldiers positioned themselves around the Boeing. The senior flight attendant was summoned to the flight deck.

"We will be leaving in a few minutes," she said to George as she returned to the cabin. She then began tidying the seat across the aisle.

Chapter 4

The black Mercedes drove onto the ramp leading a column of jeeps occupied by more of the blue uniformed guards. It stopped at the air stairs. The trunk opened, a soldier removed several bags and brought them on board the Boeing. The driver stepped smartly towards the rear of the car and opened one rear door while a guard opened the other.

Hassan Maalin stepped out of the vehicle on one side, Robert Berruda on the other. They both walked towards the aircraft and climbed the stairs. George waited, watching the cabin door. Robert Berruda's six foot frame blocked the open door to the cockpit as he came on board. He stepped onto the flight deck and spoke briefly with the Captain, nodded a final thank you to Hassan, who was still standing on the air stairs, and walked down the cabin towards George.

"Hello George, I am pleased to see you. I apologize for the theatrics."

"Mr. President, it's good to see you." George responded standing up and warmly shaking Berruda's hand.

The President turned to the flight attendant and spoke in his native tongue. She smiled and almost curtsied. Berruda sat down in the prepared seat next to George, but across the aisle. Four business suited aides climbed aboard and headed for the rear of the cabin.

"The cabin crew know they have to disappear down to the rear of the aircraft once we get going then we can talk in private."

The engines were started and the old Boeing moved on to the runway. Needless to say there was no other traffic and upon arrival at the threshold the aircraft accelerated down the runway. George and Berruda caught up with families, business and nothing in particular.

"Sir, we are passing ten thousand feet, climbing to thirty six thousand and estimating Nairobi at five forty-five local time." The captain's voice came over the cabin speaker as drinks arrived. Robert Berruda loosened his seat belt, the cabin crew retreated to the rear as promised and Berruda's demeanor became serious.

"George, in the last twenty-four hours you have seen more than I expected when I invited you. The shooting last night is the latest installment. These gangs…and at present that's all they are…have got hold of machine guns and enough ammunition to be a danger. They could get organized and start real trouble." Berruda paused and looked past George out of the window, obviously having difficulty with what he was about to say. "Hassan is a loyal and trusted friend. I am leaving today so that I will not be associated with what we have to do. Hassan and Julius Bonojo, the Minister for the Interior, are secretly bringing more troops into the city tonight and they will eradicate the gangs. But it has to be done as if it's the gangs who are doing it, not the military. I never expected to have to resort to these measures in my own country."

"Difficult decision," George offered sympathetically. 'What then?"

"If we are successful tonight I hope it will give us breathing space to deal with the bigger picture. We need money, we need aid. That's where you and I have to talk."

"We've got an hour and a half to Nairobi." George replied.

"It's not complicated George. Now, I wish I had been like so many of my fellow Presidents, and stashed millions away in Switzerland. I could use it. But I did not, I played the game straight."

"You can't be ashamed of that, Robert," George observed, only half believing that his old friend did not have a few million tucked away.

"I'm not, but it means I have to ask you for help."

"I'm listening. I'll help if I can."

Robert Berruda drew a deep breath, "It's hard to know where to start?"

George smiled sympathetically, aware that his friend was finding every way possible to delay saying what he had to say.

"My country is in desperate trouble, my people are starving and it's going to get worse. If I can't stop it, the gangsters will take over and Bakaar will cease to exist…but I think I have a chance. I have to stop being a nice guy. I have to become a threat."

"Threat to whom?" George asked.

"I would like to become a threat to Great Britain. They created us and they dumped us. The problem is they no longer have money or real power. So, I am going to threaten the United States."

George was surprised, he could see that his friend was serious. This was not a joke, but the idea of Bakaar threatening the United States did seem far fetched.

"What do you want from them?"

"A billion dollars!"

"Why do you need me?"

"I need to acquire the means with which I can threaten. It will cost money and it must be done in complete secrecy. To put it crudely, you have the money and I trust you."

"How much?"

"No more than $10 million."

"And what will you threaten. What can you do with ten million dollars to make the United States pay. How much did you say, a billion dollars? You going to buy a couple of redundant Russian nuclear warheads?"

"No, but I am going to threaten to wipe out New York and I don't need Russian warheads."

George did not know how to respond. How on earth could his friend be serious. He was not often taken by surprise but he could see that this trip to Nairobi was going to be interesting. As the two men talked, George's skepticism waned and he began to see an opportunity.

Chapter 5

George Barnard was a small wiry man with a mop of dark brown hair. He was born in the West Riding of Yorkshire, an English county about one hundred and fifty miles north of London whose natives live with the perception that their heritage is one of hard work and strife. In some strange way they see this as the fault of their disdained cousins who occupy the southern half of the country, living a life of ease and privilege. The irony is that thousands have fled Yorkshire to the soft and easy living of the south still bragging of their origins.

George had lived in London for the best part of twenty years. In spite of this and a British Public School education, he still had a distinct accent, which could pin him down to the very village in which he was born. He had inherited a major construction company from his father who had died prematurely when George was in his early twenties. In the following twenty-five years, George had built it into one of the biggest in the world.

During those years, the means and methods by which George had multiplied his wealth had been the frequent fodder of the tabloid press. George cut corners and flouted the law. There had even been the suspicion that the untimely demise of a competitor for a major contract had not been a coincidence. George was seen as a ruthless rogue, albeit a wealthy and successful one.

The Barnard companies employed six thousand people in Britain alone. The companies were responsible for billions of pounds in foreign exchange for Britain and tens of millions in taxes for the Exchequer. George received invitations to most of the functions in London not because he was a wonderful guest and not because he was one of the insiders. He was feared. No one wanted him as an enemy.

He was on first name terms with leading politicians. But, he still had a problem. In the class ridden society of Britain his fortune and his reputation were not the means of acceptance. He was not a member of the aristocracy and he would never be old money. He was colorful. A character. He said it as it was. And these attributes perpetuated his exclusion from the establishment.

However, to many in Britain his ruthless pursuit of wealth and his willingness to do anything to win made him larger than life. He was a sad reminder that in Britain the days of tough and powerful men had nearly passed. In the final days of the twentieth century, George was to many what Churchill had been during its dawn. He provided an example whereby those who were uncomfortable in the increasingly oppressive and restrictive society could vicariously live dangerously. George had become a folk hero, but that is not what he wanted. He craved acceptance.

Just three years previously, William Wickens, an old friend and fellow Yorkshireman, one of the leading lights in the Conservative Government, had asked him to become the Chairman of the Government Export Board. The Conservatives were having a tough time at the polls and needed to acquire a harder hitting image. They weighed the benefits and disadvantages and decided it would be better if George was seen to be on their side. William knew that George craved recognition and reminded him that after a couple of years in the job the normal reward was a knighthood. Sir George Barnard was acceptance. George agreed and two years later, as tradition demanded, William asked if he could put George's name forward for inclusion in the New Year Honors List.

A couple of months before publication of the list George received a call from William, now a Minister in the Government. From the moment George walked into the office, he knew something was wrong. William was sitting behind his antique Regency desk. Unusually he did not come around to greet George or to move to the comparatively greater comfort of the Queen Anne couches. They shook hands across the desk and George sat down in one of the hard-backed chairs drawn up in front.

"George, we've known each other for a very long time and I…I won't beat about the bush. I ensured that your name was put forward and was told it was actually the Prime Minister himself who made the final decision. And, eh…he's asked that I speak with you today." William cleared his throat, fidgeted and seemed to draw himself down into his chair as if to make himself a smaller target. He then blurted out the devastating news, "I'm afraid you're not going to get it, at least not this time around."

George prided himself on his ability to keep his cool, "Why not?" he asked almost in a whisper, masking an overwhelming sense of disappointment.

"It had nothing to do with me, I put your name forward…" William spluttered defensively hoping not to bear the brunt of George's wrath and wishing desperately to be elsewhere.

"Yes, I know William, I'm sure it's not your fault. But I thought I'd paid my dues, I thought this was a foregone conclusion, a nod and a wink, you know!"

"It's your record, George, your reputation. You've never denied the payoffs you've been accused of making in Africa, for God's sake!"

George's disappointment was rapidly changing to anger, his Yorkshire accent was thickening and his voice was getting louder, "Who do you think you're fooling?" A pulse thumped in his temple and his face was becoming red, "Do you believe Joe Public has any illusions about what we have to do to get work in some of these countries. Do you think the public believes we go out there like bloody boy scouts with our fingers and legs crossed hoping we're going to be the lucky lad. Well we don't! We go out there with a bloody great bag of cash—and just for the record, its not British pounds, its dollars, even the Africans don't want half a million pounds in their bank account any more. Then, if we've paid His Excellency more than anyone else and if just maybe we can intimidate the foreign competition to withdraw, we get the project and charge back the bribes in the price of the job. It's that simple, it's how the Third World works!"

"Just so, George. What do you think the opposition would make of it if you were knighted? Be reasonable, you've made a fortune, isn't that enough?"

"No, it bloody well isn't!" George shouted, "I had a fortune before I started!"

George's tone became calmer and threatening, "I could do a lot of damage William. Your precious Prime Minister could find that refusing my knighthood is worse than recommending it!"

"That's not an appropriate response George! You can't threaten the British Government." William responded pompously.

"Well then I guess there's nothing more I can say, the decision's obviously been made. There's little point in continuing this discussion." George got up and walked out.

The media carried the story of the Government's refusal to honor George. Over the weeks that followed, he became the example of how out of touch the Conservatives had become. His folk hero image shone even brighter. Whether or not the media coverage of George's snub contributed to the landslide defeat of the Conservative Government in the

General Election later in the year we will never know. But George became more bitter and willing to take risks.

• • •

On his return journey to London, George had plenty of time to ponder Berruda's proposition. It was probably not coincidence that Berruda had made the approach now. George's displeasure with the British Government was well known and he and Berruda had discussed it in London just a few weeks previously. Berruda may have recognized his opportunity, but George could see his own. If he played his cards right he would be able to influence world affairs and play a part in shaping the politics of the twenty-first century He could also see how he could make money. To hell with the knighthood.

George had given Berruda conditional agreement to an investment of up to ten million dollars. It all hinged on whether Peter Williamson would be the point man for the operation but George already knew that Peter had no choice.

Chapter 6

It was mild for March. The temperature in London had been in the high fifties and low sixties for a couple of weeks. As Peter Williamson walked along Ebury Street, the bright, new leaves were just appearing on the plane trees and the feel of spring was everywhere. It was a little before one o'clock. George had summoned him a week before and he had made the return trip to the U.K. without knowing why his boss needed him so urgently, or why they had to meet at a restaurant rather than in the office. George had made it clear he was not to let anyone know he was even in the country. Peter arrived at the restaurant, opened the heavy oak door and stepped onto the tiled floor of the entrance hallway. At a glance Peter could see that he had stepped into a haven of the rich and privileged. The Maitre D' greeted him and Peter gave his name.

"Ah yes sir, Mr. Barnard is at his table. Please follow me."

The restaurant was divided into a series of wood paneled rooms, each with a few tables well spaced around a central display of mouthwatering desserts. Statues, columns and greenery ranging from ferns to small trees were located so that it was almost impossible to overhear the conversations of the other occupants of the room. It was unlikely that a confidential conversation would become front page news. The tables were covered with pale pink tablecloths. The rooms lit by small, red shaded lamps, as well as by daylight diffused through heavy lace curtains obscuring the view into what Peter thought was a courtyard.

George Barnard had arrived early and seemed oblivious of his surroundings, completely absorbed in the Financial Times. As the Maitre D' approached, George stopped reading, looked up with a start saw Peter and half stood to lean across the table to shake his hand.

"Welcome to London, Peter. It's good to see you again." George still held the Financial Times in his left hand.

"Good to be here!" Peter said allowing his eyes to rove around their sumptuous surroundings. "This is more up market than the Chinese place we ate at when I was last here. Barnard and Co must be doing well!"

As he sat back in his seat, George folded up the newspaper and forced it between the table and the wall, smudging the ink on the pristine pink cloth. "Yes, well, the choice was a little convoluted. We needed somewhere to talk where we wouldn't be seen…and this is probably the most unlikely place I would be eating…does that make some sort of sense?"

"I guess so," Peter responded, still willing to play it for all it was worth, "but it looks just your sort of place, full of the British Upper Crust and your political friends."

Peter was careful not to cross the line, this man controlled his paycheck, but he could not ignore what he had read about George's phantom knighthood.

"Don't you start!" George dismissed the comment lightheartedly.

"I'm sorry. It's just ridiculous, the entire episode was a disaster for the Conservatives."

"You're right, absolutely right! What will you have to drink?"

George waved at a passing waiter, he was already on his second gin and tonic and desperately needed company. The waiter scurried off with the order as Peter opened the menu, and smiling broadly teased

George again, "Good God, the menu doesn't even have prices, it must be good…"

George smiled, "Mine does! Don't worry you won't have to do the dishes!"

George was known for his dislike of the pretentious, it was another of those old Yorkshire traditions. The drinks arrived.

"Your health, Peter," George toasted.

"Yours too," Peter replied touching glasses.

Peter had been in the employ of George Barnard for thirteen years and had worked his way up to where he was responsible for African Operations. Peter's expertise was not in the construction disciplines, he was a fixer. While serving in the British Military he had gained first-hand experience of working with and for, some of the worst of the African Presidents. Peter knew how the system worked and did what was necessary to keep wheels oiled and Barnard's African clients content. He lived in a company house in Nairobi, but also maintained a flat in London for his frequent visits.

In all the years that Peter had worked for George, they had never become involved socially. Peter was a lot younger than his boss and divorced. George's wife had died in an accident just before Peter joined the company and George had not re-married. Peter did not even know whether George had a social life. Their relationship had been strictly business and Peter had no clue as to the purpose of this meeting. This was a first.

He knew George well enough to know that he was not the most straightforward man and he took risks. There was no agenda and Peter was uncomfortable. He did not like the unknown. The waiter took their order.

"So how is business, Peter?" George asked

"As well as can be expected," Peter replied, "Nothing much has changed since I saw you last and just at the moment, touch wood," Peter did just that, "we don't have any major conflicts or problems."

"What about Bakaar?"

"Strange you should ask," Peter replied, "I saw a couple of reports last week, that suggested there may be trouble brewing. But we don't have anything there. They haven't got any money."

"How would you feel if we did get something going in Bakkar. Would you be prepared to spend time there over the next few months?"

"Yes, of course I would, but what about the fighting? Would we want to get involved in a project if the country's unstable...I should say more unstable?"

The food arrived and Peter began to eat. Regardless of his discomfort he had to admit the food was good.

"Well, this may be an odd ball project. It's not construction. Like your work in the Army, we'd be assisting the government...well, the President. I know Robert Berruda and he needs some help."

"Sounds like it might be more exciting than building a bus terminal," Peter observed beginning to feel that his discomfort was becoming justified. George had that twinkle in his eye, which Peter had only seen when he was faced with a challenge and decided to go for it.

One of the reasons George was successful was that he trusted his managers. So long as his guys put their all into the attempt, they could rely on backup from the boss, and if it went wrong, there was never a witch-hunt to lay blame. George's managers were able, like George, to tell it as it was and take risks.

"I heard you had a nickname in the military; 'Action Man', wasn't it?" George asked.

"Yeah, Action Man...that seems a long time ago," Peter mused.

"Weren't you involved in Bakaar, way back...?"

"Yes, I was sent to Bakaar to help out," Peter was guarded. He did not want to talk about his activities in Bakaar when he was a member of Britain's Special Services or the period after when he officially did not belong anywhere.

"What did you do?" George asked the question directly.

Peter had no intention of answering and tried to head it off with a little humor, "That's where I learned how to remove obstacles and clear blockages…"

George decided to take a different tack, "So what's your reading on Bakaar?"

"I think it's falling apart. They've had a bad run. Most people, outside of the cities, live at subsistence level or worse. There's no industry, no exports. They don't have any money and aid is pretty sparse these days."

"Is it just a lack of money or is it corruption?"

Peter answered carefully, "You know Berruda, he's a straight shooter. I don't think he's corrupt. But, I'm damned sure there's corruption, African standards are not the same as ours but compared with some of its neighbors, Bakaar's not bad."

"Mmm, I was out there just over a week ago and there was gunfire in Rapanda. I haven't seen any report here of what it was all about, have you heard?" George asked.

"Yes, it was tribal. The Witumbis and the Bwanis have always squabbled with each other over status, territory, involvement in the Government, you name it. We Brits seem to think that just because we draw a line on a map and call each side a country, it would stick. Fact is we split tribes, but the old feuds and alliances continue regardless of that line on the map. Years ago they regularly slaughtered each other. We tried to stop it but it took Berruda to be able to keep the peace. The Bwanis are now saying that what little food is handed out by the government is going to the Witumbis, that's Berruda's tribe. Some youngsters are using that as an excuse to start up the old feuds and just recently it's escalated to killing again."

George added, "I've known Robert Berruda a long time, but I've never got into the tribal stuff…it's new to me…interesting"

Peter continued, cutting across George's comment, "The Bwanis killed ten or twelve government employees one night. The next night, a bunch of Witumbis came into town armed to the teeth and slaughtered

most of the teenage kids in the Bwani neighborhood who they thought
were responsible. About two hundred were killed. It's a real tragedy,
Berruda's got to do something."

George took his cue, Peter was referring to the incident Berruda had
described on the airplane into Nairobi. George knew it was Berruda's
troops who had killed the kids, but the cover story appeared to have
worked. He was satisfied that Peter would at least be prepared to consider his proposition objectively. The problem was whether Peter's
morals would get in the way and whether George would have to persuade him.

"Berruda is prepared to do something! He wants my help and I
need yours."

"I'm all ears," Peter replied nervously.

"Berruda thinks he's got to stop being one of the nice guys. He sees
Saddam Hussein and other despots living in luxury. The Arab countries
had the oil back in the seventies and eighties and because they were prepared to get tough, be ruthless and take a risk they grabbed a share of
the wealth. Berruda says he's got nothing to lose. If he can't get some
money into the country in the next few months it'll cease to exist. As
you said, it'll fall apart."

"That's for sure!" Peter responded, "How's he going to do it?"

"He wants me to invest $10 million to provide him with the means to
persuade the United States to provide $1 billion in aid. He says he'd pre-
fer to beat up Britain. But he thinks they'd have a tough time getting a
billion dollars together!" George laughed. "I guess I'd be a modern day
Robin Hood, robbing the rich to feed the poor."

Peter was not sure if he liked the direction this conversation was taking.

"Just what will your $10 million dollars buy?" He asked not wanting
to hear the answer.

George hesitated for a moment, then looking Peter straight in the
eyes he decided to tell him the truth, "VX gas, a bomb and the means to
detonate it in New York."

Whatever Peter was thinking it was not that! He hesitated before replying. In his wildest dreams he would not have believed that his boss, George Barnard, would be seriously suggesting that he would help Bakaar build a bomb full of one of the most deadly chemicals in the world.

"VX gas! You've got to be kidding!"

"I'm not!"

Chapter 7

Peter had been married during the time he served in the Army but had spent very little time at home. He had no children and the joke among his wife's friends had been that he was never home long enough to make the arrangements. His life had not been conducive to marriage and after a few years his wife gave up and left.

Peter now lived most of the year in Nairobi. He kept the apartment he and his wife had shared in London, in what used to be South West Three, a description taken from the postal code, which in the swinging sixties, had become the common name for the trendy area south of Fulham Road. Peter used the apartment when visiting London on business and for those relatively rare vacations and duty visits to see his mother.

Since his divorce, he had had a variety of female friends and there had been times when he had friends in both London and Nairobi, but gradually the women, most of whom were looking for second husbands, had succumbed to more permanent offers. Peter was forty four and his face had that leathery, weather beaten look that comes from spending time in the open. During his youth he had always looked older

than his years but recently time had seemed to stand still and he had
changed little. He had straight, brown hair, which showed no signs of
thinning. It was always well groomed, a leftover from his days in the
army when a short back and sides haircut was the trademark of the military. He was fit and at just about six feet, still presented an image which
went down well among the young women of South West Three. He was
well paid but not wealthy. His perpetual tan, a rarity in sun starved
Britain, added to the attraction. During his short trips to London he
had usually managed to find a female companion willing to spend a
couple of weeks and have some fun. However, they were getting harder
to find and younger by the trip. This visit had been arranged at short
notice and he had not had time to run through his diminishing list. He
was alone.

Peter did not sleep well the night after his meeting with George
Barnard. At lunch, he had avoided George's question as to what he did
for Special Services, but the conversation had brought the memories
flooding back. In particular his first encounter with Robert Berruda and
Bakaar. It was in stark contrast with his present life and as he reminisced
he realized that he did miss the excitement. He missed that primeval
rush of adrenaline which only occurs when your life is on the line.

In the late seventies colonialism had, more or less, drawn its last
gasp and African nationalism was rife. In these newly independent
countries the battle was usually between warring tribal factions rather
than with the old colonial powers. Military coups, mostly bloody
affairs, were the norm.

One day he would be advising a government headed by Britain's
original choice for leader—usually an Eton and Cambridge educated
son of one of the tribal chiefs. Next day he was advising some upstart
army officer who had killed the President and grabbed dictatorial powers for himself. Peter learned quickly that it paid to be polite to young,
ambitious army officers who could become President overnight. The art

of guerrilla warfare was becoming more appropriate for potential leaders in Africa than the Eton education.

As one of the weakest and least important colonies, Bakaar had hung on. It was the last to break away from Britain. Finally the young activists won, and on a cool winter day Bakaar gained its independence in a fanfare of trumpets, and a dazzling display of uniforms, pomp and ceremony of which Queen Victoria would have been proud.

Peter got involved some years after independence. There had been reports in the London media about a small group of dissidents critical of the government, which had failed on its early promises and was seen as a puppet of the British.

Peter met with Robert Berruda, at that time the Minister of the Interior, in his London hotel suite. He was handed files on four so-called dissidents. He flicked through the files glancing at the photographs. Two of them were a married couple, the other two were unrelated. All were in their twenties and had attended the London School of Economics, a college known at that time to lean politically to the left. Berruda explained they were all members of the Bwani tribe. Berruda, who was a Witumbi, had to keep them quiet without inflaming the simmering tribal jealousies and was asking Britain for help.

Berruda needed to know whether this group had any serious support and if there was a risk that they could whip up tribal conflict and reduce the fledgling nation to a state of anarchy. Bakaar was too new and too delicately balanced to withstand any organized opposition. It was firmly aligned with the West and Berruda could not allow any disruption to provide the communists with a foothold. He wanted the problem solved and solved permanently, within three months.

Freed from the official shackles of the British Government and financed through what appeared to the outside world to be a charitable foundation, Peter could set up each operation as if he were a free agent. He hired the services of Tim Serenson, an American freelancer with whom he had worked before. Both men were to enter Bakaar as journalists.

They were provided with an unmarked Landrover, Bakaaran ID's and pistols by the Security Police, known as the SP and controlled by Berruda's Ministry. With six weeks of Berruda's original three month deadline remaining they carried out the legwork to try and establish the motivation and support of the four dissidents. Peter became convinced they were just idealistic, liberal students. In Europe or the U.S. they would have been regarded as little more than a nuisance, but Bakaar was not Europe.

One evening all four were invited to dinner by Tim Serenson. They could not resist the opportunity of voicing their opinions to an American journalist and accepted eagerly. They agreed to meet at a restaurant on the outskirts of Rapanda. Through dinner they were vehemently critical of Berruda and openly accused him of planning a coup. At the end of the meal Tim invited them back to his hotel to finish the interview.

They had all been drinking. They left the restaurant noisily and clambered into the back of the Landrover for the short journey into town. By the time they noticed they were leaving the city rather than going to the hotel it was too late. They were still in good spirits and the idea of Tim being lost amused them. They shouted at him to turn round, but he kept driving away from Rapanda in spite of their advice.

The Landrover pulled off the dirt road and stopped in front of a car parked without lights at the side of the road. The boisterous laughter and talking stopped. For a brief moment the deep black silence of the African night was all pervading. The rear door of the truck opened and a flashlight stabbed brilliantly into the dark interior, temporarily blinding the now silent occupants. As their eyes adjusted, they could see a white man holding the light that had invaded the truck in one hand and a pistol in the other. The four were ordered out of the truck one by one, handcuffed together and returned to the Landrover for the remainder of the journey to the SP headquarters where Peter, the white man with the flashlight, and Tim would question them.

It was two o'clock in the morning. Two disheveled policemen came out of the building and cheerily welcomed them. Peter and Tim were expected. The policemen opened the rear door and roughly pulled the now frightened Bwanis out of the vehicle.

The four were dragged unceremoniously into the building and Peter and Tim were told they could leave. Peter was becoming concerned over the manner in which they were being treated and was having misgivings about the entire episode. He asked for them to be put into separate cells to await questioning.

As soon as they were inside the building it was obvious there was some misunderstanding. The policemen advised Peter that the SP would be doing the questioning. Peter and Tim, were again told they could leave. The dissidents were pushed down the corridor and all were locked in a single cell. One of the policemen remained outside the door. Peter demanded that nothing be done until he had a chance to talk to his contact at the Ministry when he came on duty in the morning. Peter and Tim had no intention of leaving and made themselves comfortable for the rest of the night.

They slept fitfully, but after a couple of hours they were disturbed by the arrival of two men dressed in civilian clothes. Peter tried to talk to them but was brushed aside as they headed down the corridor to be let into the cell in which the detainees were held. After a few minutes it was obvious from the noise that the prisoners were being beaten. Peter and Tim glanced at each other, there was no choice, they had to stop it. The dissidents were their responsibility. Peter drew his pistol, checked a round was chambered and flicked off the safety. The weapon held behind his back, he and Tim approached the guard in the corridor. Peter jabbed the pistol in the policeman's abdomen his left hand over his mouth, more as a signal to keep quiet than to physically stop him speaking. Peter removed the keys from the policeman's belt and with a nudge of the pistol had him identify the key to the cell.

Peter opened the door and pushed the policeman in ahead of him. Tim followed and closed the door, his pistol now in his hand. Within a matter of seconds the two surprised and unarmed interrogators were handcuffed to the bars in the window.

Two of the dissidents were sprawled on the floor. They had been beaten but were alive. The girl was handcuffed to a chair and appeared unhurt. Her husband was secured to a support for the sink his face cut and bruised. The interrogators, caught in the act like naughty boys lying for the first time, threatened Peter and Tim with retribution and dire consequences for interfering. Peter became increasingly angry. If all that was intended was to kill them, it could have been done by Berruda's men weeks ago, without his involvement. He felt the entire project had been a sham.

During the time that Peter and Tim had been in the cell none of the dissidents had spoken. The two on the floor had recovered and dragged themselves on to the cot at one end of the room. The girl and her husband watched, not knowing what to expect.

Peter wanted to convey his feelings to Robert Berruda. The dissidents were hussled down the corridor not knowing whether they should be relieved or fearful. They had been saved from a beating and possibly worse, but they still had no idea what their fate would be.

By the time Peter and Tim got back into Rapanda it was daylight and life was returning to the streets. They drove to the Ministry and waited for it to open. Peter demanded to meet with Berruda and made it clear during a short and tense meeting that he had delivered these four people into Berruda's safe keeping. In the days that followed and before Peter departed, he was warmly thanked by an official in the Ministry of the Interior for his efforts on behalf of Bakaar. He never knew what happened to the four.

Two months later Robert Berruda, in an almost bloodless coup ousted the President and took over Bakaar. If the four had died at the hands of their interrogators and news of their death had leaked out he and Tim would have taken the blame and there would have been no possibility of tribal conflict to rebound on the newly ensconced President. After the coup the western governments hesitated for a couple of weeks and then welcomed the new regime. It was politics as usual.

During the eighties most of the dirty work required by Britain's friends moved into the hands of the SAS and Peter did not look forward to a future behind a desk. In 1985 he resigned and joined the Barnard Companies as their manager in Senegal. His considerable knowledge, contacts and experience of the workings of African government now used to further the interest of the Barnard Companies.

• • •

His thoughts returned to the present as daylight crept into the room. He could not understand why George Barnard had not discussed the details at their lunch. The idea that George saw himself as a modern day Robin Hood intrigued Peter, but he had left the lunch still unsure of what George Barnard wanted of him. He knew he wanted no part in what could only be described as a terrorist plot to extort aid from the U.S.A.

Peter was in the shower when, at eight forty-five, the phone rang. He reached for the portable handset lying in the sink.

"Peter Williamson."

"Morning Peter, George Barnard. Can you slip over and meet me this morning?"

Peter had little choice, he worked for the man, but how was he going to tell him, No!

"Sure can. What time and where?" he replied.

"At the flat in Eaton Square. How about nine thirty?" Peter agreed and was given the address.

Chapter 8

Peter left the apartment at nine, not knowing what the morning would bring. Yesterday he had felt uneasy not knowing why he had been summoned to London. Today he felt far more than uneasy.

He walked out of the building into Beaufort Street and began the search for a cab. As his mind ran over the events of the day before, it occurred to him that it might be better if there was no trace of his visit to George this morning. He turned and strode purposefully towards Kings Road and Sloane Square. No one would follow his tracks to George Barnard's on this particular November morning.

He walked through Sloane Square, turned into Cliveden Place and walked on towards Eaton Square. His mind was busy as he went over the thoughts and conclusions of his restless night. He suddenly realized that in his preoccupation with the events of the previous day he had covered the mile from his apartment and walked straight through the Square! It was not difficult to do. The major road, constructed long after the original square, had been pushed through the middle of the central garden to improve traffic flow. Houses had been built on both sides of the street and unlike many of the London Squares it now gave little impression of being one. George's apartment was in the building on the southwestern side. Peter retraced his steps and crossed the road.

The front door was massive, set off by the original eighteenth century brass knocker. It was locked electronically and access was gained through an array of twelve buttons set into the old stone wall to the right of the door. As Peter leaned down towards them he wondered why they were set so low as to make the names hard to read for anyone taller than about five feet two. With difficulty he found 'Barnard', pressed the button and waited.

George's disembodied voice crackled out of the wall.

"Hello George, it's Peter." He replied speaking into the microphone buried behind the bank of buttons. There was a low buzz as George released the lock and Peter quickly pushed the impressive door open. The interior was more modern than the outside of the building. It had been refurbished extensively and the ground floor entrance hall, adorned with mirrors and gilt, resembled the lobby of a small hotel. He entered the elevator and ascended to the second floor. He stepped out and met George waiting by the door to the apartment.

"Thanks for coming," George mumbled as he turned to lead Peter inside. Peter extended his hand but George had not noticed the gesture. Peter self consciously allowed his arm to fall back to his side. Once inside the apartment he was surprised by what he saw. He would have expected George to furnish the place with traditional decor and antiques but the apartment was ultra modern. Plain, dark stained solid wooden doors, smoked mirrors and black leather furniture on a white carpet with expensive Persian silk rugs scattered across it. They walked towards what appeared to be a study. George let Peter enter first, directing him towards the leather couch behind a low glass coffee table which was placed on one of the red silk rugs.

"Have a seat," George invited.

There was a pile of papers topped with a hard backed file on the table and on the opposite side from the couch an empty chair, where George had been sitting.

"Would you like a cup of coffee?" George asked as he walked towards the table.

It was a simple enough question, but it took Peter off guard. George making the coffee created a temporary equality.

"Please, but only if you're having one," Peter replied.

George left the study but returned in a matter of a minute or so, empty handed. Peter assumed he had turned on the percolator. George closed the door, pulled the vacant chair closer to the table and sat down. He came straight to the point. "Had any more thoughts on our conversation yesterday?"

"I didn't sleep too well last night," Peter replied with a grin

"Yes, it's not easy," George interrupted, "but I will need a commitment before we get too far into the details."

Peter still had the forlorn hope that perhaps he had misunderstood George's intentions. Perhaps it was all a dream, part of his restless night.

"One thing I should clear up at this stage," George said, "is that we will be breaking the law and there's no certainty that we'll pull it off. We might get caught."

Peter knew George was a ruthless son-of-a-bitch when he wanted to be. Defrauding an African Government or fixing a contract was one thing. VX gas and bombs in New York was something else.

"Robin Hood broke the law, but I guess his intentions were honorable." Peter said, picking up George's previous reference.

George did not reply. Picking up the hard backed file from the coffee table, he put on his steel rimmed glasses and began to study the file. As he did there was a knock at the door. Peter nearly jumped out of his seat. He could not think why he had assumed there was no one else in the apartment, but he had. So much for walking instead of taking a cab to cover his tracks. He was going to have to think a lot more quickly.

George closed the file and responded to the knock, "Come in!"

The door opened and a young woman entered carrying a tray laden with a percolator, two china cups and some cookies. Peter arrived at several conclusions in the space of a few seconds. The young woman was obviously not the housekeeper. If she was Mrs. Barnard she had to be number two or three. And he liked what he saw.

She was about five feet six inches tall, expensively dressed in pants and a sweater, which must have cost a month's salary. Her hair had a chestnut tinge and she moved in a way that made Peter feel pleasantly uncomfortable.

George's voice interrupted Peter's discomfort, "May I introduce Sarah. Sarah, Peter Williamson."

Sarah smiled, put the tray down on the coffee table and stretched out her hand to Peter, who was still sitting down. Peter stood up quickly, took it and held it just a little longer than necessary.

"Pleased to meet you," she said, her eyes disagreeing with her words.

"Me too," he replied ignoring the look and still holding her hand. He reluctantly let go and sat down again. She turned and left the room. Peter's eyes followed her, it was as pleasant watching her leave as it had been to see her arrive. Whatever the outcome of his meeting with George the day had not been entirely wasted.

George put the file down and poured the coffee. "Help yourself to a biscuit."

Peter picked up his cup, selected a chocolate covered wafer and placed it in the saucer.

"If we're going to work together I need to know more about your activities before you joined me. I had some information put together to try to get some background on you. You seemed reluctant to talk about your activities in Bakaar."

As George spoke Peter took his first sip of the coffee. The chocolate wafer stuck to the side of the hot cup as he raised it towards his mouth, it then slipped off and fell into the middle of the saucer preventing him from replacing the cup. He needed a third hand.

Peter put the cup and saucer back down on the table and removed the biscuit, getting warm liquid chocolate all over his hand. What a way to make an impression he thought as he tried to decide how to react to George's comments. His involvement was being assumed and he had to stop it.

"I think you'd better slow down, George."

George looked up from the file, said nothing but fixed Peter with a cold inquiring gaze. There was no warmth in his eyes, no movement. He waited silently.

"I can deal with the bribery and corruption to get business. I know how the world works and so far I can live with myself. But yesterday was the first time I knew that you're going to blow up New York." Peter gave an empty chuckle, "I'm not sure I can just sign on to that…I'm only sitting here in your apartment because I work for you I still don't even know what you want me to do." Peter felt a little better.

George removed his glasses and responded pedantically, "First, you're sitting in my daughter's apartment. Second, yes, you work for me but I don't know you that well. This is like the moment when you offer a government official a bribe. You have to fish around a little bit without saying it. But you need to know if he'll accept before you make the offer. What we are going to do may well be, well, suspect. But the intention is to put food in the mouths of a few million people who'll starve otherwise. That seems like a pretty good reason to me."

"And maybe you'll make some money?" Peter asked cynically.

"I wouldn't expect you to do it for nothing."

Peter could not stop a satisfied smile creeping across his face.

George noticed. "And you think my motive's money? I don't need any bloody money. I've got more than I can spend. That's not the point. It's going to cost me to do this. I'm risking $10 million. You'd want a return on your money…if you had any!"

Peter did not miss the dig. "I may not have any money George, but I still sleep at night."

"Well, would you like to make some money, real money?"

"Yes, of course I would, but I don't think I'm prepared to pay the price."

"You're kidding yourself Peter. You've already paid the price. You're just refusing to cash in." George hesitated for a minute and then decided to play his trump card. He opened the file, shuffled among the papers, pulled out a copy of a document and handed it to Peter.

"Remember that?" George asked as Peter examined it.

As he quickly skimmed through the several pages the color drained from Peter's face. As he read more of it, he read more carefully.

"What the hell is this?" he asked his eyes still scanning the pages.

"It's the contract in Angola last year. It's the one you signed. See the guarantee clause at the end. You signed that as well. Read it!"

Peter turned to the last page of the contract and read the guarantee. He remembered the contract, it was a disaster. Half a dozen Angolan workers were killed when a trench caved in. He had forgotten about it. He signed the contract about eighteen months prior to commencement of the project, as a favor to George, who was unavailable. He had little or nothing to do with it. It was small by Barnard standards and their guy in Angola had managed it.

"If you remember, Peter, the relatives of those workers claimed we'd skipped the safety measures and had them working down in those trenches without properly shoring up the sides. They said we were behind on the timing and just wanted to speed up to avoid the penalty clauses."

"That's what they said. Did we?" Peter asked.

"Well, I believe there were some photographs of the trench, taken by one of those who was killed. I've got them somewhere. Cost a bit, but I managed to limit it to just the one family. The others were told their claims were false. The Government backed us up."

"You bastard!"

"Yeah, but don't get up on your high horse. You read the guarantee, you took full personal responsibility for the contract and for the safety of those workers. It's your head on the block and I saved it for you. But I'm sure we could re-open the claims if you want."

Peter had received a bonus because the contract came in ahead of schedule and he had not even visited the site. At the time he had seen it as easy money, all he did was to stand in for George. Or at least that's what he thought.

"I'm pretty sure it's jail time if the truth came out. But it can't unless those photographs come to light." George added with an almost imperceptible shrug of his shoulders.

Peter felt like getting up and leaving, after rearranging George's face, and his daughters apartment, but he knew that was not the way to deal with George Barnard.

"How much money?" Peter asked.

"How does thirty-three million dollars sound?"

"For me?"

"Yeah, a third of the fee."

"You're going to charge Berruda a hundred million dollars?"

"No, we're going to charge the U.S.A. a billion dollars and take ten percent commission. And we're going to feed a couple of million people. Even Robin Hood had to eat, I'm sure he took his share of the venison."

"You might well get paid, but you're never going to be able to put your name to this. You're never going to be able to get any glory out of feeding these people."

George looked at him for a moment, "That depends on who wins the war."

"What war?" Peter asked not making any sense of George's answer.

"The Third World War. The third world against us, terrorism, call it what you will. If they win, you're a rich hero, if we win you're just rich. I can live with that, can you?"

Peter was calm, he knew George would do exactly what he had threatened. In a strange way Peter was relieved. All the years he had worked for George he had heard the rumors, but he had never seen it first hand, never been on the receiving end.

"I'll let you know."

"By tonight, if you will." George said as Peter let himself out of the apartment.

Chapter 9

Peter was on board a British Airways Boeing 747 out of London's Heathrow airport bound for Hong Kong with a new sense of anticipation.

During his time with Special Services he had employed a few 'freelancers'. Many of them knew each other and often worked together and every couple of years they got together at what they called a reunion. This year they were going to be in Hong Kong. Many of them were in legitimate businesses, worked as divers, engineers, any occupation which offered the ability to work on short term contracts in the trouble spots of the world. Most had been in the military. In reality they were mercenaries. Peter had only ever been to one 'reunion' since resigning from Special Services and was interested to see who would still be around in Hong Kong. It was a hazardous way to earn a living and life expectancy was short.

There was no formal agenda. The hotel had been designated and for a few days they would drink, eat and discuss old times. It was a market place, a way to say you were still alive and available. Peter heard of the get together at the end of October. He would not have gone, but for his meeting with George and his subsequent agreement to work on what they had labeled the Bakaar Project. This created a new-found need for Peter to get in contact with some of his old friends. He made a routine business trip to London, from there to Hong Kong and he would go straight back to Nairobi from Hong Kong.

More meetings with George in London had allowed them to hammer out a plan. To rob from the rich to feed the poor and like Robin Hood, to whom George repeatedly referred, expect that those who were robbed would be unable to exact retribution. The more they considered the plan the more they liked it and the more convinced they became that their intentions were altruistic. They felt they could pull it off with few repercussions and Peter satisfied himself that there was little possibility of having to carry out their threat. The U.S. could not afford the risk. They would pay.

Peter had considered his position following his meeting with George and felt he had little choice. If he refused George's request he had no doubt he would end up facing charges in Angola and would be out of a job. He had made his mistake representing George in the first place and signing that contract on his behalf. Whether or not he could refuse any of George's future requests was pretty much decided at that time.

Justifying their action was not difficult. Something had to be done, they told themselves, the third world was starving and in the international environment following the end of the cold war the world was less, rather than more, stable. Sooner or later a little country somewhere was going to get desperate and would do what George and Peter were planning.

That dark streak in Peter's character which had played a part in his past career, was again showing itself. If he was honest he was enjoying himself. A little danger back in his life was not such a bad thing.

George and Peter worked on Robert Berruda's simple pitch, which had been made to George on the flight into Kenya. Provide a small deprived country such as Bakaar, with the means to extort money, aid or favors from a wealthy one. Provide the desperation to use them and it was more likely to succeed than fail. The lesson of the eighties and nineties was that a threat to the fragile peace of the new, unstable world worked much better than the begging bowl. If it was done right the threats would never become public. It was in the best interest of the Country threatened, to pay and cover it up.

On success, George would get his investment back plus a lot more for his trouble and Peter would get a cut big enough to retire in comfort. So long as the threat, if publicized, would cause widespread panic and so long as it could be seen that the donor government, as George was already calling the U.S.A., could not prevent it, he was convinced they would pay up. The U.S. must avoid publicity at all cost. The last thing the western world needed was to tell the Third World that they would pay up in the face of a threat.

George for his own reasons wanted to make the demand for aid against Britain, to allow him the pleasure of keeping his promise to William Wickens that he would get even. But he accepted that Britain's resources were limited. The USA was the obvious donor. The question now was how to achieve the level of persuasion required at a reasonable cost.

Peter met Sarah at several of the meetings with George, but not as a participant in the project. Peter had noticed the cold look in her eyes when he had first met her at her apartment. It was almost hostile and he wanted to know why. Regardless, he was convinced there was chemistry between them and sooner or later he hoped to prove it. George had noticed Peter's interest and warned him that he did not want her implicated or involved in their venture in any way.

• • •

The Boeing climbed laboriously through the gray clouds enveloping Southern England. There were 380 passengers aboard and for the flight to Hong Kong the 747 was up around its maximum take-off weight of 820,000 pounds. At this weight the pilot could not reach his planned level of 39,000 feet until he was out over the Mediterranean. Depending on the winds, it would be about a thirteen hour, non-stop flight to Hong Kong.

The captain's customary welcome indicated there should be no adverse weather en route and he expected an on-time arrival in Hong Kong at 5.05 p.m. on the following day.

Peter settled down in his business class seat. The upgrade a goodwill gesture from George. Peter intended to spend the flight checking out the timetable for their plan. There was a lot to do in the next few weeks and the deadline could only be met if everything went like clockwork. Peter was in luck, no one sat in the adjacent seats. He was able to alternately work, eat and sleep in luxury. He enjoyed it and vowed that after he received his share of the cash he would never again travel coach.

The time passed quickly, he was surprised as he felt the captain ease the thrust levers back at a little before 4.00 p.m. local time, to commence his descent into Kai Tak Airport in Hong Kong. The aircraft finally came to a stop at the gate at 4.50 p.m. just a few minutes ahead of the scheduled arrival time.

Peter passed through customs and immigration and walked out into the warm tropical air of the late afternoon. The Chinese take-over of the island had made little outward difference. With about one and a half million people crammed into the tiny island, Hong Kong still bustled like few other places on earth. Peter joined the throng outside the airport and eventually found the hotel limousine, an American stretched Lincoln, incongruous in the heart of what was now a city in communist China. He joined a couple of other weary hotel guests and the car glided out of the airport on its way to Hong Kong island via the tunnel under Victoria Harbor.

He checked into the hotel in a daze, ordered breakfast for 7.00 a.m. and headed for his room. As soon as his head hit the pillow he was deeply asleep, as only a small child, or a jet lagged traveler can be.

• • •

Peter awoke, unsure of where he was and without any concept of time. The insistent knocking continued. He looked at his watch and realized it was just after seven o'clock. Breakfast was at the door. He was thirsty and downed the orange juice and the coffee. He had a great deal to do in just a few days and his first task this morning was to check with the front desk and see if Tim Serenson and Doug Borden were registered. If so, he wanted to spend some time with Tim today and make sure he was the right choice for the job. He also needed a specialist who could be particularly difficult to find. Years ago when he had been with the Special Services he had been given two names, Max Ryder and Rudi Van Haute. The problem was that he had been out of the business for over twelve years and in that time the law could have caught up with them or they could be dead. There was no guarantee they were around, let alone in Hong Kong this week.

Hong Kong, is situated just below the Tropic of Cancer, about the same latitude as the Caribbean Islands and enjoys a sub tropical climate. In a month or so it would be humid and almost unbearable. For Peter it was a relief from the British gray during his recent visit. He felt the cold much more since he had spent a good part of his life in Africa. He was certain that the old tale about blood thinning in a warm climate was true. The hotel, like most buildings in Hong Kong was air conditioned and Peter wore a lightweight jacket over his open necked shirt as he headed down to the front desk. As the elevator began its downward journey he felt nauseous, the thirteen hour flight and an eight hour time difference played havoc with his metabolism. When he arrived in the lobby he had no recollection of it from the night before.

"Good morning, sir can I help you?" One of the clerks asked as he approached.

"Can you tell me if Mr. Serenson or Mr. Borden have arrived?"

"Are you a guest at the hotel, sir and your name please?

"Yes. Peter Williamson."

The clerk tapped away at the keyboard watching the screen. She was reading and Peter guessed he was in luck.

"Yes, both gentlemen are here."

"Can you call Mr. Serenson's room for me. I'll take the call on the house phone."

Peter walked away towards the line of telephones on the opposite wall and picked up the white, house phone. About half a minute went by as the desk clerk tried the room and announced who was calling.

"This can't really be the Pete Williamson, Action Man himself after all these years." drawled Tim.

Whenever Peter spoke with Americans he became very aware of his precise English. He could not accept that he had an English accent, although that's how Americans described it. He was under the impression that they had the accent. Whichever way it was, he was aware that he sounded stilted.

"Yes, it's Action Man," Peter replied trying to loosen the vowels a little. "How you doing? I'm pleased you're here."

"Here? Where are you?" Tim inquired.

"I'm in the lobby…"

"Good God! Have you had breakfast? Come on up and join me."

"What's your room number?" Peter asked.

"Eleven twenty seven."

This was a good start to the day. Both Tim and Doug were around and Peter would know within an hour or so whether he could put the first pieces of the jigsaw together. He knocked on the door of eleven twenty seven. The door opened and Tim grabbed his hand with both hands and shook it like a long lost brother. "Hey, Pete, great to see you again," Tim exclaimed. "You look good!"

Peter was half dragged into the room and the door closed behind him.

"What a coincidence," Tim said as they sat down at the small table containing only the remnants of his breakfast.

"Don't worry, I've had breakfast Tim," Peter grinned, "but I'd love some coffee."

"That's lucky," Tim laughed remembering he had invited Peter up for breakfast. "We could send down for some more if you're still hungry."

"Coffee's fine," Peter reassured him.

There was only one cup on the table. Tim went to the bathroom and washed out a glass, returned and filled it with coffee from the pot and topped up his own. Beneath his obvious enthusiasm to see Peter he was trying to decide what had brought Peter to this hotel at this time. He was not sure whether Peter was there for the reunion.

"Are you on your own?" Tim asked

"Yes," Peter replied, wishing to cut the questions short, "I thought it was time I found out who's still in business."

"Then it's not a fucking coincidence. Did you know I was gonna be here?" Tim asked.

"No, I didn't know. I heard about it back in October and thought I ought to come for old time's sake. Then a couple of things cropped up and it, eh…seemed a good idea to see if you were here."

"What you up to?" Tim asked, "Are you still with that company from London, or are you back in our business?"

He was the same old Tim, just older. He was suntanned, his blonde, close cropped hair was graying, he looked fit and his handshake felt as if he was still working out. When he was in the business Peter mixed with so many of Tim's breed that he did not notice the single most obvious feature of the mercenaries of the world—their eyes. But now, as he looked at Tim, he saw what he could only describe as, 'the look'. A coldness, a hunted, open look about the eyes which, once recognized is hard to miss. It may come from the need to be aware and constantly looking for danger. On the other hand it may be more subtle—the eyes as the windows of the soul —allowing the observer a peep into the psychological make up of those who devote their lives to the world's dirty little wars.

Like many of his kind Tim was not tall, about five feet nine, but in his cowboy boots he was a good five eleven or even six feet and his muscular build looked more in proportion. Peter answered the questions, "Both, I'm still working for Barnard, but I'm also setting up a job. What are you doing these days? You still freelancing?"

Gradually they traded questions and closed the twelve year gap. Tim would never change, Vietnam had affected him as it had many who were there. He would never get over it. Peter had met enough to know that when an American of forty-five or fifty talked about the war he was talking about Vietnam. It was a war that Britain hardly acknowledged and did not suffer.

The most widespread damage was the psychological affect on the troops returning home to a country which either ignored or abused them. Peter knew of old that this was not the only problem with Tim. Tim's problem was that he liked it. Not the rejection by his countrymen—the war.

Tim could be described generously as a professional soldier or he could be seen as a killer for hire. He worked to a code of ethics of sorts. Mercenary was probably the most accurate and emotionless description. Tim saw himself as an adventurer.

Peter never considered they were friends in the true sense of the word. Tim had worked with him on a number of occasions and they knew each other. Peter considered Tim one of the best. He had never failed to complete a task and unlike some who fitted the description he followed orders and to those who paid the bill he was loyal. Most of those in Hong Kong this week would be like Tim. The sadists, the oddballs, the mentally crippled, who entered the business out of desperation or to satiate otherwise insatiable desires may have helped keep the tabloid press in business, but they did not last long. To those who did the hiring and Peter had been one of them, mercenaries were an efficient way of using force with the ability to deny all knowledge or responsibility if things went wrong.

Tim was a survivor, he had lasted longer than most, he was forty seven and knew he could not compete physically with the twenty five year olds. However, what he had lost in physical ability he more than made up in experience. In Vietnam Tim had seen young guys rush in and get blown to pieces by booby traps. He remembered seeing a little girl, not much older then ten or eleven, walk out of a village house, in which two or three Vietcong had taken cover. She walked slowly and directly towards one of Tim's new arrivals, who was not much more than a kid out of high school. From where Tim was standing he could see she was having difficulty holding something in her hands clasped behind her back. Tim suddenly realized it was a grenade. Shooting her would have made her release the grenade and would serve no purpose. She had gotten too close. He shouted for the soldier to run, but the new green recruit had a sense of morality based in a different world and could not see the danger. As Tim shouted the little girl ran the last two or three yards, tossed the grenade at the kid's feet and both were killed. You either learned quickly, or you headed for home in a body bag. Tim had learned quickly. He enjoyed the risk.

Going home tainted like most of his friends did not appeal. So after Vietnam he roamed around the Middle East together with several other Vets and was available to anyone needing a dirty job done. He became an expert in guerilla warfare and had extensive knowledge of explosives and the electronics which controlled them. He also had an expertise Peter wanted, he could operate in an urban environment.

"Yeah, still at it, but there ain't much work these days. Not legal work." Tim answered. Legal, was a misnomer, it meant work for a legitimate government and was part of the morality important to many of Tim's buddies. Over the years as the work had diminished, legal had gradually loosened its meaning and became accepted as, for a cause, and differentiated between the more abundant, but to many freelancers, unacceptable work in the drug trade.

"I've got some work. Do you want to talk about it?" Peter asked.

"May as well. That's what I'm here for," Tim answered, "What's the timetable?"

"Now…for the next three or four months. It'll mean several weeks in Africa. You interested?" Peter looked at Tim who did not seem to be concentrating.

"What's the pay? And am I gonna get killed?" Tim asked the questions not so much with an expectation of an answer, more as a means to indicate his boredom at the same routine time and time again. At this stage of every offer he always felt like a hooker checking out what the customer wanted, checking to make sure it was something he would do. Even if he would do anything, he did not want a client to think so…and anyway he wanted to get the right price for it.

"You'll be working for the President of an African country. He's got to remove some opposition, and he needs to be able to blame a white man for whatever goes wrong!" Peter smiled, bending the truth a little, "Some of the work'll be in the U.S. It's a little different, there's no running round the jungle with mud on your face!"

"Who'll I be working with?" Tim asked. "Am I leading a bunch of renegade Africans? We got an army, or am I on my own? Come on Pete, you're not giving me a fair crack. What about the big question—how much?"

"A hundred thousand dollars, plus expenses. There's no army and you'd be working with me and a couple of others—more under cover than warfare."

"Who else you got?"

"No one, you're the first I've approached and I'd want you to head it up. I thought of Doug Borden as the heavy. He's here this week. I know you've worked with him before. Do you have any problems with Doug?"

"Nope!"

"OK let's say Doug joins us, you'd head up the operation and you'd have to work with the Africans—the government, not renegades!"

Peter watched Tim's face, it was not giving much away. Peter had to get some commitment before he described the U.S. end of the operation. The description he had given Tim was not complete, but it provided all of the relevant information. "Am I supposed to be advising or am I in the front line?" Tim asked.

"We need your expertise but you'd have to look after yourself. Most of the operation would be in town. As I said, there's no jungle stuff, you wouldn't be living in a tent."

"You're full of shit, Pete! What else have I gotta do?"

"OK, I'll tell you as much as I can. Most of the operation's in the States. We need your knowledge of explosives and electronics."

There was no reaction. Peter was surprised. A few years ago none of the freelancers wanted to operate in their own countries. Opportunities must have diminished. Peter continued, "I'd like you to come out to Africa next month and meet an aide to the President, and then travel on to the U.S. to meet me and set up the operation."

"You haven't said which country we're helping." It seemed to be the only question Tim had.

"Can't tell you that. Does it make any difference?"

"Nope, not really."

"I'll tell you as soon as I've got you and Doug in the bag!" Peter was relieved, it had been easy so far.

"How long we gonna be in the U.S.?" Tim asked showing the first real interest since the conversation began.

"About a week or two for the setup, maybe a couple of weeks towards the end," Peter answered.

Tim had become increasingly subdued during the conversation. "I'll tell you, Pete I'm burned out, I'm getting too fucking old for it. Dunno what I'm gonna do when there's no more work. Managed to save a bit of cash, but the gaps between jobs just eats it. I'd like to join you. But…what are you getting out of it? I want more than a rate for the job. It's time I got a slice of the pie. For Christ's sake, if the deal's straight, we're letting this President keep his fucking country. That's gotta be worth a bit."

Peter could only sympathize with the sentiment. He and Tim had helped Berruda's coup all those years ago and all Peter got was his monthly salary from the British Government and the thanks of the Ministry of the Interior. Robert Berruda had lived like a king ever since. It did not matter what he offered as payment after the job was done, it was only the up front money he had to watch.

"Tim, I can't offer you a share, but I could agree to part of the fee in advance." Peter offered.

"Stop bullshitting, I wanna hundred thousand dollars up front, I'll pay Doug out of my share and I want another five hundred thousand when it's all over, plus all expenses." Tim could afford to play hard to get, few of his colleagues would want to work in the U.S. He was not the only one who could do it, but there were not too many left.

"I'll agree to the front money, but I can only go to a further two hundred and fifty thousand after it's over," Peter lied.

Tim knew the deal was not what he was being told, none of it added up. Peter may have been out of the business for a while, but no one paid that sort of money for a few weeks in Africa and a couple of trips to the U.S. One possibility was that he was expendable and was not expected to collect the final installment. He had some respect for Peter. There had been other times when Peter could have screwed him, but he had not. The action in the U.S. had to be bigger than Peter was letting on.

Tim was past caring, he had to find the big one to retire. He had to get enough out of it to quit. Maybe this was it, "I've said what I want and if any of it's paid after, I'll want it in escrow. It's six hundred thousand or I am not interested."

Peter could see that Tim was less concerned about what it was and more interested in how much. During the discussions in London, George insisted that they had the best people. Tim was the best. There was little point arguing about it, for six hundred thousand dollars he could be relied upon to stay the course. Bearing in mind that Tim would pay Doug, the price was well within the budget George had suggested.

"OK, six hundred thousand. Let's meet again tomorrow, Doug's your responsibility. Then we'll set up the timetable. We'll discuss the details in Africa. Go ahead and fix it with Doug."

Peter got up and walked towards the door. Tim knew he would have to watch his back for this sort of money. He had to be prepared for a few surprises. He had to be careful. Tomorrow, he would find out more.

"See you later, Pete. Hope I don't regret this. Take care." Peter left the room. Tim picked up the phone. "Can you connect me to Mr. Borden's room please?"

Chapter 10

George Barnard wasted little time. It would not be easy to persuade the other, as yet unknowing, member of the team to join them and it was now up to George to renew his acquaintance with Nirina Ghose.

Sarah was given the task of finding Nirina. She had a little information to work with. He was born in India, held a British Passport, but as a kid had moved with his parents into what was then Uganda where the family opened a jewelry business. He was sent to London for his education and had qualified as a chemist. George had met him when the Barnard Company won a contract to build a chemical plant in South Africa. Nirina had been a consultant and on more than one occasion during the construction he had visited London and met with George and his colleagues. However, George's interest stemmed from more recent knowledge of Nirina's activities.

Two years previously, a series of investigative articles in the London Daily Telegraph had described Nirina as the man whose name was linked with every Third World country which experimented with chemical weapons. He seemed to be the mastermind behind their programs. The articles carried no photographs and the name Ghose was far from unique.

It took Sarah just one week to locate him and to peak her interest in why her father would want to contact the man. She found him living in Marseilles. Sarah worked out of the Barnard Company's London offices in Mount Street, just off Park Lane. George used the office as a base, but spent little time there. He preferred to spend his time supervising or as Sarah described it, interfering in the operations overseas. There were few employees in the office, Rose a secretary of about fifty who had been with George forever and Joe. He too had worked with George since he left school. He was the same age as George and was George's right hand man and representative in the UK. Sarah had known both of them all of her life.

"Where's my dad today, Joe?" Sarah asked.

"E's in Paris luv, e'll either be in the 'otel or at the office"

Sarah dialed the Paris office

"Hello Dad. I've found him!" Sarah announced triumphantly.

George was in his Paris office with his French General Manager, tax advisor and lawyer, trying to amend the wording of a new contract written in French. George was always in a filthy temper doing business in France. He had a working knowledge of the language but he could not tackle legal French. He believed few people could, even the French had problems.

"Hello, Sarah, found who?" George asked vacantly as he continued to read the contract on the table in front of him.

"Nirina Ghose, he's living in Marseilles."

The name brought George back to life. He put the contract down and swung the chair round, away from the desk, to allow him to speak more privately.

"Have you got a phone number for him?" He asked.

Sarah gave him the number and added, "The code for Marseilles is 91."

George swung back towards the desk and scribbled the number on the edge of the contract. "What do I need to know about him?"

"I don't know. Why on earth do you want to contact him? He doesn't exactly seem to be an upright citizen. What are you getting into?"

"He worked with us some years back. I need to talk to him again."

"Yes, I know Dad, but he's into all sorts of trouble..."

"Sarah! What have you got?"

"Well it's your business I guess. He's living with his wife and a couple of kids. He's been in France for several years but spends a lot of time travelling. He's fifty-one. He's still listed in the directory as an industrial consultant and I've even got a photograph taken by one of the newspapers but not published. Are we going to see him?"

"It sounds like him, I can't imagine there are two Nirina Ghose's in the chemical business. I was coming back to London tonight, but let me see the photograph. If it is him I'll try and contact him today. If he's there I'll go down tomorrow. But Sarah, you don't need to come." George did not want Sarah involved.

"A couple of days in the South of France can't do me any harm, Dad. I promise I'll keep out of your way. I'll just eat and go shopping, but I'd like to come. Where are you staying tonight in Paris?" Sarah was not going to miss out on a little sunshine in the winter. A weekend on the French Riviera appealed.

George waited for the fax to arrive. When he saw the photograph there was no doubt—it was the Nirina he knew. He wasted no time and happily excused himself from the contract negotiations and made the call to the Marseilles number.

"Allo, puis-je vous aide?"

"Oui, M. Ghose est-il occupe?" George replied.

"Votre nom, s'il vous plaît?" the operator inquired.

"George Barnard, de la Compagnie Barnard a Paris."

There was a short pause as the receptionist inquired whether Nirina wanted to speak with a 'George Barnard' from Paris.

"Mr. Barnard, good afternoon, how can I help you?" Nirina answered in English, in the oily supercilious manner which reminded George that he had not liked the man a great deal.

"Do you remember me, from the contract in South Africa some years ago?" George asked.

"It was many years ago, Mr Barnard. Indeed I do remember you."

"Your telephone number's still listed under Consultant Industriel, I presume your are still consulting in commercial chemical production."

"Oh yes. I've been doing a great deal of work in Africa and the Middle East and it seems my reputation is growing all the time." Nirina demonstrated his total lack of modesty and a desire to ensure that George knew he had acquired some notoriety since he had last worked with him.

"Yes, I heard about your expertise. I'm about to get a contract to renovate a chemical plant in the Middle East and I wondered if you might be interested in working with us?" George did not want Nirina to even know which continent he would be working in.

Nirina was still unsure whether George knew of his current occupation but was not able to ask. "You have not consulted me for a long time, I am honored that you, yourself should call. I presume it must be a very important contract." Nirina could not resist it and added, "I wonder if you saw the articles about me in the Press a few years ago?"

The conversation had proved that Nirina was still in the business George needed, but just as Nirina could not offer his services, George could not simply ask the man on the telephone if he could manufacture VX nerve gas.

"Yes, I've read of your growing reputation Mr. Ghose. The new contract is a very different deal from the one on which you last assisted us. What we need is a very complex renovation to allow the plant to produce just one product. It will certainly need your expertise."

"When would you need my services?" Nirina asked now knowing what was wanted. He was desperate to know why on earth George Barnard would want to manufacture nerve gas.

"If we can agree terms we have to have a small quantity of the product in about three months. We're in a hurry!"

"Three months?" Nirina repeated.

"Yes, there's a great deal of urgency." George repeated. There was a pause and George waited.

"To try and satisfy your urgency may be expensive, Mr Barnard. I cannot make any promises at this point, but I would be pleased to discuss it with you. Are you in Paris? Would you like me to come up to meet with you?"

George did not want his Paris office involved and he was not going to go to Nirina's office or home. "No, I'd rather visit you in Marseilles, but it would be sensible if we met at my hotel. Could we meet tomorrow, perhaps for lunch?"

"By all means, why don't you call me tomorrow morning and let me know where we shall meet."

"Yes, I'll do that…"

Nirina interrupted, "My number is 08.63…"

"I've got the number, I'll call you tomorrow."

George confirmed the visit to Sarah, trying without success, to deter her from joining him. She had made up her mind and was going with him. She booked two seats from Paris to Marseilles early the following morning and a single for herself from London to Paris that evening. As an afterthought George asked that she send a copy of Nirina's photograph and address to Peter in Hong Kong. The mention of Peter's name reminded her that she had no idea what her father was involved in with him. He had been around every day for a week and that was not normal. Now Nirina's photograph was going to Peter. As she thought of that week and the reason for Peter's visit she could not help remembering the way he looked at her and the way he held her hand just a little too long. She knew he had been attracted to her when they first met in her apartment but she tried to ignore it. She resisted the thought, Peter was not her type at all. He would be trouble. There could be nothing long term, at best it would be a short unsettling affair, and she really did not want any more of those. She knew he would be unreliable.

George need not have worried about keeping his daughter away from the details. She had already decided to rent a car, drop George off at the hotel and drive the two hundred kilometers along the spectacular coastline to Nice.

Sarah sent the information on Nirina to Peter's hotel in Hong Kong and left the office in Mount Street at four o'clock. She picked up some clothes and headed out to Heathrow. The flight to Paris was quick and uneventful. She took a cab into Paris from Charles de Gaulle airport and checked in at the hotel at eight thirty. She dropped her bag in her room and went to find her father.

George had arrived at the hotel only a few minutes before Sarah. After their conversation the remainder of his day had deteriorated as he got back into the battle with French legalese and it had not put him in the most relaxed of moods. He was shaving when he let Sarah into his room.

"Hello Dad, where are we going to dinner?" Sarah asked, giving him a quick kiss on the cheek, pleased to see him and knowing he would not be in the best of moods.

"I thought we'd go to La Forge, the restaurant we went to last year after the conference. It's about half a mile from Notre Dame."

"I remember…it was good. Half an hour? I'll knock on the door, see you soon." Sarah returned to her room and changed.

Since her mother's death her father had taken more interest in his only child. As a little girl Sarah had hardly known who he was. He was never home when she was awake. Her childhood memories of her father were of weekends and vacations interrupted by Dad leaving just when Sarah was getting accustomed to his presence. As she grew older she became aware of who her father was. The continual critical publicity and public accusations of wrongdoing from bribery to murder did little to improve the instability of her teenage years.

By the time Sarah was in her twenties she had a love, hate relationship with him. She resented his lack of attention during her childhood. She hated him for being well known for the wrong reasons, but loved him for his willingness to deal with the world without hypocrisy. She liked that old Yorkshire down to earth attitude. Now she felt protective.

From the discussions in London it was clear to her that there was a new project in her father's life and she was not being given all the information. In fact, she was being kept out and she did not like it. So far all she had pieced together was that her father and Peter were involved in Bakaar. She had no idea how Nirina fitted into the picture. She could see that her father's involvement was approaching religious fervor and hoped it was all above board.

Sarah had sufficient money to live out the rest of her life in comfort. She had inherited a sizeable fortune when her mother died. There was no need for her father to get into any new ventures to make money.

They talked as they walked to the restaurant, small talk and odds and ends about events in the office in London and George's objections to the French legal system. After they began to eat and George was on his second glass of burgundy he had relaxed a little. Sarah decided it was a good time to find out more about his new project.

"Why are you meeting with Nirina Ghose?" she asked casually as she sipped her wine.

"I need his help on the Bakaar Project." George answered blandly.

"Yes, I know, but what can he possibly do to help?"

"Sarah, my love…" George put down his glass and reached across to hold her hand in a manner which was more condescending than affectionate, "I appreciate your assistance. You're invaluable in the business, but I just want you to help out with the research on this one." George adopted his best fatherly manner, he did not want to get into the details. Sarah hated it when he put her down.

"What are you trying to achieve? Why is it so important to you?" She paused, withdrawing her hand. "I thought you might start to take things a little easier this year. I know you feel indispensable in the business, but it really does run itself. You don't need money, do you?" Sarah suddenly wondered if there had been some catastrophe of which she was unaware.

"No, of course I don't need money," George assured her

"So, why can't I help?" Sarah continued.

George turned on his justification act. "You know me better than anyone, you know how frustrated I get when something's unfair or unreasonable. Well I've never forgotten that nonsense over my knighthood…"

"Dad, really!" Sarah sighed, "why do you always say your knighthood? It makes me so mad! Anyway, how is a knighthood connected with Bakaar?"

George had already said too much and he was becoming irritated. "I've contributed more to England than most people. I created thousands of jobs and I've paid millions in taxes and most of it when the old country was in a sorry state. You were too young to remember the mess it was in—at one time the International Monetary Fund was going to take over. Take over! The country was virtually bankrupt. I was happy to play my part, but I thought a knighthood was appropriate."

Sarah raised one eyebrow at the repeated mention of the damned knighthood. George noticed it and tried to reinforce his comments. "Don't think it wasn't mentioned. I had a lot of support. Many of the politicians I'd helped didn't want to be reminded of the connection with George Barnard. Now they give knighthoods and peerages to faceless bloody civil servants who've been overpaid to sit on their backsides all their lives. They're the biggest bunch of wasters…" George was getting heated and Sarah could see she was not going to get anywhere.

"Dad, you're not making a lot of sense. Don't get upset. I didn't realize it meant that much to you. Does Bakaar have anything to do with the knighthood?" Sarah saw from her father's face that he was not going to answer the question, "Well, at least tell me—Is what you're doing legal?"

George calmed down, but the mention of the word 'legal' brought his day back with a rush. "Legal, how do you define legal?" He paused, "I've just spent the entire day trying to agree the wording of a contract which will apply in France and I can tell you it wouldn't be accepted in England. Most of the European countries are breaking the Community Laws on a daily basis. What about politicians. I don't know how legal it was for the Americans to invade Grenada, or Iraq. But they did it. Seems to me that if there's overwhelming benefit for one party in any particular action, then regardless of the law it gets done and the rest of the world turns the other way."

Sarah did not reply. She could see that he was justifying whatever it was he was going to do, but she still had not got much closer to finding out what it was. It seemed a harsh way to view the world, but winning did seem to create laws of its own. She thought she should approach it from a different direction.

"Where does Peter fit in?"

Sarah had not mentioned Peter until now and George was not about to explain his involvement. He responded in a manner he knew would close the conversation once and for all —the patronizing father. "Don't worry, I'm sure you'll be seeing plenty of Peter in the next few months…"

"That's got nothing to do with it!" Sarah snapped back at him, "He's not my type!"

Chapter 11

The Mediterranean and the open expanse of sand and marsh seen from the airplane on the approach to Marseilles' Marignane airport provides an expectation of warm ocean and vacation. It promises the magic which only the Cote d'Azur can offer. The sparkling sea, warm sun, roads hanging on the face of cliffs and spectacular homes. However, upon arrival at the terminal building the promise is not realized. The terminal resembles an African market rather than a French airport. Regular flights arrive and depart to the old French colonies in North Africa and the airport is full of the flowing robes of the Algerians and Tunisians.

George had considered Sarah's plan to drop him off and go on to Nice an excellent idea. By 10.30 a.m. they had collected the rental car and Sarah drove the twenty-eight kilometers into the city. She had reserved a room for George at the Sofitel Vieux Port, which as its name suggests looks out over the old port, the origins of which date back to the Romans.

Beneath its glitzy exterior, Marseilles is a working, blue collar city and provides the industrial base for the French Riviera. Like most

French cities it has more than its fair share of superb restaurants and George was looking forward to one of the Marseilles traditions, bouillabaisse—a wonderful concoction of seafood in a steaming hot soup. An accurate physical description but hardly a fair appraisal of one of the world's finest dishes. It was served all over France, but the version found in Marseilles was the best.

Sarah pulled up outside the hotel, "Bye Dad, hope it goes well!"

George climbed out of the car dragging his overnight bag out of the rear seat. He held the door open, "I'm sure it will. See you tomorrow. What time's our flight out of Marseilles?"

Sarah leaned over towards the passenger door. "Half past seven tomorrow night. It'll take about an hour to get out to the airport and maybe half an hour to check in. What if I pick you up about five thirty?"

"OK, five thirty. Have a good time. See you tomorrow." George slammed the door and walked into the hotel.

• • •

If something had to be done, George wanted it done immediately. It was one of his strengths. The sooner Nirina joined the team the better. As soon as George reached his room he called.

"Morning, Mr Ghose. I'm at the Sofitel at the old port. How about meeting for lunch in the restaurant?"

"That sounds excellent, one o'clock in the Restaurant Trois Forts. I look forward to seeing you again." Nirina's oily, pedantic manner did nothing to improve George's memory of the man.

George had nothing to do for the next couple of hours. The sun was shining and it was warm enough to enjoy being out of doors. He wandered into the Parc du Pharo and spent a couple of hours looking at the boats. By one o'clock he was seated in the restaurant enjoying a bottle of burgundy.

Nirina was not difficult to spot. He arrived at a quarter after one and stood at the entrance. George began to get up from his chair, the movement causing Nirina to look towards him. Nothing more was necessary. Nirina came over to the table and they shook hands.

"How nice to see you again, Mr. Barnard. How are you?"

"Yeah, well, thank you," George responded, "would you like a glass of wine?"

"Yes, please."

George poured from the bottle on the table.

"Your health, Mr Barnard, let us hope I can assist you."

George could not say he knew Nirina Ghose. The original contact had been a passing commercial involvement. From the little that had been said on the phone during the past days George could not form an opinion as to Nirina's competence and had to rely on his published reputation. They ordered the meal and George got down to business. "I've been offered a contract to convert a chemical plant in the Middle East and from the press reports you referred to, I think you could help us do that."

"It is strange how words change. When you first called you had a contract to renovate a plant , but now you are to convert one." Nirina's manner was still supercilious and arrogant and gave every indication that George was the supplicant and Nirina the benefactor. Nirina was obviously enjoying his notoriety. If his expertise was applicable, George needed it, but if it were not, it could be damaging to have Nirina telling the media that George Barnard was trying to obtain a supply of nerve gas. George decided that Nirina had to be put in his place and had to be made to realize the danger in progressing the meeting.

"Mr Ghose, you must understand…my position is extremely sensitive. The more you know of my requirements the more dangerous you are to me. For your own protection you shouldn't ask too many questions until you're committed. I need to know before you leave this table whether or not you'll be working with us."

Nirina listened without comment, his manner remained arrogant. "I do not think you understand," Nirina responded, "with a time limit of three months and considering the expertise I think you need, there are few people in the world who can fulfil your requirements. I think I hold most of the cards. After all, here you are talking to me!" Nirina looked George straight in the eyes, challenging him.

"OK, let's move on. I can't afford to have you running loose all over the Middle East with stories of our conversation. We're talking about the production of a small supply of VX gas. Are you able to organize the ingredients and equipment to manufacture it and supervise the initial production—and do it in three months?"

"Oh my God, Mr George Barnard wants VX gas. What has the world come to! I hope you do not take the description of, 'The poor man's atomic bomb', too literally Mr. Barnard. It is not really cheap to make, not if we have to set up the plant to make it. It will take a great deal of money!"

"Can you do it and supply the product in three months?" George insisted.

"Yes I can, if we are able to agree satisfactory terms. Who will I be working for?" Nirina laughed and then added, "I presume you do not want this personally to settle a business dispute." The thought of George going to the lengths of manufacturing one of the most toxic substances in the world to remove a competitor amused Nirina. "Is VX gas the new weapon of choice in the business world?" He added still enjoying his own joke.

George had difficulty in controlling his temper, he could feel the pulse in his temple pounding, "We have the backing of an independent nation, but rest assured you will be working for me. What facilities will you require and what assistance will you need?"

Nirina stopped grinning, "I will need two or three chemists and an engineer. There is a lot of work to do. I have no idea what facilities exist. Do we have to start from scratch or is there really an existing plant we can convert?"

"Assume that we have a suitable building and availability of any equipment we choose to purchase and the capability to manufacture or adapt existing equipment."

"Do you have a totally safe environment. The gas will have to be tested and there cannot be any risk of contamination for the people involved."

George had to fly by the seat of his pants. He had no idea what could be utilized in Bakaar. But he could not believe it would be too difficult once Berruda had agreed to go ahead. "We may well have to create a suitable laboratory." George answered.

"When you say a small supply, how much do you mean?"

"Perhaps a few gallons."

"Gallons? That is not commercial production Mr. Barnard."

"I know that. Can you do it?"

"Well…it's a question of my fee. I cannot be held responsible for the cost of the plant. I will assume we have the facilities you describe and that money is available and in that vein I would need a fee of one million dollars."

Sarah had learned from her research that Nirina had not been in the news recently and given that he was in Marseilles it was reasonable to assume he was not working. His fame was a double edged sword. It attracted a few customers who would pay highly, but it was unlikely that anyone would want him consulting on an innocuous chemical production problem, for fear that his presence was misinterpreted. George was prepared to believe he was not busy.

"We'd need you to start work as soon as possible. You'll be away from home for a couple of months I would guess."

"I usually am when I'm working, Mr Barnard. You have not said where I will be working."

"No I haven't. The Middle East will have to be good enough for the moment, I'm sure it makes little difference." George had no intention of letting Nirina know where he was going and the Middle East was going to suffice until Nirina was on a plane to Bakaar.

"But you must appreciate, Mr Barnard, that working in Beirut would be very different to Baghdad. The location would affect my fee."

If Nirina was a different character, George would have felt more inclined to be reasonable, but he knew he could not trust him. However, he had to accept that he could do the job. In one sense Nirina was right. If they had to start looking for another chemist they would never make the deadline. George had to clinch the deal.

"We can't pay you a million dollars, Mr Ghose, but we will pay you $250,000 for the work and a bonus of $250,000 if we get the amount of gas we need. We'll ensure that you receive a substantial down payment so that your family will be comfortable while you're away."

"You insult me Mr. Barnard, I cannot work for such a sum, it is out of the question!" Nirina was scathing but he did not leave the table.

"Mr. Ghose let me remind you of my original comments. Once I'd disclosed what I wanted, you didn't have a choice. We'll be fair and pay you well for a few weeks work, but you will be working for us and you will be paid $250,000 plus all of your expenses. I need your agreement so that we can plan your timetable."

"I told you I cannot work for such a sum!"

"As I said, we will also look after your family while you're away."

"What does my family have to do with anything?" Nirina asked.

"Well, we have an excellent benefit package. We have another professional who works for us. He specializes in protecting our associates families. He'll make certain that your wife and your two lovely children are well looked after. Mind you, if we felt you weren't being cooperative, he might not look after them as well as otherwise and then, in this unpredictable world, you never know what might happen."

"Do I understand that you are threatening me?"

"No, I'm just advising you of the position. You have joined the team. I trust you'll go home and prepare to work with us. You'll make a great deal of money for just a few weeks work. We'll be in touch…and don't breathe a word of this conversation to anyone."

At that, George stood up, took out a bundle of notes, counted out the cash to pay the check, and walked away. Nirina remained seated at the table staring out over the harbor, unable to enjoy the view. That evening, having eaten little at lunch, George decided he would go out and have the bouillabaisse he had promised himself. Later he would call Peter and make sure that the promises he had made to Nirina could be kept.

Chapter 12

Peter was disturbed by the insistent bleeping. He rolled over still half asleep and picked up the phone. "Hello," he mumbled.

"Peter it's George. How you doing?"

"Apart from being asleep, I'm doing fine." Peter was quickly becoming conscious. It was the end of a busy day for George in Marseilles, but for Peter it was just seven o'clock in the morning and the day in Hong Kong had not yet started.

"Sorry to wake you up. Sarah found our chemist more quickly than we expected. Did you get the information she faxed yesterday?"

"Yes, I did. You've met with him?"

"I saw him today. He's going to need coaxing. He's an arrogant bastard and although the money should get him interested when he thinks about it, we're going to have to send in the troops," George paused, "which raises the question...do we have any troops?" The speed with which events were moving was good from one point of view. The deadline might well be achieved. But the risk that the various segments of the operation would get out of step was making George nervous.

George had learned something in the past twelve hours. He pretty much knew who and what he was, his strengths and weaknesses. He tended to bear grudges. He could be a hard negotiator and he could be ruthless when it suited him. But what had transpired with Nirina was different. Ruthlessness in George's life tended to be financial. Credibility might be on the line and a decision might put a few hundred people out of work, but he had always employed other people to make physical threats. George hoped he had convinced Nirina, but he was far from happy with his performance. He felt uneasy and tense. This was Peter's world and George was uncomfortable in it.

"Yes, we've got some troops," Peter reassured him. He had no intention of expanding on the statement. It was better that George knew as little as possible about those involved. "We've got a good team, I've finished here and I'm leaving today. What do you need?"

"I need the Chemist to be persuaded that it's in his best interest to assist us. He knows what we want and he knows he's probably the only person we'll find at short notice to do the job. Unfortunately that's made him think he's valuable." George continued and relayed the details of his lunch with Nirina.

Peter confirmed that he could set it up. "I had better get back to Africa as soon as possible and get to see the man. It's moving along quickly." Peter was careful not to mention any names. He knew they should not use the names of the team on the phone.

International phone calls were now routinely transmitted via satellite at some point along their route and there was no great difficulty in them being intercepted. Government's computers were programmed to look for certain trigger words or names, and as soon as one was recognized the conversation could end up transcribed and on a desk in any one of a dozen security centers around the world within twenty four hours.

"How much cash do you want our man to deliver to the Chemist?" Peter asked, "And what about the travel arrangements?"

"I think his family should have $50,000 while he's away. If I were his wife I'd be delighted to see him gone and if she gets money as well, she may never want him back. Tell him he'll have to travel in two weeks, the quicker we get him out there the less time for him to run or hide and the longer he has to make the deadline. He won't know the location until he's on the damned plane. Your man will have to use some persuasion, our Chemist has got to see we're for real, but I don't want anyone hurt at this point. Is that too tall an order?"

"No, I'll explain it. I'm sure we can persuade him to come along quietly."

"Where do you want the cash delivered?" George asked.

"I'll fax you an address. Have it delivered by courier addressed to me, I'll instruct our man to sign for me. I'd better get going, I've got a bit more to do before I leave. Where are you going to be later…tomorrow?" Peter added as he remembered the time difference.

"I'll be in Paris tomorrow night," George answered, "then I'll be in London the following day."

"I'll let you know when I hear the Chemist's in the bag and I'll check back with you when I've spoken to our man in Africa and have a date for a meeting. By the way, how's Sarah?"

"Sarah's not involved in this!" George snapped defensively.

Peter was taken aback, "I was just asking after her health."

"Yeah, she's well. I'll expect your call, good luck!"

Peter had been successful. Tim had recruited Doug Borden and after a couple more hours of discussion, had confirmed the deal. They ironed out the details and Peter got a phone number where he could reach Tim for the next few weeks. Peter was to confirm the travel arrangements as soon as he had a date. They set up the bank which would be used for the deposit of Tim's up front payment and worked out an escrow arrangement for the bonus. Tim and Doug would go to Bakaar and meet with Peter and hopefully someone from Robert Berruda's government. It now all rested on whether Robert Berruda would finally accept the plan.

Peter knew it could fall flat on its face. Then they could lose the payments made to Tim and Nirina. But that was George's risk, He had made the statement that only people with a lot of money are able to make with a straight face, 'It's only money.'

A couple of days after his meeting with Tim, Peter had followed up the other leads. He had found that Max Ryder was long gone. No one knew what had happened to him. He had not been seen for years. But Rudi Van Haute was in Hong Kong. Peter was amused at how easy it was to find someone who had the reputation of being a well known assassin. Peter phoned Rudi Van Haute's room and arranged to meet him in the coffee shop.

Rudi was a survivor. He had been in the business for more than fifteen years. He was short, lightly built and had the smooth rounded features so typical of many Dutchmen. Apart from wisps of hair above his ears and around his neck, he was bald. He spoke English with that unmistakable and attractive Dutch accent in which the s's are slightly slurred and the r's have an Irish or American twang. Rudi was forty three and in his younger days had been a member of the Amsterdam police force.

No one seemed to know how he got started. He had a reputation for getting the job done. He spoke, English, French, Spanish and German. Peter knew of him from his Special Services days. Rudi had been linked to a number of disappearances of prominent people. However, there had never been enough evidence to convict him and on a couple of occasions, after he had been arrested, political pressure was brought to bear and he was released. Rudi had some powerful friends.

Rudi often worked legitimately as a body guard. Everyone who hired him knew that in a tight spot he would not hesitate to pull the trigger and worry about the consequences later. He was a good man to have on your team.

Peter entered the busy coffee shop and joined Rudi who was already sitting at a table against the wall. "Good morning," Peter greeted him.

"Hi there," Rudi replied.

"I believe you may be able to help me."

"I'm always pleased to help someone. What can I do for you?" Rudi asked.

"I knew your name when I served in the British Special Services. I also think you know Tim Serenson. He's working with me."

"Yes, I know Tim. What help do you need?"

"Can you go down to Marseilles for us—to deliver some cash and ensure we get some cooperation from a guy who's working for us ?"

"When do you want me to go?"

"Next week?" Peter replied.

"Why don't you tell me exactly what you want and I can get back to you in a day or so."

Peter explained what was required and gave Rudi the faxed copy of the photograph and newspaper article. They agreed the address to which George would send the cash. Rudi excused himself from the table and left. Peter felt unsatisfied. A fifteen minute virtually monosyllabic conversation did not provide sufficient reassurance. Rudi said very little. Peter had not expected an instant answer, the guy had not survived in his business without checking out who he worked for. But the delay would be a nuisance. Peter left the coffee shop concluding that Rudi was not being hired for his conversation. Anyone working as a professional killer had to be different.

• • •

Nirina's house was typical of the older, more expensive village houses in the South of France. It faced directly onto the street, perhaps only twenty feet back from the sidewalk. It was built with tall narrow windows, flanked by wooden shutters. It was finished in rough pink painted stucco and surrounded by a low wall topped with spiked metal railings. The space between the wall and the house provided a barrier, a little like a moat, but instead of being filled with water, it was crammed with a thick growth of lush shrubs and trees which grew well in the warm Mediterranean climate.

Rudi had been in Marseilles for two days, most of his time spent watching the house. He had called Nirina's office twice. Once posing as a courier service needing to deliver a package requiring a signature, and once as a potential customer wishing to make a date to meet with Nirina. Rudi had confirmed that Nirina was going to be around all day Wednesday and Thursday. The chances were that he would be at home on Wednesday evening. On Tuesday Rudi had followed Mrs. Ghose. She took the kids to school in the morning and picked them up again in the afternoon. He knew from Sarah's research that only the family lived in the house, no nannies or live in help.

He had remained near the house on Wednesday watching the activity and had seen Mrs. Ghose bring the kids home. At about seven Nirina returned from his office, drove through the open gates and around the back of the house, Rudi heard the car door slam and a few seconds later Nirina appeared and closed the gates. It looked like a night at home for the Ghose's. Rudi decided he would wait until a little later in the evening, when the kids would be in bed.

Rudi rang the doorbell. The door was opened by Mrs Ghose, she was still wearing the bright blue, silk dress she had been wearing when she collected the kids in the afternoon.

"Bonsoir Monsieur." The greeting was relaxed and the door was held wide open. There was nothing to suggest any caution.

"Bonsoir," Rudi replied. He was carrying a molded fiberglass brief case and as he responded, he placed it down in the doorway stopping the door from closing. He was going in, invited or not. He reached into his pocket and took out a business card, which showed his name as Jacques Dupres, a Private Investigator from Lyons. He handed it to Mrs. Ghose and speaking in French asked to see Nirina. It could not have been easier. He was invited in, the front door was closed behind him and he followed Mrs. Ghose into a sitting room.

He quickly sized up the room as he entered. There were curtains drawn along one wall, which from his external survey on Tuesday he knew covered windows. The wall along the left hand side of the room had a fireplace with a closed door to the right of it. A wing chair was placed on each side of the fireplace. Nirina was sitting in the one facing him reading a newspaper. There was a couch between Rudi and Nirina facing the fireplace and a small table was positioned at one end of the couch. A heavy glass vase full of flowers was sitting on it. Rudi looked for a telephone but could not see one. There was no sign of the children. He assumed they were in bed. Rudi entered the room, knowing it would look odd when he closed the door behind him but he had to try and keep any noise from disturbing the kids. It might make the Ghose's uneasy, but the door had to be closed.

Mrs Ghose handed the business card to her husband and introduced Rudi, "Nirina, Monsieur Dupres, he's a private detective from Lyons," she smiled and added, "what have you been up to?"

"A private detective?" Nirina folded the paper and looked down at the card. Without standing up he waved in the direction of the couch.

"I don't know what I've done," he answered his wife's question and then addressed Rudi, "Do sit down Monsieur, how can I help you?"

Rudi did not sit down. He remained standing between the Ghoses and the door through which he had entered. He could not be sure where the door by the fireplace might lead, but he had to cut off any access to the door behind him.

"I believe you had a meeting with an Englishman at the Restaurant Trois Forts and that you're expecting an initial payment for the contract you agreed."

By the time Rudi had finished the sentence Nirina was looking shaken and was becoming angry. He moved as if to stand up. Mrs. Ghose sensing that all was not well, moved closer to her husband and further away from the door. Rudi had to assume that Nirina still did not want to work for Peter and the task was going to be difficult. Rudi had hoped he might be able to hand over the cash to a willing recipient and that Peter's fears were not justified. Rudi remained close to Mrs. Ghose as she stood by her husband's chair. He had to take control and quickly put a stop to any resistance. In a single sweeping movement he swung the brief case, clasped in his left hand, upwards and forwards until the flat surface delivered a glancing blow full in Mrs. Ghose's face. He then let his arm fall back towards the ground and half dropped and half placed the brief case on the floor.

His action was so sudden and unexpected that the brief case made contact before Mrs. Ghose could even raise a hand to protect herself. She exhaled making a slight grunting sound and fell backwards sprawling on the couch with blood oozing from her nose. Nirina had almost finished rising from the chair but was still off balance when Rudi planted his now empty left hand squarely in Nirina's chest and pushed him back. At the same time he drew the silenced pistol from the holster under his left arm and by the time Nirina settled back in the chair the pistol was firmly pushed into Rudi's left cheek. Mrs. Ghose began to groan. She was clasping her nose with both hands trying to prevent the blood from running down her face. The blow had not been hard enough to break her nose, but the edge of the case had caught her forehead. A bruise was already forming, getting darker and swelling by the second. Rudi grabbed Nirina by the collar, the pistol's silencer still pushed into the side of his face, dragged him out of the chair and pushed him onto the couch beside his wife. Rudi stood back.

"Sit still and look after your wife. Don't stand up!" Rudi ordered. As he said it he grabbed the vase of flowers and poured the flowers and the water onto a cushion in the chair in which Rudi had been sitting and rolled the vase away towards the far corner of the room. He picked up the now saturated cushion and threw it at Nirina, "Use that!"

Nirina flinched and raised his hands to protect himself from whatever Rudi had thrown. He just managed to catch the wet cushion. He looked at Rudi with a helpless expression on his face.

"Stop the bleeding! Use the cushion!" Rudi instructed.

Nirina began to try and wipe the blood from his wife's face and dress with the entire cushion.

"For Christ's sake tear it up. Take the cover off. Use some common sense!"

Finally, as Nirina began to recover from the attack and began thinking again he tore off the cushion cover and applied the cold wet cloth to the bridge of his wife's nose. In the lull Rudi listened, there was no sound from the children. While Nirina was occupied assisting his wife, Rudi stepped behind the couch and with his left hand he roughly wrenched a handful of Mrs Ghoses's long black hair. He dropped to his knees jerking her head backwards and downwards against the back of the couch. She cried out and Nirina dropped the cloth as her head was pulled away from him. Rudi almost gently placed the muzzle of the pistol against her temple. Nirina twisted round on the couch as if to get up and Rudi quickly delivered a blow to the side of his head with the fist holding the pistol. It hurt his knuckles but it knocked Nirina down against the end of the couch. The Heckler and Koch pistol itself was not particularly heavy, but the silencer and the eighteen rounds in the magazine added nearly twelve ounces to the weight and provided a substantial club.

"Keep still, we don't want you injured. If you move again I'll shoot your wife!"

Now that Rudi had them both on the couch and still had his grip on Mrs. Ghose's hair he felt the situation was under control.

"I've got your initial payment of fifty thousand dollars in that brief case. I'll need you to be ready to travel in two weeks...I'll deliver the tickets and escort you to the plane. There'll be no notice, just be ready to go in two weeks. Do you understand?"

Nirina nodded, none of the arrogance showed now, even though he had begun to regain his composure.

"You'll be paid the remainder of the two hundred and fifty thousand dollars when you get back here and if you have been successful a bonus of $250,000. That was the deal wasn't it?"

Rudi nodded.

"If you finish on time you'll be back here in five or six weeks. According to our mutual employer I'm the benefit package. I make sure that your wife and family are well protected while you're away." As Rudi mentioned Nirina's wife, he gave another tug on her hair. "Am I to assume you will be working with us?"

"Yes, I will work with you." Nirina replied in a whisper.

Mrs. Ghose had not said a word since she had introduced Rudi. "Do we have your cooperation Mrs. Ghose?"

"Yes, just leave us alone!"

"Don't be worried. So long as your husband does what is expected of him you should look on me as a friend of the family. I'll be around while Nirina's away just to look after you and your children."

"Don't you dare touch the children!"

Rudi pulled her hair a little tighter and pushed the gun into her temple, "I won't be touching anybody if your husband behaves himself. I think you should have a long talk with him after I leave this evening. Your children's health is entirely in his hands."

Rudi looked at Nirina, "Open the brief case!"

The case was on the floor where Rudi had dropped it. Nirina could reach it, but he did not want to risk getting up off the couch. He leaned back and pulled it closer with the edge of his foot. When it was within easy reach he picked it up.

"Don't pick it up, open it on the floor." Rudi instructed.

Nirina did as he was told. He bent over and opened the case on the floor by his feet. He saw the neat bundles of hundred dollar notes.

"Take the money and sign the receipt. There's a pen in the case."

"Sign the receipt?" Suddenly the entire situation seemed unreal to Nirina, "Sign the receipt! You come in here and threaten us. You're holding a gun to my wife's head and now you want a receipt. How do I know how much money's there?"

"Would you like time to count it?" Rudi asked without any expectation of a positive answer. "Just sign the receipt and take the money Mr. Ghose, before I begin to think you're doubting my honesty."

Nirina picked up the neatly typed receipt and the pen and signed it. He threw the receipt back in the case and picked up the cash.

"Now close the case, leave it on the floor and push it away from you."

Nirina obeyed, his resistance had gone, "Leave us alone, I will do the job for you. I 'll be ready in two weeks." Rudi could see he had achieved what he had come for.

"Good! Welcome aboard. I'm sure you'll enjoy your time with us."

Rudi released his grip on Mrs. Ghose's hair, moved cautiously around the front of the couch and picked up the case without taking his eyes off them. He backed toward the door and was gone.

Chapter 13

Peter left Hong Kong and returned to Nairobi via Bombay. He had just a few days to reorganize his life, before he was due to meet George in Bakaar.

Peter made a date to meet with Julius Sifolo as Berruda had requested. Peter had met Julius back when he helped Robert Berruda deal with his opposition. Julius had remained Berruda's right hand man and he was now the Minister of the Interior. Peter had made a point of seeing him whenever he was in Rapanda and the two men were if not friends, acquaintances.

The final jolt as the captain applied the brakes upon arrival at the parking space sparked off the usual desperation in the few passengers to leave the aircraft. Those who could, got out of their seats, stretched across those who could not, to retrieve their possessions from the overhead lockers and then crouched, baggage in hand to try and see out the windows. Peter knew it would take a while. Nothing happened quickly in Africa and the wait for the airstairs was the reminder Peter needed to slow down. He remained seated quietly.

As he walked down the stairs, nearly twenty minutes after the Boeing had arrived on the ramp, he felt the nostalgia wash over him as it did every time he returned to a backwater in Africa. In Rapanda, the clarity of the air could be felt. It reminded him of his childhood. It did not matter whether it was day or night, the sky was brighter and clearer and Peter always had a sense of going back.

There were now cities in Africa where progress had made it difficult to tell which continent you were on. Nairobi was one of those. Whatever the reason, Nairobi was more like Europe than Africa. But in Rapanda it was not only the unpolluted air that sparked Peter's nostalgia. It was the familiarity, the look and feel of a British town. Rapanda was designed and built in the days when Bakaar was a colony—a member of the British Empire. The buildings looked as if they had been picked up in England a hundred years ago by a giant hand and placed on the African coast. It had changed little in that hundred years. There were few private cars but most of the cabs in Rapanda were early sixties, pre-independence British cars. Austins, Morris Oxfords and the odd Ford. The cars of Peter's youth. Many of them had little original paint, broken windows and the upholstery was torn and patched.

All of the privately owned vehicles were maintained by a form of cannibalism. Spare parts were bought at the open air roadside markets from the owners of vehicles which had finally given up the ghost. In the inflationary economy of Bakaar, the owner of a defunct vehicle would often receive more from selling the parts than he paid for the original car. It was the final return on the original investment, not sufficient to replace the car, but enough cash to feed the family for a few more months.

Peter walked out on to the street. As soon as the cab drivers caught sight of the arriving passengers emerging from the terminal building they began to shout and wave to attract customers. Peter was virtually assaulted by an aggressive, ragged young man, the proud owner of a broken down 1962 Morris Oxford. The young cabbie grabbed Peter's bag and reluctant to let go, Peter was dragged towards the awaiting antique. The driver tugged the front passenger door open and Peter half fell and was half pushed into the sagging patched seat. Having caught his customer, the young man unceremoniously threw Peter's luggage onto the back seat.

Before he was subjected to the, 'Do you want a tour of Rapanda?' routine, Peter told the driver his destination in Witumbi which immediately labeled Peter as someone other than a tourist and stopped any more selling. It also disappointed the young cabbie who would have been better off with another passenger, perhaps one of the now rare tourists who could have been sold the grand tour and who would have been good for a big tip. Silence fell, the starter whined and the old car coughed into life. Peter was on his way to the faded Presidential Hotel.

But choosing Peter as opposed to a tourist was not all bad news. The cabbie was a Bwani, spoke both languages and had understood Peter's request. Peter did not know there was growing unrest just beneath the surface and that it was becoming more organized. Peter's fluency in Witumbi meant that the cabbie could earn something simply by reporting Peter's arrival and his language skill to the local Bwani militia.

The temperature was still in the high seventies and Peter enjoyed the certainty that it would be well over eighty-five degrees Fahrenheit every day during his stay. Until May rainfall is unusual and recently this had remained the pattern for most of the year. So long as hot, dry weather was to your liking, Bakaar was a great place to be.

Peter's most important task was to set up a meeting with Robert Berruda for himself and George as soon as possible. He unpacked and spent a couple of hours making notes and sorting out his timetable. He hoped to make a date with Berruda within the next week or so.

"Hello Peter, my friend, when did you arrive?" Julius responded as Peter announced himself on the phone early the next morning...

"I got in yesterday and I need a favor."

"What can I do to assist you?" Julius asked. Julius had been briefed by Berruda following the phone call with George. All of the details would be handled by Julius.

"I'd rather meet with you to discuss it. How are you fixed today?"

"I'm free this morning, how about meeting down at the old Colonial Club at the marina, at about…when can you make it?"

"Around eleven." Peter replied.

"O.K. I'll see you in the bar."

Peter assumed that George Barnard was now in London. He needed to know how Rudi's visit to Nirina had gone and felt it was time to check in. He called Rudi to confirm if his visit had paid off. Yes, Nirina was ready to leave for Africa. Peter called and told George the good news and George confirmed that given a day or two's notice, he would come to Rapanda to meet with Berruda.

After the call to George, Peter headed for the hotel desk to see where he would find the Jeep Wrangler he had rented when he reserved the hotel room. Peter knew of the trouble that had been brewing and of the shooting spree that occurred in Rapanda when George visited and he was interested to see if Berruda's action had eased or worsened the tension.

Peter was told the Jeep was parked behind the hotel waiting for him. He completed the paperwork at the desk and went to inspect his rental. As soon as he saw it he wished he had inspected it before signing. It must have been ten years old and looked as if it had been driven across the Sahara.

He knew only too well that he would not be able to swap it today, if at all, and with some misgivings, convinced himself it would be alright. As he drove the two miles down to the harbor to meet with Julius, he saw the soldiers guarding the banks. The traditional policeman outside the police barracks had been increased to about half a dozen, and barriers had been erected around the building.

When he arrived at the harbor, within sight of the club, the road was blocked by another barrier manned by soldiers. Peter stopped behind a car that was being slowly and laboriously searched. When it was finally waved on its way, one of the soldiers beckoned him through with a friendly wave, not requesting him to stop. He drove on and parked behind the club building. He noticed a police car parked outside the front door, the driver lazily leaning against the passenger door avoiding the heat in the car. As he entered the building it was eleven fifteen. The club was situated at the back of what had been the commercial dock during the British colonial days. Over the past few years there had been attempts to improve the area and there were now a few private boats tied up in the limpid, oily water. The dock was now called the Marina and it was the exclusive domain of the Witumbis. The building had been constructed by the British military and in the days of Empire was the officer's mess for the occupying regiment. It was well built of bricks, with a tile roof, and would have been more in keeping in Aldershot, the Home of the British Army, than in modern day Rapanda.

It was not air conditioned, but the small windows and the large paddle fans hanging from the vaulted ceiling did a good job and even with the temperature inside hitting eighty five it was reasonably comfortable. Julius was sitting dressed in just a shirt and pants at one of the circular cane tables with another Bakaaran, who, in spite of the heat, wore a jacket. Peter did not recognize him. As he approached the table both men stood up and as Julius moved forward, the other man stepped back and sat at another table just a few feet away.

"It's nice to see you again, Peter my friend," Julius greeted him, shaking hands, "I understand we may now relax and that Mr. Barnard will cater to all of our needs!" Julius was obviously referring to the reasons why George Barnard and Peter were going to meet with Berruda. Peter had been told he could discuss anything with Julius, but this cynical greeting suggested there might be less support for the plan from Julius than George had suggested.

"Seems things are less settled than when I was here last." Peter observed wanting to know the cause of the currently increased security.

"Things have become more tense my friend. We've had a couple of unpleasant incidents over the past few weeks. Just showing the flag as you British would say."

"Who's your friend?" Peter nodded towards the Bakaaran sitting at the nearby table, "Is he prejudiced?"

Julius laughed, "He's not a racist either. He's my…eh, assistant." Julius could not bring himself to say bodyguard, it would be a loss of face to admit to Peter, a foreigner, that he needed a bodyguard. In deference to Julius, Peter let it go.

A waiter came over to the table, tray in hand. "Will you have a drink?" Julius asked.

"Yeah, I'll have a beer," Peter replied.

Julius was far from the usual Bakaaran and did not need to spend hours on small talk before getting down to business. "How can I help you?"

"I need to make a date for myself and George Barnard to meet with Robert Berruda." Peter replied.

"When do you want to meet him?"

"As soon as possible."

"As you have seen, we have some problems and Robert has been very busy, but he is here next week. Could Mr. Barnard come out next week?" Julius answered.

"I thought you'd sorted out the problems?" Peter asked ignoring the question.

"No, the Bwanis are becoming more vocal. The economy's in bad shape and they think we're weakening. They've been trying to gain support by showing they are not afraid to oppose us. They shot up one of the Minister's cars when he was on his way home the other night…they're flexing their muscles. If we have any hope of survival we have to stop it now. So, we must show we're prepared to respond with force. We have to raise the stakes."

Peter continued, "Well we've got some news we think the President will want to hear. Following President Berruda's discussion with George, we think we can put the project together and persuade the United States to pay Bakaar the $1 billion in direct aid—cash!"

Julius eyes opened wider and he showed interest, the Government needed a boost in popularity for Robert Berruda to remain in power. If the President was able to offer the Bwanis in Rapanda a better chance for jobs and medical care and provide enough food for those in the rural areas, he could stop the rot.

"Over what period would they offer the aid and what strings would be attached?"

"No strings whatsoever, we go for it all at once."

"No strings?" Julius looked doubtful and his cynicism returned." I guess this is going to be the deal of the century! My friend, if Bakaar receives $1 billion in a single payment without strings, it would indeed be a miracle." Julius laughed.

Peter felt that he had said enough.

"Which of your colleagues do you wish to join you?" Julius asked.

"Just George Barnard," Peter replied.

Julius did not respond and his attention began to wander.

"Is the police car here with you?" Peter asked feeling the need to say something. The club was beginning to get busy, the elite of Bakaar met here at weekend lunchtimes and Julius had nodded to a number of people as they entered and filled the surrounding tables. Julius' 'assistant' had moved from his table to make way for the increasing number of patrons and to improve his view of the room. He was now leaning against a column.

"Yes, I came in it," Julius answered automatically. He was becoming more distracted and uncomfortable as the bar filled. Suddenly, he looked straight at Peter, "O.K. meet with us next week, I'll arrange a date with Robert today. When will Mr. Barnard arrive?"

"How about Tuesday?"

"I will try and arrange Tuesday." Julius was becoming more uneasy as the bustle increased and he beckoned to his assistant. "I'm leaving and Mr. Williamson will leave with us."

As he spoke, the familiar and increasing background hum of voices, laughter and chairs scraping on the hard tile floor, was shattered by the sound of an impact. It sounded like a car crash, followed immediately by distant shouting. At the same time there was an increasing roar from the street outside. A car or truck was approaching the club at high speed. There were several short bursts of automatic gunfire.

A car containing two men had driven straight onto the dock, hitting the metal barrier and scattering the soldiers. One man drove the car, the other sat in the rear seat on the drivers side with the window lowered. It could have been Chicago in the thirties, but in place of the gangsters' Tommy gun, the passenger was wielding a Kalashnikov automatic rifle.

The car sped on towards the club one or two of the startled soldiers fired at the fast receding car others fired into the air. The soldiers dusted themselves off and re-assembled at the broken barrier. As the car drew level with the entrance to the club the passenger opened fire and allowed the speed of the car to rake the entrance to the building as it passed. In less than two seconds the magazine was empty, but in that time thirty rounds had hit four or five people around the door including the policeman who had been leaning against Julius' car. The car had also been hit in several places. One round smashed the windshield.

As the sound of the gunfire burst into the club Julius' bodyguard rushed towards them knocking tables and people aside as he went. As he ran, Peter could see an Uzi machine pistol swinging from a long strap under his jacket. By the time he reached their table, both Julius and Peter were flat on the floor. During the burst of fire several bullets had entered the room through the open door. The flat 'plop' as they struck the columns and woodwork seemed harmless in comparison with the raucous noise from the gun outside, focussing the danger in the wrong place. As the gunfire stopped, panic erupted. The bodyguard was crouching protectively over Peter and Julius, facing the door and now had the Uzi firmly gripped in both hands.

No one inside the club knew how the attack was launched, no one knew who was waiting outside, but people were running for the exits. Some, in their panic, even ran towards the open door through which the bullets had entered.

As Peter lay on the floor he was not entirely sure if Julius' bodyguard offered protection or whether he added to the danger. If the attackers came into the building and were after Julius, it gave them some protection. But if the first people through the door were the police or soldiers, how would they know that the guy waving the Uzi was on their side. Peter remembered the times in the past when innocent people had been killed by confusion and nervous, trigger happy troops. He felt that it was a good idea when conflicting armies had their positions marked out on the battlefield and wore distinctive uniforms.

The noise of the car's engine receded into the distance and no one followed the bullets into the building. And as if to answer Peter's unspoken thoughts, both Julius and his assistant were struggling to remove something from their pockets while still lying on the floor. Julius managed to remove a package from his trouser pocket and shook out a bright green, nylon vest which he succeeded in stretching over his head and pulled down over his shirt. The bodyguard was trying to retain access to the Uzi as he pulled the vest over his head. On the back of the vests the letters 'SP' were printed in black.

The sound of sirens was now wafting in from the street and two soldiers who had been at the barrier ran into the club. As they entered, Julius' bodyguard cautiously waved the Uzi in the air. On seeing the vests, the soldiers made straight for them and one spoke quickly, in Witumbi. Peter knew enough to understand.

"It was a car…they fired from a passing car…they've gone now it's all clear outside…it's O.K."

They all stood up and cautiously walked out, shadowed by the body-guard who seemed far from convinced that all was well. By the time they reached the road there were several police cars, a truck full of soldiers and the crew of an ambulance was beginning to tend to several people who had been hit.

Julius' car was in no condition to provide transport and they were all bundled into another police car and driven off at top speed towards the Government buildings. Bakaar had changed in a short time, but Peter had to believe it was probably to his advantage so long as it did not get much worse, too quickly.

Chapter 14

Peter met George at the airport on Monday afternoon. On the drive back, knowing it was unlikely to have made the news in England, Peter described the shooting at the club. By the time Julius, President Berruda's right hand man, arrived at the hotel on Tuesday morning, both George and Peter were convinced that Robert Berruda had little to look forward to except probable loss of office. It would not be long before the problems grew to the point where he could be overthrown. The threat was real and with a worsening economy and little improvement to offer, the end would be inevitable.

Julius arrived in a police car, escorted by another containing four security guards. Peter and George rode in the car with Julius and they headed into the center of Rapanda. The car pulled up at the Presidential Palace, Peter and George followed Julius into the building and were ushered into a waiting room. Julius went on, presumably to confer with Berruda. Regardless of George's friendship with the President, it was traditional that they would be kept waiting. It was seen as part of the display of power, not so much to impress the visitors, but more to demonstrate to the aides and staff in the building that their President was powerful.

George and Peter said little as they waited. After only twenty minutes Hassan Maalin, Berruda's private secretary appeared with a security officer, apologized for the need, and asked if they would object to being searched and proceeded to pat them down. After they had been frisked he led them into Robert Berruda's office.

It was a large, imperial, opulent room conflicting with the man of the people image Berruda tried so hard to cultivate. A massive desk sat in the center which Peter guessed was French, from the time of Napoleon. The legs and frame of the desk were golden, it might have been gold paint, but Peter thought it looked more like gold leaf. The top was covered in unmarked, dark red leather and apart from a set of antique ink wells and a statuette of a toiling African, the top was bare. The floor was covered with oriental rugs and the walls were decorated with Bakaaran art—carved masks and paintings.

Robert Berruda stood up and smiled. He was dressed in a very non-African pin stripe Saville Row Suit. He acknowledged Peter, "Good morning gentlemen. First I must apologize for the incident on Saturday, I am pleased you were not injured." He then turned to George, "It's nice to see you again George."

"And you." George replied.

"Please be seated," Robert Berruda waved his hand toward the chairs spread around the front of his desk and George and Peter sat down. Julius and Hassan walked away to one side and sat down slightly behind them.

George began. "We've done a great deal of homework since we spoke last. We will be able to do it."

"Good. What is the timetable?" Berruda asked.

"We should have everything in place by early July. But we must operate out of Bakkar. We'll require premises, labor we can trust and proper documents…"

"Yes, I would imagine we can do that." Berruda cut across George and was looking uncomfortable. "Julius will provide you with whatever you need. He knows of our conversation and is aware of the action you intend to take."

Berruda stood up, nervously straightened his tie and brushed down an immaculate jacket. George was surprised, Berruda was distant, not enthusiastic. He was, without a doubt, uneasy.

Julius spoke first, "We'll go to my office if you have a little more time."

In his enthusiasm to relay the news it had never occurred to George that Berruda would remove himself from the action. Berruda had cut off the conversation before there was any discussion of the details. Berruda gave the operation his apparent blessing but Julius was going to be the political fall guy. This plan was in the hands of the Ministry of the Interior. If all went wrong Julius would take the heat and Berruda could walk away. If it succeeded, Berruda would take the credit and the up-side for Julius was probably a few million dollars!

They were ushered into an office at the end of the corridor.

"We can talk in here, we are alone and I will not record the meeting," Julius reassured them with a fleeting smile as he sat down at the desk.

"Obviously Robert cannot discuss the subject any further. I will handle the details. The President will not be involved, but I can assure you that he will be working with us and we have his support."

Peter was surprised that they had even met with Berruda. He was used to dealing with the cousin, brother or trusted aide. Peter had experience of the problems created when politicians tried to distance themselves from particular actions or policies. There were dangers for all concerned.

They sat down, more comfortably than with Berruda, jackets were removed, cold drinks were served and George and Peter laid out the plan. Bakaar would provide a secure location, capable of use as a laboratory. Julius suggested the old fertilizer plant a few miles outside Rapanda. It was still in use but there was a good deal of unused space.

George and Peter confirmed they had recruited the expertise required to manufacture the VX nerve gas. And that they would develop a simple explosive device capable of dispersing the gas over an area the size of a city block. The bomb would have to be constructed in Bakaar, then disassembled and transported piecemeal into the U.S.

Peter's team would assemble it in a high rise building in New York and it would be designed to be detonated remotely. Once the device was in place, Berruda would have the means of creating wholesale panic in the city and by careful manipulation of information could probably create panic across the entire country. As George explained they would never have to reach the point of detonating it. It was unlikely that its existence would ever become public knowledge.

The U.S. government could never allow such a threat to become public. If it were, it would demonstrate their vulnerability and confirm that it was impossible to defend against such an act. If publicized it would be the precursor to a myriad of copycats. It would be a repeat of the aircraft hijacking spree of the seventies.

When a societal threshold is breached those less desperate or less courageous than the original perpetrators are prepared to follow and use what they now perceive as an acceptable means to their end. Nerve gas in a city had not yet been unleashed on the Western World, or at least not made public. That threshold had not yet been passed. Bakaar's action could destabilize the West and quite apart from kicking off this unholy means to an end, it might be the catalyst that hardened attitudes in Iraq, Libya and the other hot spots of the world. There was also the potential for escalation. Bakaar's threat would be a real disaster for a city block, but relied more on fear, the unknown and being first. The escalation could be multiple locations and even atomic bombs in city centers. It could be the beginning of the Third World War, the war between the have's and have not's. It was in everyone's best interest, particularly the U.S.A., to keep it quiet.

George and Peter had little doubt that the success of the venture was timing. It had to be done quickly. Regardless of the fact that they thought they were the first they could not be certain. Sooner or later, someone was going to do it, in some form or other. It no longer required the massive cost of the arms race, no longer the delicate maintenance of a balance of terror. Now any little country could produce and deliver massive damage to a densely populated city. Regardless of their plan to use nerve gas the availability of both expertise and material following the breakup of the Soviet Union made it inevitable.

They discussed the details of the plan with Julius and the risks were assessed. They had to be careful how they assembled both the team and the material. If the U.S got to know what was going on, they would try and stop it covertly by any means available. Security was going to be the name of the game and Peter knew, even assuming success, there were dangers far beyond the success or failure of the venture itself. Berruda might try to cut off the risk of any post operation leaks and the U.S.A. would not take kindly to parting with a billion dollars.

On the other hand Peter mused, aid would acquire a completely new look at the beginning of the millennium—the underdeveloped nations making a play for their share of the peace dividend. It would be a case of first come first served. The end of the cold war, far from providing greater stability would be seen to have returned the world to the tinder box of the sixties. The Americans knew, and they expected they would have to maintain the delicate peace by balancing their ability to use military power on the one hand with cash and aid on the other. The Iraqis, Iranians and even the Libyans were now in a more powerful position than ever before. All they have to do is be prepared to strike the match and the result would be the same as if the Soviets had launched a missile. The little guys possessed more power than they had ever imagined possible.

Peter thought back to the seventies and the massive oil price increase demanded by the Arabs. It was unacceptable, but in the end the potential damage if the West took aggressive action was considered an even greater problem. The West objected but paid up. The financial structure of the world was changed forever. The action Peter and George intended to take would be different, but in principal it had been done before. As if he had read Peter's thoughts George was on the same subject.

"On a smaller scale, we believe that the Chilean grape incident may have been a successful payoff," he said to Julius.

"What was the Chilean grape incident?" Julius asked, puzzled.

"The U.S. imports a large portion of the Chilean grape harvest. Some years ago, two people were poisoned eating the grapes. There was an immediate ban on imports and much of the crop already in the U.S. was destroyed. However, almost as soon as it started, the grapes were back on the shelves and a very positive statement was made by the Government that all was well. No prosecution followed, no explanation. We believe there was a demand for payment not to poison or to identify what was poisoned. We think the U.S. paid."

"So we may not be the first," Julius responded.

"We'll never know!" George smiled.

Chapter 15

George and Peter were pleased with the outcome of their meeting with Berruda. They were headed back to the hotel and it was just becoming dark as they turned on to the wide, deserted road that ran along by the park.

An old Ford Zephyr had been following them most of the way from the Ministry and it made the turn behind them. It was not unusual to be followed. Most of the old cars had little power left in their two and three hundred thousand mile engines. The lack of power and broken roads did not provide an opportunity for overtaking. Peter was driving and paid little attention to the old car.

There was a screech of tires from behind and the Ford disappeared out of Peter's rear view mirror. In just seconds it was alongside, passing them at a speed that defied belief. Peter glanced towards it. There were four men dressed in T-shirts. All except the driver were watching the Jeep. As the Ford began to pull ahead, Peter saw the driver adjusting his grip on the steering wheel.

Peter could see it coming, they were going to either cut in front or side swipe him. He shouted to George, "Hang on! We've got trouble!"

He hit the brakes as hard as he could. The Jeep skidded and fell back from the Ford, just as the driver pulled the wheel hard to the left to cut across in front. Peter swerved to the right, the Jeep rolled badly and passed by the tail end of the Ford which now had its near side wheels off the road, spewing out clouds of dust. The driver, having missed the target, was trying to get back on the black top.

Peter managed to control the Jeep and kept going. He had missed the turn to the hotel and was heading out away from the city. The road had rapidly deteriorated and there was little habitation. Peter looked in his rear view mirror, the Ford burst out from the cloud of dust as the driver regained the road and was closing fast. The Jeep roared and whined as Peter pushed it to over sixty, its worn four wheel drive screeching in complaint.

The Ford was catching up and Peter could go no faster.

"Who in the hell are they?" George shouted above the whining of the transmission.

"God knows, they were following us from the Ministry! Got any ideas—they're going to catch up!" Peter shouted back.

As he spoke the old Zephyr pulled alongside again. The passenger in the front seat pointed a pistol out the window and signaled for Peter to slow down.

"You're going have to stop!" George said, hanging onto his hurriedly fastened seat belt. "If we keep going they'll start shooting. If we stop we may be able to talk to them. We have to stop."

The pistol was being waved more aggressively and Peter removed his foot from the gas pedal. The high pitched whine from the transmission dropped an octave and the Jeep began to slow down. The Ford remained a little ahead and slowed with the Jeep. The dusk had quickly become dark and there was no sign of any other traffic.

As the Jeep slowed, Peter pulled it off the blacktop, braked and stopped.

The doors of the Ford flew open and three of its occupants ran back to the Jeep. The front seat passenger still brandishing his pistol, the other two had automatic rifles.

"Out of the car! Get out of the car!' the pistol brandishing youth shouted standing off about ten feet from the side of the Jeep. The rifles were leveled at George and Peter and even if Peter had been armed there would have been little point in putting up a fight.

Peter climbed out keeping his hands conspicuously in sight, George did the same from his side of the vehicle. As soon as they were clear of the Jeep, they were grabbed by the rifle carriers, and pushed to the ground. A rough body search convinced their captors that neither George nor Peter was armed. The pistol owner rummaged in the Jeep and found George's brief case.

"In the car!" The pistol pointed in the direction of the Ford.

George and Peter were bundled in and squashed between two of the gang in the rear seat. The front doors slammed and the car roared into life heading away from Rapanda.

Peter and George said nothing as their four captors spoke to each other quickly and desperately during the journey in what Peter knew to be the Bwani language, but he could not understand most of what was said. The car turned off the broken highway onto a dirt road and a several miles further on turned again and continued for two or three miles. In the dark all Peter could ascertain was that they were perhaps eight or ten miles out of town. Peter saw some dim lights ahead and as they grew closer he could see they were a group of houses and buildings, almost a small village. The driver turned into the open area between the mud brick houses, lit by kerosene lamps. The car stopped and George and Peter were pulled out and led towards a building that looked like a barn. One of their captors took a lamp off its hook on the outside of the building and lit their way inside. George and Peter were handcuffed to a metal bar secured in the wall above what appeared to be an animal trough. Once secured they were left alone and the Bwanis retreated to one of the houses taking the lamp and George's brief case. They were left alone in the darkness.

"What the hell's going on?" George asked Peter as if he might know and as if it were his fault.

"I have no idea! Just feel lucky. If they wanted to kill us, I think it would have been done by now. My guess is they want information—but about what?"

"I'm trying to remember what's in my case," George said, thinking what value it might have to the Bwanis and whether it would be a problem for him. "My passport's in there. My calendar will show the meeting with Berruda."

"Damn!" Peter exclaimed. "I don't think that's good!"

Peter and George slid their handcuffs down the bar and sat on the edge of the trough.

There were sounds of conversation and argument coming from the houses. An hour passed. Peter had no clue as to what these people wanted. If only he knew the motive behind their capture he would at least know what not to say when the time came.

Suddenly the distant noise of voices drifting in from the house increased and light from the lamps bobbed around as they were carried toward the barn which was now Peter and George's prison.

Eight or ten men entered the barn, most carrying lamps. The four who had captured them were still carrying their weapons. The remainder were older–mostly in their forties and fifties, one man was probably sixty. Their faces were gaunt, the deep shifting shadows cast by their lamps exaggerated their hollow cheeks and sunken eyes. They all wore ragged jackets or sweaters and some had blankets draped around their shoulders, seemingly to keep warm. It was still far from cold but they looked hungry.

One of the older men approached George, "Who are you?" he asked in good English.

George felt relieved for no better reason than that they could at least talk to each other, "George Barnard and this is Peter Williamson." George responded not knowing what else to say, but guessing this was not the answer they sought.

"Why are you here in Rapanda?"

"We came to meet with your Government."

The young man with the pistol pushed forward out of the group and speaking agitatedly to the questioner in Bwani, grabbed Peter and pointed the pistol at his temple.

"What do you do with our Government?" the young man screamed in his face.

Peter had decided they were not a bunch of thugs, but the youngsters were like coiled springs. Say the wrong thing or even move in the wrong direction and one of these guys could pull the trigger. Peter did not underestimate the gravity of their situation. Apart from the fact that he and George had been forcibly removed from their car, they had not been badly treated and some of their captors' English was better than they would have learned at high school. Peter was prepared to bet they were in the presence of the leadership of the Bwani militia. He had to try and get these kids out of his face and deal with the older men. "We're here to negotiate aid to provide food for Bakaar."

The young man looked confused and loosened his grip on Peter's neck. The older man looked at Peter more closely. "We have his papers from his briefcase," he said tipping his head towards George. "He's not a representative of your Government. Are you?"

"No, I'm not." Peter responded, "We are both representatives of a corporation, we are trying to generate aid commercially."

One of the older men, Peter guessed to be around forty-five, stood in the center of the group. He had been watching intently and had not taken his eyes off Peter since arriving in the barn. He had been gradually moving closer and as Peter spoke, he came out of the crowd, the lamplight sparkling off the blade of a machete in his right hand. He walked to within a couple of feet, too close for comfort—the machete held loosely by his side. Without taking his eyes off Peter he started speaking in Bwani for the benefit of his colleagues. It seemed from the tone of his voice that the man was making a case, perhaps suggesting what to do with Peter and George. Peter grew apprehensive, the glinting machete was all that he could see. He was beginning to doubt his confident statement to George, that if their captors had wanted them dead they would already be. Maybe the group had decided they could not let them go.

Peter had been in tight spots before, he had looked down the barrel of a gun on more than one occasion. As far as he could remember that had not made him screw up his toes and the palms of his hands had not been as cold and clammy as they were now with the prospect of being hacked to pieces with a machete.

The orator stopped and looked into Peter's face, "Have you been in Bakaar before?"

The question surprised Peter, "Yes, many times."

"But before President Berruda, during our first government."

Peter realized he might be talking about the time when he was working for the British Government. He had only made one trip into Bakaar at that time, just before Berruda took over.

"Yes, I did make one visit just a few weeks before President Berruda came to power."

"You mean grabbed power," the man responded quickly, still with a puzzled look on his face. He thought for a moment longer and then very slowly said, "I think we've met. If I am right, we met in a Landrover one night in Rapanda, many years ago. I was with my wife and two friends." He continued more confidently, "You were both my captor and my savior on the same night".

Peter would never have recognized him, but given what he knew of that night, there was little doubt that this man was the husband of the girl Peter delivered to the mercy of Berruda all those years ago.

"I am pleased to see you survived," Peter said cautiously, "I was not going to let those thugs beat you to death."

Peter had no idea how he might be regarded by this man. He might see Peter as the reason for his misfortune or he might accept that Peter saved his life. Gradually a smile spread across the man's face. He shouted something to the group and one of the younger members ran out of the barn. The young man with the pistol who had remained by Peter's side fumbled in his pocket, produced a key and removed the handcuffs. Peter rubbed his wrists still not sure whether he was free.

After a few minutes the young man who had run out of the barn returned, pulling a woman by the hand. She was probably in her late thirties or early forties, but looked more. Three small children followed in her wake, trying to hide behind her, but at the same time wanting to see Peter. The man carrying the machete took the woman's hand from the youngster and pulled her forward. Still with the smile on his face he looked at Peter, then expectantly at the woman. Peter was the first to speak, "Your wife?"

The smile grew wider, "Yes!"

The woman had not recognized Peter and her husband explained. She looked more closely realization dawning.

A smile spread across her face also, "Thank you," she said softly, her acceptance triggering a sense of relief throughout the group. The children took their cue and came out from behind her legs having sensed they were safe and free to demand attention.

David, the man Peter had freed, beckoned him to follow and they went towards the houses. A shouted instruction to one of the wired young men prompted George's release.

Peter thought that the people in this group, living just a few miles from Rapanda, had to be in better shape than those living in the rural areas. But it was obvious from the condition of these houses that there were few of the benefits of the twentieth century and food was in short supply.

• • •

In the house Peter and George were seated on rickety chairs at an old table, David and his wife also sat at the table. The remainder of the group pushed into the corners of the small room, some stood, some crouched, some held their children. The room lit by the same lamps they had carried to the barn.

"Why did you bring us here? Who did you think we were?" Peter asked.

"Berruda has been trying to gain support from outside the country and we believe he has been seeking the sort of assistance you provided all those years ago. We have security forces which Berruda controls, but we don't have a substantial army as such. History is repeating itself, but instead of a coup to grab power, our President is looking for a way to keep it." David replied. "After the massacre down by the park, we are more determined. We know of every foreigner entering the country and if we consider them to be a threat to us...we interview them. In the end it will become too dangerous for foreigners to come here and in that way we may protect ourselves. Berruda has to have foreign assistance to succeed."

"Did you come here to assist Berruda?" David asked Peter.

Peter explained saying little more than he had in the barn, but saying it differently. He indicated that both he and George would be in and out of Bakaar for the next few weeks and that others who worked for them would also be in the country. He told them he was confident they would be able to persuade the United States to provide enough aid to change their fortune. He did not explain how they were going to do it.

Peter learned what had happened following that night when he had driven David his wife and their two friends to the Ministry. Berruda had been embarrassed by the incident and whether or not out of fear of what the British might do if the dissidents were harmed, he had imprisoned them until he had taken over the government. Afterwards in a show of magnanimity he released all of the political prisoners. Whether Berruda knew of the potential fate of the four on that night, who could say.

Once the past had been laid to rest it was obvious that David and his wife accepted Peter as their savior as opposed to blaming him for their imprisonment. Others began to speak and it became clear that this group was the core of the Bwani opposition to Berruda. Peter and George learned that David and a couple of the others in the group would be running as candidates in the upcoming elections.

Now that Peter and George seemed to be out of immediate danger Peter could think again. He was unsure if their plan had been compromised. George had said almost nothing since they had left the barn. He was strangely quiet and Peter could get no reading as to how he was holding up.

An hour later Peter heard cars arriving and the youngsters who had grabbed them came into the house. Peter had not even noticed their absence, but David had sent them back into Rapanda to pick up the Jeep.

"For the moment I have no reason to doubt what you say," David said to Peter. "You are free to go back to Rapanda. Just follow Boco". David pointed to the youngster who had wielded the pistol. "He'll show you the way back".

"However, you now know who we are. I hope we don't regret this decision. We need any help we can get. Please get the aid for us and make sure that Berruda distributes its benefit evenly. Once again, Peter, you have our lives in your hands."

"How do we contact you?" Peter asked.

"We will know when you arrive or leave and we will contact you".

Peter and George departed and drove the several miles behind the Ford. As the lights of Rapanda appeared the Ford slowed to a crawl and Boco waved Peter past.

George had still said nothing since they had been released from the handcuffs and Peter feared he had been badly shaken by the experience. As the old Ford Zephyr made a U-turn and headed back, George spoke thoughtfully.

"That's the first time I've been at the mercy of another person. I mean, unable to effect the outcome. I had no way to defend myself. In just a couple of seconds, on a whim, any of those people could have killed me!"

"Sobering isn't it." Peter enjoyed George's revelation. "Now you know how I felt when you roped me into this craziness!"

George seemed not to hear the comment, "I thought our end had arrived when that man, David, approached us with that machete. Why did they let us go? We can go straight to Robert Berruda and get them arrested."

"Who knows. Maybe they think it's better to trust us. That we may well be able to improve their lives. I hope they're right."

"What do you mean, when I roped you in…"

"What choice did I have, George?"

Chapter 16

Nirina received the call from Rudi on the fifteenth day after their first meeting. Rudi advised him to be ready to travel immediately and Nirina dutifully packed and waited expectantly. Nirina had no idea how his travel arrangements would be made but he expected that an itinerary and tickets would arrive–somehow. Two days passed, then on the Sunday, unannounced, Rudi arrived at seven in the morning. Rudi was let into the house and did not leave Nirina's side while he gathered up his bags. Nirina wanted to know where he was going and in an attempt to discover the destination, all but threatened Rudi with not travelling. Rudi did not disclose any information and after a tearful parting from his wife, Nirina left the house with Rudi almost dragging him by the hand.

They drove in the rented car to Marseilles airport and departed for Paris. Nirina badgered relentlessly to know their final destination. Rudi ignored him and hardly spoke a word during the entire journey to the airport.

In Paris they transferred to Charles de Gaule airport for the international flight into Africa and Rudi handed Nirina the ticket as they passed through security and headed for the gate. Nirina eagerly examined it. The destination was Nairobi. He knew that was unlikely and he would not now be able to let his wife know where he would be. He had hoped that her knowledge of his whereabouts would provide some protection should things get difficult for him.

• • •

The meeting with Julius had gone well but George and Peter were well aware that if anything went wrong Berruda would do everything possible to make sure they took the blame. George returned to London and Peter moved out of the Presidential Hotel and into the apartment Julius had provided.

Over the next week there were daily meetings. Peter requested what they needed. Julius acted as the liaison with the agencies which were involved, taking care that none of them were aware of the project. Peter inspected and approved the construction of the laboratory in the old fertilizer plant. Mr Jaffar, one of the senior civil servants at the Ministry, was appointed as the man responsible for providing manpower and supplies.

Nirina need not have concerned himself. There were well qualified chemists and engineers available to work with him. Regardless of the fact that Bakaar was virtually broke, it was a sovereign state, an independent country and that provided advantages which were not possible commercially. As George had explained to Sarah at their dinner in Paris, whatever the morality might be, the question of legality, of right or wrong, becomes moot when acting with the authority of a government, however insecure it may be. Anything Peter wanted was available and could be purchased through Mr. Jaffar at the Ministry.

Julius put the wheels in motion to clean up one of the houses at the fertilizer plant for Nirina and agreed to make a Ministry apartment available for Tim and Doug. A telephone only accepting incoming calls was installed in Nirina's house to make him accessible to the rest of the team.

Julius joked about the fact that Tim and Doug's apartment had been originally prepared for visiting British dignitaries during the independence celebrations and at that time the Bakaarans had secretly bugged it. Peter accepted the comment as a friendly warning. He doubted that the bugs would work, but maybe they had been replaced.

On the following Monday, Peter contacted Tim Serenson and confirmed the operation was on. Tim asked where he would be based but as with Nirina all Peter would tell him was, get to Nairobi and he would be met at the airport. Nairobi was safe, it was possible to get anywhere from there, it provided no clues. Tim and Doug would be met by Julius' security staff and would be escorted into the country. There was no need for visas or permits. The same applied to Nirina. Rudi would hand him over to Julius' security staff and Rudi would return to Europe. There was no need even for Rudi to know where they were going.

Peter felt that he had covered everything. None of the team knew where they would end up until they reached Nairobi and were safely aboard the Air Bakaar Boeing 737. From that moment they would remain in the company of Julius' men and would not have the opportunity to call or contact anyone. Once inside Bakaar, Nirina would be under virtual house arrest. But once Peter had briefed Tim and Doug, they would be free to come and go as they pleased.

By Wednesday, Peter felt that the operation was well on its way. Rudi and Nirina were leaving Marseilles today and Peter would meet with Nirina on Friday, after Julius' men had installed him in the house at the fertilizer plant.

Peter needed electronic expertise to construct the telephone switch and the arming device. Frederick D'butu was the senior electronics engineer employed by the Security Police. He was responsible for their surveillance equipment and computers and after a couple of conversations Peter decided he was capable of doing the job. Julius gave his permission and Peter set up a meeting to brief Frederick on what was required. He dropped in at the apartment on Wednesday evening.

Peter greeted Frederick as he opened the apartment door and led him into the sitting room. It had been a hot day and the temperature still hovered around eighty five degrees. Frederick was dressed in a bright red, open neck, short sleeve shirt, a pair of crumpled dark blue pants and leather sandals without socks. He did not qualify for a Ministry car and driver. He had walked from his home and from the knees down, his trousers were covered in fine red dust.

Frederick stepped inside and followed Peter.

"Would you like a drink?" Peter asked, not knowing if Frederick was a Christian or Moslem but as he worked in the Ministry it was most likely he would be Christian.

"A beer, if you have one," Frederick replied. His education and three years in England made him one of the privileged and relatively well paid few. But the education and experience had created difficulties, particularly when he was in the company of Europeans and Americans. Should he act like a European, as he had for three years in England, or should he behave like an African? Since returning from university both seemed wrong; he was no longer comfortable in either role.

Peter returned from the kitchen with two ice cold beers. Unusually, the electricity supply had been on all day and the refrigerator was working. He placed them on the low wooden table in front of two easy chairs and invited Frederick to sit down.

"From our conversations you know roughly what I want?" Peter said. There was no need for Frederick to know what the devices would be attached to, he just had to design and construct them.

"Yes, I think so. You need a switch controlled from a telephone."

"Yeah, I need two. But we don't want to go into the market outside of Bakaar, looking for a commercial product. We need to construct them here. One switch has to be inserted into a small, computerized, American phone system. The phone systems will be multi-line and our first switch will be attached to an extension. That extension must be able to be used normally regardless of our switch. But on receipt of a code entered at the phone making the call the switch will connect us to the second one."

"That's O.K. I can do that," Frederick was eager to help.

"The second switch will operate a device we will install and it too has to be activated from the phone making the call. It's vital that the second switch can't be triggered by mistake, there's got to be a second code needed to activate it."

"Yeah, that's O.K., I can build in a requirement for a further code to be punched in by the sending phone." Frederick was enjoying the challenge, "I think it could work like this…"

Frederick began to draw an electrical circuit on the pad. "A call on the incoming line would ring out like any other. The call could be answered manually or automatically. Then you would dial or ask for the extension."

"Would it matter if the extension was answered?"

"No, if it wasn't answered the switch would respond after say ten rings, more than anyone at that extension would permit. The eleventh ring would activate it. Then you'd need to punch in your code, say 1.2.3.4. which would provide access to the second switch. Then you'd require a code, dialed in from the sending phone, say 5.6.7.8. to activate the second switch. If the extension was answered, you'd just punch in your first code and the rest would follow in the same way."

"You make it sound easy," Peter responded.

"It's not difficult. The problem is reliability. With so many stages and codes, noise on the line might affect it. An electrical short somewhere might bypass the security codes, but I could put in some protection for that."

"We'd need to," Peter said with concern showing in his voice, "It has to be foolproof."

"It can't be guaranteed, I might get it to 99.99% certain that it can't go wrong, but it'll never be 100%."

Peter thought he was laboring the point, "I can live with 99.99%"

"If we use a four figure code for each stage and a one second delay between digits it could not be triggered by accident," Frederick assured Peter.

"I have to be able to set or change the codes by telephone. Can that be done?" Peter asked.

"Yes."

"Would the switch work in a telephone system still based on pulse signals?"

"Ah, I don't think so, I think the telephone making the call would still have to send the signals to the switches by tone. I'll have to check that out, which system do you want?"

"I want the tone system. The first priority is to make it work with the tone system." Peter left it at that. He did not want to complicate the issue.

"I'd like four of each switch and I need them as soon as possible. Do you have all the components you need or will we need to buy anything in?"

Frederick thought for a moment while his eyes carefully followed around the drawing of the circuit on his pad. "It would be easier if I could buy in some ready made components." He replied.

Peter had already set up the procedure. Any questionable component would be purchased through George's company in France. It was the time that might be a problem.

"Let me have a list of what you need as soon as you can. Now, are you going to be able to have them finished in three weeks?"

"Yes, so long as I get the components in a week or so we should be O.K."

"We have to be O.K. Frederick. There can be no doubt about it. If there's any chance that you can't make it within three weeks, say so now. A delay could jeopardize plans far beyond these switches."

Frederick was left in no doubt that he had to get it right.

"We'll make sure that the sample phone systems come straight to you when they arrive and I'd like you to keep me posted on progress. Ideally I'd like to see the first version and check it out before you get on and assemble the remainder."

"O.K. I'll try and have one working within three weeks after I get the components." Frederick answered hesitantly concerned that he was being over optimistic, but not prepared to lose face.

Everything in Bakaar sounded positive. The fact was that time had little or no meaning, Peter knew he could be promised the earth, but to achieve anything on time would be a miracle. He had already built slippage into the timing, but he wondered if he had allowed enough.

"Thank you, Frederick, I know where to find you. I'll come by in a week or so and make sure you have the phone systems and the components."

Peter stood up, indicating the end of the meeting. Frederick packed his pad back in the old brief case. Peter walked him to the door and watched as he descended the outside staircase to the ground floor. The compound was well lit, but he quickly disappeared into the darkness on his way to the gate.

• • •

Tim and Doug arrived on Thursday and were taken to their apartment where they waited for Peter's briefing. During the week Peter obtained an American passport which he would need for his trips to the U.S and a Bakaaran Security Police identity card in the same name. The ID card was circulated throughout the Ministry and the Security Police so that Peter would be able to move through the increasing security on the streets and gain access to the fertilizer plant. If he had been black there would have been no need to take any more action than issue the ID card. But it would be unusual for a white man to turn up at what were becoming sensitive locations.

In view of the increasingly violent opposition to Berruda's government Julius suggested that Peter should have a bodyguard and a ministry car. Peter graciously declined the offer, but accepted the suggestion that he carry a pistol. After the shooting incident in the club, Peter did not want to be defenseless.

On Thursday afternoon, Peter headed into the City to meet Tim and Doug. The apartment they had been allocated was one of four in a large converted house within the wire fence surrounding the police barracks. There was little doubt, particularly with the increased security, that Tim and Doug were going nowhere without the knowledge and approval of the government.

Peter tested his new ID card for the first time on arrival at the gate of the barracks. It worked. The guard examined it, saluted and let him pass without a murmur. He drove around to the house. He was not looking forward to this meeting. He was now going to have to admit to Tim that the task was not quite as described when they met in Hong Kong. The armed policeman at the door to the apartment repeated the performance of the guard at the gate and the door was opened and Peter entered.

"Hello, anyone home?" Peter called as he walked down the narrow, gloomy hallway. The original house was a Victorian structure built of brick and tile, a design which the British had exported to half the world during the days of Empire. As Julius had said, it had been converted into the four apartments just before independence, in order to provide accommodations for some of the visiting British dignitaries. The decoration was the original, now peeling, brown and cream paint. The furniture was 1960's English, not the best period of furniture design in the history of that great country. The apartment smelled stale and oppressive.

Tim stuck his head around one of the doorways and peered at Peter through the gloom. "My God, it's Action Man!"

"Hello, Tim. How was the journey?" Peter asked trying to sound upbeat as he walked into the room that Tim had chosen. At least the bed was new and the room was clean, even by American standards. Tim's expensive but worn leather luggage was on the floor and he was still in the process of unpacking.

"Where the fuck are we?" Tim asked aggressively as he raised his eyebrows and spread his hands in apparent incredulity. As he spoke Doug Borden walked in and extended his hand to Peter.

"How you doin?" Doug asked with a look on his face that said, let's cut the crap.

"More to the point how are you?" Peter asked as they shook hands.

"I've been better, it's not the Hilton for Christ sake." Doug looked critically around Tim's gloomy peeling bedroom.

Peter was surprised, he thought Tim's comment applied to Bakaar, but it was the accommodations which were upsetting him.

"What did you expect?" Peter asked becoming angry with their child-like behavior.

"We should've been at a hotel. I'm not staying in this fucking place long. You'd better find somewhere more upbeat next time we're in town!" Tim sat and bounced on the bed, which really was not too bad.

"I couldn't ask earlier but have either of you been in Bakaar before?"

"No, thank Christ, and we may well not be coming back!" Doug answered.

Tim had swung his cowboy boots up on the bed and rested them on the rail at the foot.

"I'd like some coffee, let's talk in the kitchen." Peter led the way and sat down at the kitchen table.

Tim heaved himself off the bed with a sigh and followed Peter into the kitchen. Doug came in and opened a couple of drawers and noisily rummaged through the cabinets.

"Is there any coffee?" Doug asked dejectedly looking at Peter.

Peter knew there should be. He had been told there were basic groceries earlier in the week.

"Of course there is." Peter began to open cupboards, " It's here in the bloody cabinet at the end!" Peter decided to fight fire with fire. "For

God's sake cheer up, you're not going to be here for long. Don't try my patience, there are only two ways out of here. You co-operate and you go home standing up with money in your pocket or you leave in a box!"

"We'd go out in a goddamned box, would we!" Tim kicked round a chair to face him and sat astride it. The familiar Smith and Wesson automatic pistol appeared from nowhere in his right hand.

"Jesus Christ, you're full of shit Peter!"

The only reason Peter was wearing his jacket was to cover the shoulder holster containing the small Browning 380 he had received from Julius. He suddenly became very aware that he was carrying it.

"How the hell did you get that in here?" Peter asked Tim. He suddenly remembered Julius comment about the bugs and he raised his finger to his lips to indicate silence and pointed to the lamp, the radio and several other places trying to indicate that the room was bugged. It may well be that they were defunct and that Julius' warning was unnecessary. Whatever their state he did not want there to be any risk that Julius' men might discover that Tim had brought a gun in with him. Peter knew the tricks that had worked a few years ago, but with today's airport security he could not imagine how Tim could have got it through. From Nairobi Tim had been accompanied every step of the way by security police and they had instructions not to even let him pee on his own.

"Same ole tricks still work, Peter," Tim drawled answering Peter's question, "I take it everywhere. You can't carry it in your hand luggage any more, but by the time it's broken down into its components and wrapped in metal foil, who the hell'd recognize the bits." Tim sat with the gun held loosely in his right hand, "So no one's gonna blow us away without a lotta grief."

Doug was about to fill the kettle with water from the faucet. "Can we drink this stuff?" He asked.

"Yes, it's alright, the British built the plumbing and it still works." Peter answered.

The atmosphere was a little better. Tim and Doug had made their point and their anger was dissipating.

"Come on gentlemen, it's Africa, you knew it wasn't going to be five star hotels." Peter tried to get away from the petty complaints and get down to the real business.

Tim sighed, "Yeah, we know! We just figure it'll get better, but it never does." He looked slowly around the dismal kitchen. "Fucking place should have been demolished…" Then in what was almost a whine and with a perceptible shudder, he added, "I hate cockroaches, I bet the place is full of the bastards. They keep me awake."

Peter laughed, he had never seen Tim flinch at anything, but it was obvious he was scared to death of cockroaches. "Keep you awake! How the hell do they do that?"

Tim did not reply and looked sheepish. Cockroaches had been one of his childhood terrors. It was hard to justify his fears to anyone else.

"How do they keep you awake?" Peter asked again, enjoying Tim's discomfort.

"They fall out from behind the cabinets, you can hear them all night. They land on their backs and make a hell of a din, plop! plop! plop! all fucking night."

"They won't hurt you! You're just a big kid!" Peter scathingly shut him up.

The kettle whistled, Doug with the image of cockroaches still dancing vividly in his imagination, turned the last cup he was holding upside down and shook out a couple of dead flies. He placed it down on the surface to join the other two, spooned in the coffee and poured on the hot water, sliding the steaming cups down the surface to the other two. He gave Peter an evil smile and as he sat down he raised his finger to his lips imitating Peter's earlier gesture concerning the bugs, reached into the back of his pants and from under his shirt produced his gun and placed it on the surface.

"What works for him, works for me!" Doug laughed.

"Oh no!" Peter looked at them both with a mixture of despair and humor.

"You said you needed the best Peter, you've got 'em." Doug said with a leer.

Tim had spotted Peter's pistol as soon as he had walked into the bedroom. "Now, if you just rest easy and put yours on the table we'll all feel better. Then you can tell us your story and we'll make believe you're telling the truth and maybe by the time it's dark we'll all know what the fuck we're doing in this Godforsaken place."

Using the pistol like a pointer as he spoke, Tim gently lifted the lapel of Peter's jacket with the tip of the barrel, exposing the grip of the Browning.

Peter exaggerated his movement and very gently took out the gun holding it between two fingers as if it were dirty and placed it down on the table.

"That's much better," Tim smiled and laid his own pistol down on the table with the others.

"O.K." Peter sighed resignedly. "Once upon a time…" the humor finally removed the tension, Tim and Doug laughed and began to relax. "In fact, for the first time in your lives the reality is going to be easier than the story I gave you in Hong Kong. It's certainly different."

Whether the Ministry was listening was irrelevant as far as the operation was concerned, the Ministry knew all about it. However, Peter had brought a pad and pencil with him and every time there was a comment he did not want to be overheard he scribbled it down.

Peter explained Doug's task. He was the in-house bodyguard for Tim and himself in Bakaar all he had to do was to keep an eye on both of them. After explaining much of the operation, Peter wrote on his pad:

'LET'S GO OUT AND EAT TONIGHT AND WE'LL TALK IN DETAIL THEN. DON'T BRING THE DAMNED GUNS WITH YOU UNTIL I'VE ARRANGED PERMITS.'

Peter returned to the apartment that evening, picked up Tim and Doug, and they went to an Indian restaurant. During dinner, Peter filled them in on Nirina, the work they needed to do in Rapanda on this trip and the timing of the task in the U.S. Both Doug and Tim seemed satisfied, and Peter did not even have to offer them more money. Their only grouse was the standard of the accommodations.

• • •

Nirina arrived on time and Peter went out to the fertilizer plant on Friday. Peter had not previously met him, but the reports from George had prepared him for an arrogant, unpleasant man. The SP had almost finished putting a barbed wire fence around the plant. A barrier had been placed across the entrance road and a guard house installed at the gate. To accommodate the extra bodies needed to guard the plant round the clock, men were erecting temporary buildings of the sort seen on many construction sites. Peter used his ID card for the fourth time in two days and was admitted into the wire compound. He drove over to the house and could not help chuckling to himself as he thought of it as Nirina's summer residence.

The house was relatively modern, built of drab concrete blocks with metal window frames, reminiscent of those used in subsidized housing in the fifties. It was topped off by a corrugated iron roof that at one time had been painted white, but the filth that belched out of the fertilizer plant chimney had turned it into a permanent gray. In the old days, it was cleaned once a year by the torrential rains of early summer. But it had not rained much in the past few years and it would now take a lot more than rain to remove the grime.

Peter entered the house and found Nirina sitting in a chair in the sparsely furnished bedroom, reading. He must have heard Peter arrive, but he had not moved nor made any attempt to inquire who it might be. Nirina glanced up from his book, but still said nothing. Peter introduced himself and Nirina started bleating. 'George Barnard had said nothing about a fertilizer factory…he was told it was to be in the Middle East…he had to contact his wife…the house was dirty…the food was inedible.' Peter ignored the avalanche of complaint and reminded Nirina of Rudi's presence in Marseilles.

Once Nirina had stopped moaning, Peter explained the program, or at least that part of it he needed to know. Over the next few days Nirina would be introduced to the team of Bakaaran scientists who would work with him. Peter explained that time was the most important factor and the job had to be finished in just a few weeks. It was up to Nirina to work night and day to set up the laboratory and get the job done.

Once Nirina was up and running, Peter would have little to do with his work. All Peter wanted was to hear that there was enough of the VX gas loaded and ready for shipment by the deadline.

As Peter left the plant, he felt relieved that he did not have to deal with the impossible man on a daily basis and he heartily agreed with Georges' description.

Chapter 17

During the next few days Tim and Doug picked up ID cards and permits for their pistols and were provided with new American passports for their return trip to the U.S. and their future travel. There would be no trace of Doug Borden's or Tim Serenson's entry into or departure from Bakaar. Their names would not appear on any passenger list with the Bakaaran airline. Tim and Doug could be traced arriving in Kenya, on their way to Bakaar but from there they simply disappeared. In future they would travel on the new documents.

The plan was for Tim and Doug to remain in Bakaar to meet with Nirina and the Bakaarans with whom they would be working. Peter would return to London and they would all meet in New York in two weeks. Peter needed to see George in London and he felt he had earned a little recreation.

Upon arriving in London Peter phoned George's office. Anyone in the office could have told him George was in Paris, but he really did not want to speak to George, he wanted to make contact with Sarah. He asked for her.

"Sarah, how are you? Is your father around?"

"No, I think you'd know where he is better than I. You seem to be living in each other's pockets." Sarah was sarcastic. She did not like the thought of Peter knowing what was going on, while she was kept in the dark. "I hope you're not keeping him awake at night," she added petulantly, then paused for a moment. Peter did not respond and she continued, "He's in Paris, do you need him?"

"Yes, I'll call him later. But I'd like to see you."

Sarah had known since that first day in her apartment that Peter could mean trouble. Sooner or later an invitation would be extended and she would have to say, Yes or No. She knew she should say, No.

"How about dinner tonight?" Peter asked.

"Yes, fine. Nothing special—Italian or something. Will you pick me up at the flat?"

"Sure, how about eight o'clock?"

"Eight o'clock it is." Sarah replied.

She put the phone down and could have kicked herself, why say yes? She just could not resist it. For the rest of the day she convinced herself that she had agreed only to find out more about the Bakaar Project.

Promptly at eight o'clock, Peter pressed the door bell.

"Hello, I'm on my way down." Her voice floated out of the speaker in the wall.

"O.K." Peter said, finding it awkward to respond to the disembodied voice. She may not be going to let him in, but he was damned if he was going to stand there looking at the door. He walked back down the steps and began to pace the pavement. It was ten minutes before the heavy door opened and Sarah emerged. He was only about fifteen feet away and just beginning another circuit of the now familiar pavement. He turned back to greet her and his impatience was forgotten. She was dressed in black pants, a cream shirt and a leather jacket. Peter had decided weeks before that sooner or later there would be a right time and place. As he watched her walk down the steps from the front door there was little doubt in his mind that it was the right time. All that remained was to decide the place.

"Hi, Sarah," he said as he took her by the arm and led her towards Kings Road, "You look gorgeous!"

"Thank you," she replied, all pretense of discussing the Bakaar Project had gone. Sarah was going to have a good time. As usual, there was not a cab in sight and they resigned themselves to walk. It was a pleasant early summer evening and the daylight was slipping away into the red of the setting sun. Peter had reserved a table at eight-thirty at an Italian restaurant just off the Kings Road, beyond Sloane Street. From the moment Peter took her arm he knew there was not going to be any awkward small talk, no pregnant pauses while each tried to let the other make the first move. The first move had already been made weeks ago at Sarah's apartment.

After they had walked about a quarter of a mile, Sarah gave Peter a mischievous, sideways glance. She walked round him, maintaining her hold on his arm, turning him around, and without comment, they began to walk back towards her apartment.

Peter's adrenaline began to flow. Tightness in his chest, a shortness of breath, the tingling at the back of his neck. It was the same sensation as fear, a heightened awareness, life slowed down and he noticed every-thing as they walked at an ever increasing pace towards Eaton Square. He could hear the rustle as her shirt rubbed on the lining of her jacket. Her perfume filled the air. He felt her tighten her grip on his arm.

As they climbed the steps to the door she released him and searched her bag for the keys. As she did he slipped his arms under her jacket and around her waist from behind. She could not concentrate on the search for the key and turned to look at him over her shoulder, one hand still clumsily holding the open bag, the other hand inside. He kissed her as she turned her head back to look at him, she playfully bit his lip. She pulled away and laughed, "Let me find the damned keys. I'm not doing it in the middle of Eaton Square!"

She found the keys and opened the door. The elevator was waiting. They entered and Sarah pressed the button. Peter stood apart from her looking into her eyes and began to undo the buttons of her shirt. Sarah smiled. She could not participate, her hands were full, the bag in one and the keys in the other. By the time they had completed the short journey to the second floor her shirt was undone. Peter helped pull her jacket protectively around her as they walked the short distance from the elevator to her door. In her haste to open the door she fumbled with the keys and it took two attempts to get the key in the lock.

They stumbled into the apartment and Sarah slammed the door shut. "Blasted bag!" she exclaimed, throwing it on the floor and freeing her hands. She took off the jacket, dropped it and turned to Peter, grabbed him by the tie and playfully pulled him into the bedroom. Maintaining her grip on his tie with one hand, she pulled her shirt free from the waistband of her pants with the other. She jumped onto the bed and pulled Peter on after her. He fell awkwardly beside her, his legs hanging over the end. She released her grip on his tie and removed her shirt. She rolled backwards on the bed, kicked her feet up in the air and took off her pants, just for a moment Peter hesitated watching her.

"Get them off!" was all she said. He needed no second bidding and started to undo his pants without sitting up. It was not easy. As Peter discovered it is not easy to elegantly remove your pants while lying on your back with your legs dangling over the edge of a bed and your shoes on. Sarah was quick to assist, she hopped off the bed, crouched at his feet and roughly removed his shoes and pulled at both trouser legs from the bottom. Definitely not elegant, but effective. Pants removed, Peter sat on the edge of the bed and it took just seconds for his jacket, crumpled tie and shirt to end up in a heap on the floor. Sarah down to her bra and pants climbed over his legs and knelt on the bed facing him, one leg on either side of his, her arms around his neck.

The bedroom was illuminated only by the subdued light filtering in from the hallway through the almost closed door. Sarah's dark chestnut hair formed a frame for her flushed face, her eyes were bright and in the semi darkness they seemed to glow like a cat's and she was becoming impatient. She pouted and began to sway her shoulders from side to side. The effect was hypnotic, all Peter could see were her breasts still encased in her bra.

"Interested?" Sarah whispered, the swaying becoming more of a shudder.

"You're gorgeous," Peter replied huskily as he quietly reached behind her with the intention of demonstrating his interest. As soon as the garment was undone Sarah shook herself free of it, but her movement finished Peter. He fell back on the bed pulling Sarah with him and in a matter of moments it was over.

Sarah lay quietly snuggled against his shoulder, he was gently stroking her hair, neither had said anything for many minutes. Peter spoke first, "That was better than an Italian dinner."

"Yes, but I'm hungry now. Are you hungry?" Sarah asked looking up but not changing her position.

"Yes, I could eat a horse." Peter answered honestly, "What have you got to eat here?"

"We could rustle up something from the freezer." As she spoke she rolled over and got off the bed, walked into the kitchen and opened the freezer. "I've got some spaghetti, or it looks as if there's some frozen pizza. We can still make it an Italian evening. What do you want?"

Peter could not remain in the bedroom and allow Sarah to prepare the food. He reached for his clothes, but how the hell could he get dressed while Sarah did the cooking stark naked. There was no choice, he climbed off the bed and walked self consciously into the kitchen. He made no sound as he approached the door. He could see her standing with her back to him, still contemplating the contents of the freezer and waiting for a reply. There was no doubt that Sarah was never meant to wear clothes. It was hardly spring, she did not have a tan, but even so her skin was far from white. He noticed the slight freckling and felt mean. He could not stop himself from thinking that it probably meant her chestnut hair was real. As he walked towards her, he wondered what her mother had been like, George had no freckles and no sign of red in his hair.

Sarah turned as he approached, "You look sweet," she said mockingly, not boosting his confidence. As she said it she felt cruel. He did not look comfortable. She moved towards him leaving the freezer door ajar, "I'm sorry," she said as she slid her arms around his neck and kissed him. She intended it to be a reassuring kiss, an apology for the harshness of her comment, but it lingered. As she kissed him the only points of contact between them were their lips and her nipples, just brushing his chest. Peter had never had any problem with his power of recovery, but he thought this was ridiculous as a fourth point of contact made itself evident. Sarah smiled, he picked her up and carried her back to the bedroom. All thought of dinner had gone. This time it was slower, much slower.

Sarah awoke suddenly and collected her thoughts, Peter was still fast asleep beside her, the light in the kitchen was still on, she looked at the clock it was 2.10 a.m. Then she noticed the noise, like the dripping of a leaky tap.

"Oh my God, the freezer!" She exclaimed jumping out of bed and running into the kitchen. There was water all over the floor and the thawing packages on the higher shelves were dripping over everything.

Peter had not heard the words but her shout awakened him. He followed her into the kitchen. The first he knew of the problem was cold wet feet. "We must stop meeting like this," Peter suggested as he paddled through the water and took the mop Sarah had removed from the closet. They both began to laugh.

• • •

The telephone rang. Sarah was again awakened and leaned over and answered it. The sun was coming into the room, she glanced at the time it was nine thirty. "Hello, Sarah, how are you?"

"I'm fine Dad, where are you?" she replied.

"I'm back at home, I tried the office and thought you might not be well," he added with the implied criticism that she should have been in the office by nine thirty. He should have known better, she had been his daughter long enough for him to know she would not react to that sort of intimidation.

"Have you heard from Peter?"

"Yes, he called me yesterday," she said truthfully, "He said he would call you today."

"Are you going into the office today?" he asked.

"I'll be there later this morning, are you coming in?"

"Yes and when I hear from Peter, I'll get him to come over. I need to talk to him. I'll see you later."

The few words exchanged with her father and the hard brightness of the March sun streaming through the window, brought home the fact that she and Peter had a lot to talk about.

Peter was stirring. She got out of bed, showered, dressed and finished clearing up the mess from the freezer. She made some coffee. Peter's head appeared around the door, he was dressed in her robe. "Hi, I guess you've seen the time." He yawned, "do you have a razor?"

"Yes, there's a packet in the bathroom," she tried to walk past him but he took hold of her arm and kissed her. "Last night was great, why did we wait so long?" Peter had not fully surfaced and he was still enjoying the thought of the night before, but for Sarah the call from George had revived all of the reasons she should have said 'No.'

Sarah did not pull away but rested her hands on his shoulders, "Peter, we must talk but I have to get into the office to meet my old man. He's also expecting to hear from you today."

"Well, I suppose we have to decide if it was a one night stand. If it was, we can just avoid the issue and it won't make any difference." Peter did not consider it a one night stand, but he was not going to complicate the issue if Sarah was already regretting it.

"Like hell it was a one night stand!" Sarah said forcefully.

"Seriously Peter, we have to decide what to tell Dad. I don't have any reason for him not to know, I'm over twenty one. I'm more concerned how it might affect whatever you're doing with him."

"Well…I don't think it's going to create any problems. I know he's keeping you out of the Bakaar project and he'll be concerned that you don't get involved through me."

"I want to know what it's all about, but I'll promise not to grill you…but Peter, I want you around." She leaned closer to him her hands sliding up around his neck.

"So who's going to tell him?" Peter whispered.

"I will when I see him this morning. Why don't you call the office and make a date with him. I'll tell him before you arrive."

"O.K., show me where the razors are and I'll get cleaned up."

They left together, Peter went back to his apartment, Sarah headed for the office.

Chapter 18

"Hello, it's good to see you." George greeted Peter alone in his office. Sarah was nowhere to be seen.

"How was Paris?"

"Fine, the phones and all the electrical components are on their way to Bakaar and New York's set up for next week. How did you get on with our scientist?"

"I don't like him. I'm sure he'll do the job, but it's going to be hard work all the way."

"Yup, afraid it is. Any problems?"

"No. Frederick's going to be able to make the switches we need. The pulse system in Bakaar could cause us a bit of difficulty, but that's the least of our problems. I assume Bakaar is not the main issue at the present time. Generally, the troops are raring to go!"

There was a knock on the door.

"Come in!" George called out.

Sarah came in and smiled at Peter, "Hi, Peter, I've confessed, Dad doesn't seem too surprised..."

George looked at Peter disapprovingly, "It's none of my business, but for God's sake keep bloody romance and business apart. I don't want to lose you if she kicks you out of bed and I don't want Sarah involved in the Bakaar project. I've explained why. No pillow talk."

'Trust him to think of it that way round,' Peter thought as George gave his un-required fatherly approval. Nothing must affect business, but what about Sarah if he and George had problems over Bakaar. Peter left well alone. Sarah departed suggesting that Peter meet her that evening for the promised, but as yet undelivered, Italian dinner. Peter agreed.

After she left, George got out a street map of New York City. "As I told you, a company I have no visible connection with has an office on the fifth floor of a twenty story building up towards the northern end of Manhattan." He pointed on the map, "It's similar to this office, a bit bigger—as are all things American," he smiled. "It's the home office for the Eastern U.S. and the building's air conditioned with vents on the roof…and it's old…"

"Old?" Peter raised an eyebrow.

"Well, old by American standards. Built about forty years ago…bound to be wiring all over the place, just what we'll be looking for."

Peter looked at the map. George continued, "One of this group of companies is a distributor of electronic equipment—computers, phones, all sorts. In August, we're going to make our customers in New York an offer. A special deal to replace their old telephone systems with the latest version—more bells and whistles. That should give us a pretty wide choice of buildings. Your team can then work through the list and pick out the most suitable. I hope your lads won't mind the work, but I think it would be sensible if they worked legitimately for a week or two and installed as many normal systems as possible, just in case they're checked out later on. They also have to make sure they can install them properly, it'll give 'em plenty of practice."

"Sounds good to me! I've got a list of the kit we'll need. Tim's working with Frederick and keeping the pressure on. We should have a sample of the switches for Tim to bring with him."

"How's the cash going?" George inquired. He had been providing Peter with substantial sums over the past weeks. Peter had given Tim and Doug an advance and he now needed to buy tickets for the trip to the U.S.

"It's going fine, I don't like carrying it around, but I'll need some more for the U.S. next week."

"O.K., I'll arrange to have some dollars for you on Wednesday." George scribbled a note to himself, "What are your plans for the rest of the week?"

Peter thought for a moment, "I've got my normal job to do. I'm still responsible for affairs in the rest of Africa. I've got to catch up. I'm coming in tomorrow, Rose has been keeping tabs on things for me. Depending on what I find, I'll probably be in and out all the week. I'm leaving for the States on Saturday. How about you?"

"I'll come over on Sunday. Let's meet at the office in New York on Monday morning at about nine, that's Monday, May 18." George entered the appointment in his calendar and then for the first time asked after Peter's welfare, "By the way, how are you? Do you still feel you were roped in or do I get the sense that you're warming to the project?"

"Well, thirty-three million; it is thirty-three million isn't it, seems to have a warming effect."

Over the past few weeks Peter had thought of little else but his originally unwilling involvement in this affair. He had finally justified it on two levels. One to salve his still uncomfortable conscience, the other more complicated.

His conscience rested more easily based on the fact that he already risked conviction for his unintended responsibility in Angola. So now he would be at risk for God knew what on the Bakaar project. But this project had a humanitarian face. If he succeeded, a few million people would eat. He had been at greater risk in the past but this time he just might make thirty-three million dollars. That was a lot of money. He would be rich. And that was far more complicated.

All of his life Peter had served and worked for others and received a salary for his effort. When he worked for the British Government more often than not one or more of his charges received millions of pounds in sweeteners to tow the British line. Often he had been the reason some despot retained his wealth and power. And forget the risk of jail time, more than once his life had been on the line. Faced with the need to reconcile his conscience with what he was doing in Bakaar, he realized he resented that others had got rich off his risk and effort in the past. This time it was his turn. There was no turning back. He was going to get rich no matter what and God help George if he tried to welsh on the deal.

Next day Peter got a cab to Mount Street. He climbed the stairs to the offices, rather than take the elevator, just to convince himself he was still in shape. Rose, greeted him. Rose was well into her sixties and had worked for George longer than any of them. She was a small wiry lady, little more than five feet two inches tall. Her gray hair was drawn back tightly against her head which exaggerated the angular shape of her face. She looked severe.

She had known Peter ever since he joined the company. She liked him and although she was old enough to be his mother, she occasionally allowed herself to fantasize, 'If only I was twenty-five again.' She found Peter attractive.

"Well, well, it's the return of Action Man," she said playfully as Peter walked into the office, "It's so nice of you to come and see us. You avoided us yesterday."

Her manner became sympathetic, "We hear you nearly didn't make it. Did they really try to shoot you in Rapanda? What's going on?"

George and Peter did not try to hide the fact that they had visited Rapanda, it was more or less routine that they should. Rose was only concerned for Peter's safety. She had no clue as to the reason for the visit.

"Yes, it's getting dangerous, Rose. I'm thinking of handing in my cards if it gets much worse." Peter answered nonchalantly.

"We're all dying to know what you've been up to for the past few weeks…you've been very quiet." Rose looked at him intensely.

'So much for thinking Rose had no clue.' Peter thought to himself. Peter had only slightly changed his pattern of behavior for a few weeks and already questions were arising. It was going to be difficult to keep his and George's involvement under wraps but Peter decided that no one should know of any further visits to Bakaar. They would have to arrange their own tickets and keep quiet about it in future.

"Not a lot," Peter said flippantly, smiling but trying to ignore Rose's question. The last thing he needed was to have Rose getting involved, seeking a mystery and questioning his every move. "We're just re-assessing our role in Bakaar, there's a lot of work to do with the Government, and between you and me, and strictly off the record, Rose, we can't be sure which Government we'll be dealing with. Even if there were any projects we wanted to have a go at. We're having to pay so much under the table that we'd have to be sure they'll be in power when we need them." Peter gave her a conspiratorial glance to let her know he was sharing a confidence.

"So, that's what it's all about ?"

"That's about all I know, Rose."

"Well, you'd better be careful, that's all I can say."

Peter did not want to say that Barnard was bribing officials in Bakaar, but on the other hand, telling the staff nothing of his visit created even more of a problem. Peter hoped he had said enough to ensure that Rose felt included and that she would not start looking at every detail to try and keep herself in the picture.

As usual when Peter worked out of the London office he borrowed a desk and spent most of the day on the telephone. He spoke to Muli, his right hand man in Nairobi, and caught up on his day to day responsibilities. He also spoke with Tim and as he expected, the delays were beginning to build up. The much promised efficiency was rapidly turning African. Tim reported that Frederick had disappeared for the past few days. He had wandered off on a family matter, leaving the switches unfinished and Tim had been chasing all over Rapanda trying to find him.

Peter met Sarah for dinner as planned, but they still did not make it to the Italian restaurant. They spent the entire weekend at Sarah's apartment and it was not until the following Wednesday that they finally got their Italian dinner. Tim called on Thursday and confirmed that Frederick had returned and that he and Doug would be in New York on Monday complete with the switches which Peter wanted to examine.

By the time Peter left for New York he felt every day of his forty-five years and he was tired, very tired. The Bakaaran version of the American passport meant that Peter should pass through immigration into the U.S. without difficulty. The only paperwork he was required to complete was the customs declaration. He carried only $9,900 of George's money into the U.S., less than the permitted $10,000, which meant he did not have to declare it or risk lying about its origins, his tax status and a whole sheaf of questions he did not need. George was bringing in a similar sum and additional cash would be wired into a local account as needed.

It was pure luck, but the first name on Peter's new documents was still, 'Peter'. Getting used to a new name was no easy matter it could easily trip you up. When using false documents the real danger was an unlucky break. Getting involved in an accident, or witnessing one or even being stopped for speeding. Anything requiring the formal provision of personal information may not check out.

George had provided them with some protection. They were each employed by the electronics distributor and the Bakaaran consulate had somehow produced New York driving licenses for them. Peter considered their cover was deep enough to survive if they were careful and just a little bit lucky. George traveled to the U.S. every couple of months and his continuing to do so would attract no attention. Peter was also concerned about the need to pay for everything in cash. These days any self respecting traveler presents an array of plastic not cash and as opposed to ensuring anonymity cash has the reverse effect. On the other hand, a credit card transaction creates a traceable record. George came up with a solution. He ordered each of them a credit card in their new names, on the account of Electronic Communications, the New York company which he indirectly controlled.

Peter flew Delta to New York and upon arrival at Kennedy, he carefully followed the arrows on the floor to immigration for U.S. Citizens. Peter stood in the short line waiting at one of the many glass booths occupied by immigration officers. He watched others at the booths on either side enter and present their passports. Most got a pleasant, 'Welcome home!' and were on their way in a minute or two. But one young man, ahead of him in his own line, who looked a like a student, was having a rough time. After an intense conversation another officer arrived and escorted the young man into an office at the rear of the hall. Peter could not help feeling some anticipation. He had no knowledge as to what information was presented on the screen when the officer slid the document into the scanner. He had been assured by the Bakaaran intelligence officers that it would work without a problem. It would check out. The original owner was the U.S. citizen whose details were shown, the only difference was the photograph. Peter hoped that the Bakaaran's craft in compiling the photo page and resealing the document was as good as it should be.

The family ahead of him moved into the booth and Peter waited, toes on the red line. After just a couple of minutes and multiple stamps, the family gathered up its hand baggage and moved out of the booth. Peter was beckoned to go forward. He handed his new passport and customs declaration to the immigration officer who, hardly glancing at it, slid it into the scanner. He studied the screen for a moment. He hesitated and looked at Peter, who fought not to swallow or turn his head away to avoid the gaze. The split second seemed an eternity as Peter maintained his best impression of a citizen returning home. The officer removed the passport from the scanner, arranged the Customs Declaration, picked up the stamp—bang, bang, a stamp on each document and Peter was on his way to the customs area to await the arrival of his baggage.

He was lucky. He spotted his bags among the first on the belt. He picked them off and joined one of the lines to pass through inspection and out into the terminal. As he waited, he noticed a number of Customs Officials talking to each other in the passenger area, away from the inspection desks at the end of the lines. He had only been in the line for a few moments when one of the officers looked straight at him. Their eyes met. The officer walked towards him. The last thing Peter wanted was a detailed inspection of his baggage. He did not know how well he could play the part of an American. Should he try and imitate an American accent? Peter could not understand what triggered the official's interest in him. Peter hoped he would get waylaid by another passenger, but as he came closer there was no doubt that Peter was the officer's designated target.

The customs officer held out his hand. Peter was unsure what he wanted, he looked as if he wanted to shake hands, but Peter knew that was not likely.

"Gudda declaration?" he asked in a strong Bronx accent.

Peter's customs declaration was tucked into his passport. He struggled to free a hand, withdrew the declaration and handed it over. The officer glanced at the U.S. passport still in Peter's hand.

"Returning home?" the officer asked rhetorically.

"Yes," Peter kept it simple and did not try an American accent.

"Where ya bin?"

"United Kingdom."

The officer did not look at him at all, he did not seem to be interested in Peter, so why had he picked him out?

"Purpose of the trip, bidness or vacation?"

"Just a short business trip."

"D'ya have any samples, ya importing anything for bidness?"

"No, nothing." Peter answered.

The officer scribbled on Peter's declaration and handed it back to him with continuing disinterest.

"Hand it to the officer at the door," he said pointing around the inspection desks to the door out into the terminal. As Peter made a point of not hurrying towards the door he could see similar inspections taking place all over the area. It was obviously intended to speed up the process for anyone who did not fit any of the profiles which required a search. If he were a tourist he would be delighted with the service, but in the circumstances it had rattled him. He hoped Tim and Doug knew the system—their luggage was full of electronics.

• • •

"Peter West for Mr. Barnard," Peter announced the name on his American passport to the receptionist as he arrived at George's New York office exactly at 9.00 a.m. on Monday morning. The first name being the same was just a lucky fluke.

"Do you have an appointment?"

"Yes, nine o'clock."

"Please take a seat and I'll let him know you're here."

Peter sat down, choosing a chair furthest from the only other visitor, who in spite of the no smoking signs was smoking an evil smelling cigar. He picked up a copy of Time Magazine from the table and began to thumb through the pages. A couple of minutes passed. The reception phone buzzed and was quickly answered.

"Mr. West, Mr. Barnard will see you now," the receptionist called as she replaced the phone.

The man with the evil cigar looked up and glanced at Peter. Peter did not respond, he continued reading the magazine. The receptionist walked around the desk and towards Peter, "Mr. West..." She leaned forward almost in front of Peter. The movement caught Peter's eye and he suddenly realized she had called him by his new name. He got up and followed her along the corridor. George greeted Peter formally and the receptionist left and closed the door.

"No problems with the travel documents?"

"Everything was fine, no problems." Peter answered aware that he needed to practice using his new name.

"I've got the driver's licenses from the Consulate and the credit cards." George took an envelope out of his desk and handed it to Peter. It contained the documents for himself, Tim and Doug. Apart from the photographs which Peter had supplied, the documents told George nothing. He still did not know who David Schwartz or William Barnes really were, they were Peter's business, and it was better that he knew nothing about them.

George took out another packet. It contained business cards, some decals and two bundles of the embroidered name tags seen on almost every work shirt in the U.S., one said 'David' the other 'Bill'.

"When do your lads arrive?" George asked.

"They're coming in this afternoon. In fact I've got to get out to Kennedy to meet them," Peter looked at his watch, " I'd better get going."

There was little more to say. Peter repacked the decals, picked up the package and left quickly.

Peter got a cab to the airport, collected the white Ford truck at the Hertz Rental center using his newly acquired credit card and driving license. He then returned to the terminal and parked to await Tim and Doug's arrival. Tim had to get the electronics through without inspection. Although Peter was apprehensive Tim and Doug had an advantage. They were not the Americans stated in their passports, but they were American and they knew the system.

Peter watched passengers as they entered the terminal from the customs area. He caught sight of a luggage tag which corresponded to Tim's flight. It would not be much longer. Fifteen minutes passed and more passengers from Tim's flight were greeted by awaiting relatives and friends. Thirty minutes and still no sign of Tim or Doug.

Peter's apprehension deepened. Had they been stopped. If the electronics were questioned or confiscated the entire project was in danger.

As Peter's apprehension began to become worry Tim emerged, closely followed by Doug. To Peter's partial relief their smiling faces suggested all was well.

"Hi, boss!"

"Hello, Doug. How are you?" Peter inquired anxiously. "All well? Have you got it?"

"That's, I'm well and two yes's," Doug replied answering all three of Peter's over anxious questions. "God, it was busy as hell in there, it took nearly thirty-five minutes for our bags to arrive."

Peter's unasked question as to the time it had taken answered, he continued with his grilling, trying to remove all areas of uncertainty as quickly as he could. "How did it go? I assume you've got everything we need."

"Yeah, we've got it all, and it worked when we left the Dark Continent," Tim answered, "I hope the crash course in phone engineering is enough for me to install this babe."

"This is just a rehearsal. You're going to get a lot more practice before you're back next month."

The baggage was piled in the back of the van and Tim drove into Manhattan. Peter was dropped off and Tim and Doug took the truck uptown. They had to have a hotel out of the city center so that they could park and have easy access to the van. Later that afternoon they went shopping.

Chapter 19

Paperwork had already been created for Tim and Doug's employment. Files existed in the personnel department of Electronic Communications Inc., in their new names showing that they were hired in Chicago and being transferred to New York. They were to help out with the workload on test marketing phone system upgrades. New York expected Tim and Doug and Peter was the imported marketing man in charge of the test.

On Tuesday morning, Peter sat in the reception area waiting. He had already introduced himself to Michele, the receptionist and had obtained a key to the office. He was early and while waiting for Tim and Doug he decided to take a preliminary look at the phone system. He stood up and asked Michele where it was located.

"It's at the back of the general office. Follow me. You're English aren't you?" She asked as they walked through the office.

"I was." Peter answered.

"I thought you were but I didn't say anything. I can always tell an English accent, I'm French, well my grandfather was. I'm also half Russian, my mother's parents came from Russia. You've got a great tan.

That didn't come from around here. I bet you've been to the Caribbean? I'd love to go but my husband doesn't like the sun…"

They reached the closet and Michelle opened the door to display the control unit. The action created a break in her soliloquy. Peter was relieved that she could not sustain the flow of incessant chatter and open the closet at the same time. He thanked her quickly hoping to avoid another verbal onslaught. Mercifully the phone on the reception desk began ringing and she ran to answer it providing no opportunity for her to continue talking.

At ten o'clock, Tim and Doug arrived dressed in jeans and blue work shirts proudly displaying their new names—the result of their shopping expedition and some late night sewing in the hotel. Each carried a tool box labeled with decals George had supplied—"Electronic Communications Inc.—Telephone Service Unit" and Doug carried several small boxes containing new additions to the system.

"Hello, gentlemen," Peter said, "I'll show you where the system's located."

Peter then left them to get on with it, advising that he would be back after lunch. When he returned they were nearly finished.

"How the fuck did you persuade me to do this?" Tim asked as Peter arrived.

"Having problems?" Peter replied, hoping they were not serious.

"Not really, it's just such a goddamned fiddle. I think we've done it right. I've gotten it wired into extension one two six five. It sure as hell better be right, now I need to test it."

"Leave it until the office closes," Peter advised, "We don't want anyone to see what you've done." Peter looked in Michele's direction as he said anyone. Tim and Doug having suffered the endless chit-chat during the entire day knew exactly what he meant.

They returned at six forty-five and like a group of excited kids, crowded into the closet to look at Tim's handiwork. Peter gazed at the circuit board not really knowing what to look for.

"Where is it?" Peter asked after about fifteen seconds of silence.

"There's the little bastard," Tim pointed to the small flat metal box now attached to the backboard. "Looks simple doesn't it. Given more time I could hide the extension wires in the duct behind the wall and you'd never see 'em, but for the test I'm gonna connect 'em in the open. Doug, you got the switch?"

"Yeah," Doug took the second box out of his toolbox. It was no bigger than a pack of cigarettes and had a small light and a test button on it. Doug pressed the button and the light glowed red. "It's got a battery in it," he said knowingly.

Peter took it from him wondering just for a moment if he had made the right choice of backup in Doug. There was not much to see. A couple of wires extended from each end of the box and a row of numbered dip switches ran along one side.

Tim pointed to the switches, "You just set these to the code number you want to use. This is just a test kit. You can set and change the number by phone on the working versions. The hooks and adhesive pads look rinky-dink. You know, a bit like the lunar module back in the sixties—all aluminum foil and sticky paper, but it worked. You can hang 'em or stick 'em in almost any goddamned place."

Having completed the installation Tim was enjoying himself. It took him just a couple of minutes to connect the switch to the trailing wires from the control board.

"Somebody better go make that call…Doug, I think that's a direct line." Tim pointed to a phone on one of the desks in the office. Doug was sifting through his tool box, like a child looking for toys. He was not paying attention. Peter left the closet and picked up the phone. "I'll dial into the office. What's the number, Tim?"

Peter dialed the number and waited for the automated attendant to pick up. He was amused. He had finally found a way to make use of the detested human-less system. 'If you know your party's extension you can dial it now....' He dialed the extension to which they had added their switch, 1265. It began to ring.

"OK, you gotta wait ten rings then you'll get a bleep, like an answering machine on the eleventh. Dial 1.3.5.8. then wait ten seconds. It will bleep twice more and you have to dial 5.7.9.6. If the red light goes on we've got ourselves one hell of a tragedy!"

Peter scribbled the numbers down on a scrap of paper. One, two, three, four, he counted the rings. 'Bleep!' He dialed 1.3.5.8: It took exactly ten seconds then bleeped twice more, 5.7.9.6…The little red light glowed.

"Bang!" Doug shouted, slapping his hand on the desk as he said it.

"Alright! We did it!" Tim shouted, "I'm a fucking telephone engineer. Do I graduate? Do I get my degree?" Tim was pleased with himself. When the excitement died down, Peter produced a utility plan of the building. "Now we have to get real. We've got to see where we could take those cables. We've got a lot of work to do tonight."

Doug started to clear up. Peter eased Tim out of the room. "What's the matter with Doug? Is he O.K.?"

"Yeah I guess so. He's just acting up. He's not as stupid as he's making out. He knows we're trying to get $1 billion for our efforts and he's been making noises about how much he's worth and he's not getting enough…"

"How much are you paying him?"

"He's getting $100,000. That's more than he's ever earned on one job."

"What's his beef? Why doesn't he think that's enough? I guess he accepted it at the start."

"He's just looking at a $1 billion and I guess he can't even imagine that much money. He's just whining."

"Yeah, maybe. But we don't want a problem. Keep me posted."

"Yeah, OK. I'll deal with it."

They worked all Tuesday night finishing early Wednesday morning. This installation was strictly practice. There was no intention of using it; it was intended to check out the problems and allow them to be better prepared for the real thing.

The exercise provided vital information on the type of building that they should seek. They required accessible ducts and trunks through which to run the wiring. The office they chose had to be as close as possible to the mechanical floor, preferably adjacent to it.

They made one major mistake. They bought and used new cable. In most of the older buildings, the wiring for long gone tenants was disconnected but remained in the ducts. Tim's bright new cable stood out like a sore thumb. If anyone got as far as to check out the building they would see the new cable and then either risk cutting it or could follow it through the ducts to its eventual destination. An immediate task was to obtain used cable. It had to disappear into the morass of old wiring they would find in their old buildings, removing the possibility that someone could easily track down the location of the bomb from the phone system.

Peter got back to his hotel early Wednesday morning and wearily slumped down on the bed. Less than a minute after he laid down the phone rang. He stretched his hand out above and behind him trying not to have to move his weary body, but he could not reach. He shuffled nearer to the top of the bed and still lying on his back was able to pick it up.

"Hello." he said in a resigned, tired voice.

"I want to talk dirty." The female voice at the other end of the line sounded familiar, "I've been without you for nearly a week and if I don't get laid…"

"You'll have to wait," Peter replied, a smile crossing his face, but without joining in the spirit of the call, "Hello, Sarah, otherwise how are you?"

"You guessed! I thought you might say Carol, or Pat and drop yourself right in it. When are you coming home?"

"It looks as if we'll be finished by Thursday, we've got some details to tidy up but I expect to be out of here on Friday. Should be back on Saturday with any luck."

"Will I get you quicker if I pick you up at the airport on Saturday?"

"Give me a chance," Peter replied. "I've only just recovered from last week!"

"So, what's your problem old man? Are you going to spend the weekend with me, or not?"

"Yes, I'd love to. I'll call you and let you know the flight number."

Sarah would not be put off that easily and she continued to whisper in his ear. Peter was uneasy talking sexy on the phone. Sweet nothings were not his thing. He felt like an observer, watching himself and he was embarrassed by what he saw. Somehow, Sarah managed to hit on all of his hang-ups. After several more minutes, he persuaded her to put the phone down. He dragged himself off the bed, cleaned up and went back to bed to sleep.

During the following days, Tim rented a mini-storage unit near the airport. They were going to store the tools, clothes, credit cards, everything they would need again in June. Peter had to return to London. He called Sarah, confirmed his flight number and headed for JFK.

Doug and Tim were remaining in the U.S. They needed to buy used cable, lots of it, and more tools. Their last day in the City was warm. One of those May days when the jet stream obligingly kinks and allows the wind to blow gently up from the south pushing the mercury up above seventy degrees. They set out with the rush hour, fighting the incoming traffic as they headed uptown. Doug drove, weaving and cursing his way across the traffic to Route 95 and the George Washington Bridge. By the time they hit the bridge there was as much traffic heading for New Jersey as there was coming into the city. Finally they drew alongside the tollbooth on the western side of the river, paid the toll and turned south for Union City. They had decided that anything they purchased should be second hand. Once they were on the job in New York for real, they had to look as if they had been installing phones forever. Their tools and equipment should not look new. They would visit every junkyard they could find until they had what they wanted. Apart from Doug's cursing, little had been said since they left the hotel.

"Did you speak to Peter?"

"Yeah I tried, but it's not his problem. You're working for me."

"I need more money, Tim. Hundred thousand goes nowhere. For Christ's sake they're getting $1 billion and I'm taking all the risks."

"What do you think I'm doing. I'm in this thing too."

"Sure you are but how much are you getting?"

"None of your fucking business. You accepted a hundred thousand. I can't go back to Peter and start pleading for more money. A deal's a deal."

"Whatever you're getting, it's not enough. I got no beef against Berruda and his guys, but I want a bigger share. It's not for me to talk to Peter, but you got to get more money. Hey, if we walk away they ain't got nothing. No bomb, nothing. Now's the time to put the squeeze on 'em."

"You know Doug, sometimes I think you are stupid. We may be the guys doing the work down here. But this thing involves governments, it's big time. You try putting the squeeze on and I'll tell you now, you'll end up back in that pissing river with a couple of neat round holes in your head."

"Fuck you, Tim. We're gonna have to get more money."

Chapter 20

Bakaar was not one of the countries considered sensitive in the modern world. The harbor in Rapanda was the only asset that might have strategic value, but it was no longer of any military use. Due to neglect, it had silted up. Robert Berruda had, by necessity, continued his close association with Great Britain. There was no interest from the U.S. and following the demise of the Soviet Union, Bakaar could not even play the East against West card.

The CIA tried to keep abreast of developments and trends in low priority areas through reports from businessmen, journalists or anyone who could provide regular and objective comment. These were often copies of trip reports or news stories sent back to the businessman's company or the journalist's paper that may or may not be destined for publication. The trip reports provided little more than second hand accounts of the economic or financial situation and the news stories rarely provided any real political insight. However, every now and again a couple of reports might cover the same subject in a single week or highlight a trend which might suggest a need for greater attention. Occasionally, they could be early warnings of changes that might affect

U.S. interests in the region. The latest report concerning Bakaar was one of those rarities:

> 'The opposition to Robert Berruda's Government is becoming organized and armed. A Minister's car was machine gunned and on Saturday, April 11, another armed attack was carried out. This time a building at the harbor was fired upon, killing three people and injuring others, including a police officer. There is a suspicion that the Chief of the Ministry of the Interior might have been the target. There are now troops on the streets and Rapanda, the capital, is tense. It appears that the situation is worsening and there is the possibility that these events are connected.'

The report was from an American Investment Banker, Ron McDade, who was in Bakaar during the shooting incident at the docks. His name was well known to the analyst at the CIA offices in Langley, Virginia. McDade traveled frequently for his bank in Africa and the CIA received his reports. Over the years the reports had proven to be accurate and reliable. Short but to the point. McDade visited Bakaar several times each year and he noticed some of the subtle changes as well as the more obvious ones. His reports provided a uniform viewpoint which made it possible to establish trends. This time the comments were sufficient to warrant the CIA analyst's supervisor to prepare a report. It was sent to the operations officer responsible for Bakaar. The situation was unlikely to adversely affect any U.S. interests, but the British were still involved in Bakaar and a copy of the report was sent to London for the Embassy to pass on to MI5. A little transatlantic cooperation.

The assessment was that Berruda's Government was not strong. The country was weak economically and if there was an organized and persistent opposition they might well be able to topple Berruda. It was not likely that the opposition had any substantial following and also unlikely that any other government was trying to muscle in on Bakaar.

But African politics was a constant puzzle and it was just possible that another of the African nations might have reason to become involved.

The bank that submitted Ron McDade's report was asked for more detailed information when someone next made a visit. They were asked to pay particular attention to anything, which might suggest an organized effort to overthrow Berruda's Government.

• • •

During a routine examination of satellite photographs at the National Reconnaissance Office which showed the area around Rapanda it was noticed that a number of new buildings had been erected at an industrial plant outside the city. Lynn Parsons, the officer responsible for Bakaar, spotted them and knowing that Bakaar was virtually broke and was not building anything new, felt it just might advance her career if she were first to identify a new problem. She made out a report and enhancements of the photographs were requested.

When they arrived, Lynn examined them and could see clearly that there were additional sectional buildings stored on the site. The area was examined on several consecutive passes of the satellite and the progress of the construction could be seen. Knowing that information on Bakaar was of little interest to anyone her first inclination was to take it no further. It could be an innocent commercial construction and who would care? However, nothing else in Bakaar was expanding and the building was relatively remote and like a dog with a bone, she could not leave it alone. She decided to have one last look. As she examined the photographs again she noticed that one of the new buildings was very small and had been erected on the side of what seemed to be the entrance road. She looked more carefully. There were some vague shadows which might just be a fence of some kind. A not very substantial fence, perhaps a wire fence—a barbed wire fence? Going against all her training her imagination began to run away with her. If she stretched it just a little, the new building could be a guard house on the road and that suggested it might well be more than commercial expansion. She decided to report her idea. Her supervisor was pleasant but firm. His imagination was not that flexible. The report was filed.

• • •

Tom Jacobson was making only his second trip for the bank into Bakaar. As requested following Ron McDade's report he had been specifically asked to keep his eyes open. The bank wanted a detailed report of the situation in the country. What were the whispers around Rapanda. Tom had a number of appointments spread over four days, but he had plenty of time to look around.

He noticed the increased security from the moment he arrived at the airport. There were more troops and policemen than he remembered and there were armored personnel carriers guarding the entrance to the airport. In Rapanda, all of the Government buildings had armed troops at the doors and there was a road barrier at the entrance to the harbor near the club which had been shot up back in April. There was no doubt that the tension was greater than when he had first been in Bakaar a year before.

Tom discussed the situation with one of his contacts in the Bank of Bakaar. He thought the Government knew who had carried out the attacks on the Minister and on the club at the docks, but did not want to arrest them for fear of polarizing the opposition along tribal lines. The Government appeared content to demonstrate a show of force to deter further adventures and it seemed to be working. There had been no serious incident since the attack on the club.

Tom had rented a car from the airport. Several of his appointments were outside the city and although he would normally have used one of the famed Rapanda cabs, he felt that the detailed report requested of him warranted the expense of a rental. It would enable him to look a little further and wider. In fact, he had a second agenda. When he had been in Rapanda the previous year he had joined a bus tour. He had seen some wooden carvings in a small village outside Rapanda at about a quarter of the price asked in the shops in the city. As soon as he left the country he had kicked himself for not buying them and he was determined to find the village and buy something like them on this trip.

The next day his first appointment was in what he remembered to be the general direction of the carvings and he set off in good time to make the detour. He turned off the paved road he thought to be the route the bus had taken to the village. It was a dusty dirt road and the car lurched and rattled as he slowly negotiated the rutted surface. So long as he kept moving he could see ahead, but when he slowed or stopped to avoid potholes the following dust cloud caught up, overtook him and enveloped the car in a choking reddish brown fog. His view of the road obscured he had to wait for the cloud to disperse before moving off again.

After driving for about twenty minutes the car, his shirt, his hair, everything was a reddish brown and he could not get rid of the dry, bitter, gritty taste of the all pervading dust in his mouth. When he had first turned off the paved road on the outskirts of Rapanda, there had been a good number of people walking along the dirt road. At times it had been difficult to avoid hitting them as they loomed out of the dust cloud. Now the road was deserted. No one was walking and there was no traffic. He realized he was lost, he must have taken the wrong road or missed a turning off this one. His wooden carvings were not out here. Just before a sharp bend he decided to return to Rapanda. He braked and stopped, waiting for the dust cloud to dissipate. As it cleared a police car and a small truck passed by, slowly negotiating the ruts and once again raising the dust.

Obviously the road went somewhere and curious, he moved forward intending to go just a little further. As he rounded the bend he was faced with a straight stretch of road blocked by a barrier and a small hut. The barrier was raised and the police car and the truck had just passed through. Beyond was an impressive old factory building. He drove on, the factory was surrounded by a shiny new barbed wire fence complete with flood lights. It could have been a prison.

As he drew near, a soldier came out of the guard house and directed him to stop. Tom wound down the window. The soldier approached and spoke in English, he had an automatic rifle slung over his shoulder, "You can't go further. You turn round." As he spoke he made a circular motion with his left hand.

"I'm lost and I'm trying to get back to Rapanda," Tom advised in what he considered to be a good impression of a British tourist.

"You can't go further, turn round. That way!" This time the tone was less casual and the left hand pointed vigorously back down the road, the way he had come.

"Yes, O.K. But is that the way back to Rapanda?" Tom needed a little more time to make sure he could remember the layout and report it accurately. Before the soldier replied he counted the new buildings and tried to see what was going on. He was uncertain of how good the soldier's English might be. He probably did not understand it as well as he appeared to speak it. Tom's question did not receive a reply. Instead the soldier slipped the rifle sling off his shoulder and came towards the car with the weapon pointing uncomfortably at Tom's head. Tom decided it was time to comply, turned the wheel and started a hurried three-point turn. The movement covered the soldier in dust but seemed to satisfy him. The rifle returned to a less threatening position and the soldier backed off. Tom drove back to Rapanda.

There was no way he could clean his clothing or hair and by the time he arrived late for his appointment, he looked as if he had been on safari for weeks. He excused his appearance, described where he had been and asked if his hosts knew of the old factory.

"Oh, yes!" one responded, " It's the fertilizer plant. Produces agricultural fertilizer. Built by the British."

"Have you been out there lately?" Tom inquired.

The younger man replied, "No, but we understand the Government's started doing something out there. All the workers were screened by the police, some were laid off and the rest provided with ID cards. They've put up some new buildings and we believe soldiers are living out there now. No one who works there will talk about it."

"If you look at the fence, you'd think it was a prison. Do you think it could be?" Tom could not think of anything else and given the brief he had received about the opposition to Berruda, he could only think that perhaps the old fox was locking up the troublemakers.

"No, if you look at it, the fence is designed to keep people out." The older of the two men said indicating that he must have been out there.

Tom returned to his hotel and after removing the red grime from every orifice in his body, he started to make notes. It took nearly two weeks for Tom's report to find its way to Langley.

On Monday, May 11, the officer at the CIA studied Tom's report with interest. He referred back to the first report which had sparked his interest and his request for more information. There was no basis for any conclusions. But the fencing of the factory suggested there was a new reason to keep people in or out, either way, something different was going on. Tom Jacobson had made a pointed note that his banker contacts considered that the security was designed to keep people out. The reader considered that it was worthwhile to check whether the NRO had carried out any reconnaissance that might confirm when the factory had been fenced and whether there was any other activity which might arouse interest. The British had not responded to the report sent in April and a follow up was sent to London to see if they had any input.

The inquiry from Langley finally arrived on Lynn Parsons desk on May 19. She immediately gained access to the information filed back in April and this time her supervisor agreed that they had reason to ask for a more detailed examination. Lynn felt excited, but sadly noted that there was no praise for her original interpretation of the photographs, which seemed to be correct. The request for an investigation was granted and an examination of satellite photographs of the entire coastal region of Bakaar began. Through the Director of Central Intelligence, to whom both the CIA and NRO report, a request was sent to the National Security Agency for any communications that may have been picked up during electronic eavesdropping. Ever so slowly, the wheels of the most extensive intelligence organization in the free world were beginning to turn.

• • •

To the British Government, Bakaar was just one of many ex colonies which had offered little except a financial drain on the exchequer. It produced nothing, received some aid and was of no strategic value in the nineties. A British warship had once sought refuge in the docks at Rapanda for some urgently needed repairs and the harbor was used to make transfers of personnel during the famous meeting between Harold Wilson and Ian Smith during the Rhodesian crisis. Currently Bakaar was of little interest to anyone.

There had been some inconsequential discussions between the CIA and the British in London when the inquiry had first been received from Langley, but no official response had been made, nor had one been sought.

The British had an embassy in Bakaar and to save cost and time, the CIA based in the U.S. Embassy in Grosvenor Square in London requested assistance from their British counterparts. This time they asked specifically for a report on the fertilizer plant. The British report arrived at the U.S. Embassy on May 27.

'CONFIDENTIAL:

As requested we have carried out a physical survey of the fertilizer plant situated ten miles north of Rapanda.

It has operated for many years, using labor from local villages and Rapanda. At the end of March, this year, a barbed wire fence was erected, floodlighting was installed and the road into the plant was blocked off by a gatehouse and barrier. Many workers were laid off and security ID's were issued to the remaining workforce. A number of temporary buildings were erected during April and May and there is now a substantial contingent of troops living on site apparently providing security. Although wearing standard issue Army uniforms the troops are apparently under the direct control of the Ministry of the Interior. The already sparse brush has been cleared for a distance of about 200 feet from the fence.

There have been deliveries of building materials which appear to have been utilized within the old factory suggesting that some substantial structure has been built inside the old building. There has been an increase in vehicular traffic on the access road. Although we have not been able to confirm their nature there have been a number of heavily guarded shipments from the docks to the plant. There has been no attempt to conceal the delivery of building materials and we must therefore assume that the content of the other deliveries was sensitive. We do not consider that the plant is used as a prison. We consider that security is intended to secure the factory from outside access.

We consider that some form of extension to its industrial or commercial potential is being completed and that the purpose is being concealed. Output of agricultural fertilizer has continued although at a lower volume than previously. It is not possible to see all of the temporary buildings from the road and security is such that we could not carry out a more detailed survey without the risk of being observed or of placing ourselves in some jeopardy.

Please advise if more information is required.

> *Commercial Attaché*
> *British Embassy*
> *Rapanda*
> *Bakaar*
> *25th May*

The report was sent immediately to Langley and the wheels turned a little faster.

Chapter 21

Spring had become summer and time was passing quickly. Peter made several trips to the U.S. and ordered the cradles—the metal basket into which each of the components would be installed. Great care had been taken to ensure that the protective clothing, breathing apparatus and some of the remote handling equipment was bought through friendly African and Middle Eastern sources, not from Europe. This equipment was kept locked up and guarded around the clock. Peter was present when the three shipments were taken from the airport to the fertilizer plant. He supervised the loading of the trucks and joined the convoy for its short journey. He could confirm first hand that no one had access to the contents.

Peter knew that little could be done in secret. In Bakaar, the attempt to maintain secrecy fed the rumor mills and the attempt at secrecy became the center of attention. As Peter said, they could have shipped the equipment hidden in the building materials, but it would be more dangerous. Every shipment arriving in Bakaar gets rifled to some extent, someone always thinks they have a right to a little of everything which passes through their hands. If one of the trucks carrying the equipment had an accident and was not closely guarded, it would not be knowledge of the contents all over Rapanda, it would be the contents themselves. Kids on the street would be playing space games wearing protective bio-suits by the end of the day. It was decided that complete secrecy and rumors were the best bet. Peter knew their operation would be discovered, he wanted that. It was necessary that it would be. But when it was discovered was crucial. Peter had to retain control of 'when'.

The laboratory had been built and Peter saw it complete for the first time when he accompanied the final delivery to the plant. In the first few weeks, the project had become larger than life and in the same way as meeting an idolized film star, the reality was smaller than the image. Peter had imagined the laboratory to be substantial, long benches and gleaming, polished surfaces taking up the entire ground floor of the massive old factory. In fact it was a building within a building and was quite small. The need was not for bulk manufacture, they required very little of the product.

The laboratory had no common walls with the existing building. It stood alone in the center of what had been a storage area for fertilizer and was manufactured from reinforced concrete blocks designed to withstand a moderate earthquake. The laboratory contained just two small rooms each measuring about sixteen by fourteen feet. A substantial wall separated the safe room, in which the technicians worked, from the area in which the VX gas was mixed, tested and stored. Benches ran along both sides of the wall and above them a heavy, armored glass screen was set in the wall. Remote handling equipment, operated from the safe side of the glass screen allowed the technicians to safely mix and test the two agents.

Nirina's value was his knowledge of binary production, the safe method of producing the gas. Two virtually harmless chemicals, isopropanol and methyl phosphonyl difluroride, are produced separately and only when mixed do they become the toxic gas, VX. The description of the substance as a gas is misleading. VX is not a gas at all. It is an oily, viscous liquid, but when vaporized, it remains suspended in the air and can be carried for miles by air currents. It is not new. It was discovered in the fifties when the world was still trying to improve on the recently realized horrors of the atom bomb. The military needed a weapon which would have the same devastating affect on troops on the battlefield as the atom bomb. One which was able to be narrowly targeted, kill people, but leave buildings and the infrastructure intact. Preferably it should not create a radio active, no-go area for friendly forces.

The scientists struck gold. VX provided the terror of an almost certain and horrific death and in spite of more than forty years of research no one has found a more toxic, useable product. Just one drop the size of a pin head absorbed through the skin and even smaller amounts if swallowed or inhaled, are fatal. Regardless of the manner in which the gas is absorbed, it begins to take effect so fast that treatment is almost impossible. Within ten minutes anyone receiving a lethal dose suffers severe cramps and vomiting followed by paralysis and death from suffocation.

There is an antidote, self injection through clothing, straight into a muscle. The problem is, VX is so fast acting that the antidote has to be administered almost before contamination to have any chance of success.

For George and Peter, VX offered the best possible threat. It cannot be seen and upon contact it is almost certainly fatal, a silent killer of the worst kind. If the gas were released high above a city it would drift in the complex air currents between the buildings, eventually finding its way onto surfaces in the streets below. As long as the weather remained dry it would remain for days on the surfaces of vehicles, door handles, fire hydrants, parking meters, waiting for its innocent victims. Simply opening a cab door could prove lethal

It was this unavoidable indiscriminate nature of VX which was valuable as a terrorist tool. The awful inevitable death would be played up by the media if it got wind that use of the gas was threatened. You could even argue that the threat was the ultimate use of public relations. If the threat became public the terrorist could rely on the target country's media doing most of his work. That assumed it became a public threat. The expectation was that the government would try and ensure that it never happened, they would pay up rather than demonstrate their vulnerability. There should be no need to kill anyone.

George and Peter had to prove to the U.S. Government that Bakaar had the capability to produce the gas. They also had to get it into a U.S. city in a form which could distribute the gas in such a way that it could kill thousands. The amount of gas and the size of the actual bomb were almost irrelevant. The task was to appear credible and demonstrate that the provision of aid was the only reasonable way out. If the U.S. Government tried to evacuate the city on some less threatening pretext, then Bakaar would leak the news to the media They would announce the presence of the gas before it was exploded. There would be panic. If the U.S. allowed the bomb to be detonated without announcing the nerve gas content, hundreds, maybe even thousands of city residents and workers would return to their cars, climb in a cab or open a door and in ten minutes they would die a ghastly death. It needed only one death and an announcement from Bakaar and once again there would be panic. It was not only fear of panic in a major city, it was the need to maintain the illusion that U.S. citizens in their everyday lives are safe from such attacks. Far better for the Government to provide a billion dollars in aid than face the cold, hard, undeniable fact that they and their President were powerless.

· · ·

Because Nirina had been virtually kidnapped Peter dared not trust him. Not that Nirina would do anything for the sake of mankind, but he might hold back on the manufacture as a means of protecting himself until he was released. Peter had instructed one of the Bakaaran chemists to watch him and supervise the testing of the gas every step of the way making sure Nirina did as he was told.

Toward the end of May Peter received word in London that the gas had been tested on animals in the laboratory. Unfortunately for the animals it worked. They had the gas. Peter was anxious to get on. He was due to leave on Sunday, June 7, and would spend the next three weeks with Tim and Doug. At the end of this time they would be able to rig the phone system and set up the detonator. The electronics were finished and Peter confirmed that the cradles were ready. He had personally delivered four of them to the storage unit at Kennedy Airport and shipped two, the larger one and one other, to Bakaar.

Peter left Sarah's apartment early on Saturday morning to do some last minute shopping before his departure for Bakaar. He walked down the steps into the square, crossed the road and turned into Elizabeth Street heading towards the shops at Victoria Station. It was a beautiful morning, mild and still. The sun-dappled sidewalk was dry and the sounds of the waking city had that unique early morning echo that would be lost when the traffic noise rose to its normal deafening roar. He became aware of steel tipped heels on the pavement behind him. The sound was getting louder echoing off the high walls of the houses facing directly on to the street on the southern side of Elizabeth Street. He realized it was the echoing footsteps that had made him aware of the stillness. The ringing heels had been with him since he left Sarah's. Someone was following him, he turned at the exact moment the footsteps caught up with him.

"Mr. Williamson?"

Peter was confronted by a tall, solid man in his mid thirties, overdressed for the mild morning in a beige raincoat, unbuttoned and flapping open as he came to an abrupt halt. Crowning his red, sweaty face, he wore a brown felt hat and the ringing heels were a component part of a pair of heavy, well polished, brown brogue shoes. Apart from the raincoat, the clothes were all shades of brown and green an odd assortment of tweeds and checks. It was the unmistakable weekend working uniform of a civil servant.

"Yes," Peter responded.

"Peter Williamson, of the Barnard Company ?"

"Yes, that's me."

"Good!" the man said with obvious and heartfelt relief. "We've been looking for you for a couple of days, but you're a hard man to find. You haven't been at your flat for some time."

"Who's we?" Peter asked.

"Oh, sorry, my name's Turner, Brian Turner. I'm with your old department at the Ministry."

"Do you have any identification?" Peter asked knowing that he would not have any official identification if he was part of the old department.

"I'm not the police," Turner said reproachfully, "I've got a driver's license somewhere." He began to delve, with difficulty, beneath the raincoat into the inside pocket of the tweed sports coat. "Damned raincoat! I've been outside Miss Barnard's flat since five this morning, it was bloody cold then. Never know what the weather's going to do, do you?"

"Don't worry about it," Peter added, stopping the search. "How can I help you?"

Turner gladly gave up, straightened his tie and rearranged the clothing. "Well, I wondered if you could meet my boss. We need some assistance and I understand you're going back to Bakaar tomorrow. We'd very much like to talk to you before you leave."

"It's Saturday, do you chaps work on weekends now?"

"Well, yes. To be honest I can do with the overtime."

Brian Turner was a typical example of Peter's former colleagues and it was easy to accept that he was who he said he was. He had an understated, simplistic, polite manner, but Peter knew this was the public front. He had little doubt that if he refused to cooperate Mr. Turner would rapidly become less obliging. It was no coincidence that the Department suddenly wanted to talk to him after all these years. He would have to speak with them but he felt he should try and give himself time to talk to George first. He needed time to think through the possibilities.

"I've got some shopping I have to get done this morning. Can we meet later today, perhaps after lunch?" Peter inquired.

"Yeah, how about the Intercontinental Hotel in Park Lane. We could meet in the foyer. How's two o'clock?"

"Sounds fine. I don't know what help I can offer?"

"Well, I can't really say. I'm just the messenger, but my boss will explain this afternoon. I'll be there. I'll look out for you at two o'clock. Are you staying at Miss Barnard's tonight?"

"Yes, I'll be there." Peter knew he was being boxed in and effectively told that he had better be at the meeting that afternoon.

"...and you're travelling on British Airways tomorrow to Nairobi?"

Now he was certain he was being boxed in.

"Yes, I am. Don't worry, I'll be there!"

"Good,! Look forward to seeing you."

Peter walked on towards Victoria Station where he completed his purchases. Outwardly he was calm but his mind was racing. 'What could have gone wrong? How on earth could they know what was going on? There was no way they could know. How did they know he was at Sarah's flat? Had someone in Bakaar double-crossed them?'

Peter returned to Sarah's apartment. She could see he was upset when he arrived. "What's the matter?" she asked almost before he had shut the door.

"Nothing!" he answered, intending that the single word should indicate questions were out of order.

"Obviously there is something wrong." Sarah responded irritably, "Can I help?"

"No!" he answered abruptly, "I've got to speak with your father, do you know where he is today?"

Sarah backed off, "I think he's at home, shall I get him for you?"

"No! I'll get him. May I use the phone in the study?"

"Yes, of course you can."

Peter disappeared into the study to make the call. He had to speak with George and he might try and contact Julius in Bakaar. He had decided not to ask Julius any questions but see if he mentioned anything that might indicate there was a problem. He had to make contact with as many people as possible. He would see if any of them could give him a lead as to what the afternoon meeting could be about.

"George, I'm glad I've caught you. We need to talk, have you got a minute?"

"Yes, what's the problem?" George replied sensing Peter's concern.

"I've just been approached by one of the guys from my old department in Whitehall. I've been asked to go to a meeting this afternoon, to provide them with some assistance. They knew I was traveling back to Bakaar tomorrow and the guy I met had been waiting outside Sarah's flat half the night."

"Did they give you any more details? Did you get any hint of what they want?" George asked.

"No, I didn't, but I believe they genuinely want help. I may be grasping at straws, but it was the way he said good when he was sure he had found Peter Williamson. He was really relieved. I wonder if I should call Julius to see if anything has happened there. Just to see if he can throw any light on it."

"No, I wouldn't do that. I'd just go to the meeting with an open mind and listen."

"Perhaps Tim or Doug have been arrested or have talked to the wrong people."

"Just go to the meeting. They can't have any hard evidence. Play it by ear."

Peter had called more for reassurance than anything else. George was probably right. Any action might cause more problems than it would solve. It was against his nature but he would just have to wait and see.

"Yeah, you're right. I'll go along and help this afternoon and we'll deal with any problems when I've had a chance to assess them."

George felt he had calmed Peter down and did not want to expand the conversation. "Give me a call when you get back. I'm going to be here all day. Say, hello to Sarah for me." George rang off.

The Intercontinental Hotel is squeezed in between Hamilton Place and Park Lane, overlooking the southeastern end of Hyde Park. On the ground floor there is a large open foyer with windows from floor to ceiling which look out on to Hyde Park Corner. From these windows many visitors got their first glimpse of the British driver's road craft. Long periods virtually parked on the road, followed by gear grinding dashes to reach the next intersection. The foyer serves both as a meeting place and a corridor to the coffee shop at the far end. Peter arrived deliberately late at ten minutes past two. He walked towards the coffee shop. The area was full of people, but he could see Brian Turner and another man sitting on one of the leather couches. Turner saw him and half raised a hand to attract Peter's attention. Peter acknowledged and threaded his way between the legs and luggage that covered most of the space between the furniture.

Brian Turner stood up as Peter arrived, "Hello again. Thanks for coming, may I introduce Mr. Gordon, Mr. Williamson." He turned towards his companion who rose from the couch and stretched out his hand toward Peter. Gordon was probably in his early sixties. His silver hair was thinning above a ruddy complexion. His neck was slightly too small for his collar and loose jowls had replaced his jaw line.

"Nice to meet you." Mr. Gordon said as Peter gripped an unexpectedly cold hand.

There was a chair opposite the couch and Brian Turner stepped back and sat on it beckoning Peter to the seat he had occupied on the couch.

"I have no idea whether I can be of any help, but I'm happy to listen." Peter said wishing to get into the meat of the matter as soon as possible.

"I don't want you to take this the wrong way," Mr. Gordon looked almost apologetic, "but we don't know anyone else who might be able to help. It's a bit of a unique situation."

"I've never thought of myself as unique!" Peter joked.

"Well, maybe not unique, but I'd be grateful for your assistance." Mr. Gordon seemed to be having difficulty asking for a favor and Peter was not helping. Peter was relieved and quickly becoming convinced that the approach was exactly what it seemed, they wanted help. He began to relax.

Mr. Gordon continued, "As a member of the Department you signed the Official Secrets Act, and would you believe that document is still on file. I'm sure you're aware it still applies."

"My goodness, you must have been going back a long way." Peter answered, "Yes, I know it still applies."

"Everything I'm going to say is confidential. It's a very sensitive matter." Mr. Gordon was laboring the point.

"I understand." Peter was impatient for him to get on with it.

"It's your operation in Bakaar…"

Peter's ease left him in an instant, the adrenaline pumped around his body, his heart began to thump. He tried to give no outward impression of his concern. They knew! How?

"…the fact that you're there for Barnard from time to time and that you'd have every reason in the world to be traveling around could be very useful to us. It's all probably a waste of time, but the Americans have given us some information and asked if we can help. You know what they're like, up and down like yo yo's—quite excitable. They're all fired up over some satellite photographs but they don't have anyone on the ground in Bakaar and thought we might have a better chance at checking out what's going on."

"So what do you need from me?" Peter asked, his pulse rate remaining at a rapid ninety-five.

Turner reached into his brief case, which had been lying on the floor by his feet, and took out a large brown envelope. He handed it to Mr. Gordon, who opened it and took out a bundle of photographs. He sorted through them and handed one to Peter. Apart from the odd one printed in the press, Peter had not seen satellite photos before, and certainly not with the definition of the one in his hand. Mr. Gordon leaned towards him and pointed, "This area is apparently a few miles from Rapanda, I think I've got the name right, I've never been there myself. In fact I've never had any involvement with the place."

As Mr. Gordon spoke Peter recognized what he was looking at. The fertilizer plant was very clear and he could see Nirina's summer residence and the new buildings for the troops. He could even see the guard house on the road.

"How far away was the satellite that took this?" Peter asked genuinely interested.

"Oh, I've no idea. Miles, probably hundreds." Mr. Gordon replied showing no interest in the technical details of what he considered a nuisance.

"This is amazing, I know where this is, it's the old fertilizer plant."

"Yes, we know that. Apparently, the buildings around it are new and recently there's been all sorts of activity along the road. The Americans are all up tight. They can't get their minds off Iraq and they're seeing missiles in the woods and chemical weapon plants are springing up everywhere. They're looking for reassurance."

"How am I supposed to reassure them?" Peter asked, feeling a little more comfortable as he again became convinced that Gordon had no idea of his involvement.

"We'd like you to have a look at the plant when you get out there. Try and get a chance to look around and let us know if you feel there's anything going on which might concern our American friends, or us for that matter. I suppose the question is whether the plant is being used to manufacture anything other than fertilizer. We'd like to know what's in the new sheds they've built and what the traffic's all about."

"Can't you just ask them. I thought Britain was on good terms with Robert Berruda?"

"Yes, but we don't want to create any problems unless we have good cause. You know what it's like. We like to know the answers before we ask the questions…officially that is," Mr. Gordon responded with the flicker of a smile.

"So at the moment all you've got is the photographs?" Peter wanted to know whether there was more. "What about the Embassy? They're a good bunch, can't they help you?"

"We don't want to go through the Embassy. They've already produced a preliminary report. Anyway, there's no one there with any training. They're all diplomats and clerks for a change." Mr. Gordon smiled again.

Peter felt certain he was getting the true story. The British thought it was overreaction by the Americans. If he thought about it, who else traveled frequently to Bakaar and could freely move about the country. Peter was beginning to see opportunities he could not possibly have planned. Assuming neither the British nor the Americans were following any other leads, Peter's task provided a degree of security. He could probably control the timing of the investigation and the eventual discovery of what he had been doing in Bakaar. It was an enormous advantage to know what the other side was doing. It was now Peter's turn to smile as he considered the possibilities.

"Yes, I'll have a look for you. How quickly do you want a response?"

"If it was just us, we'd be in no hurry. But some crank phoned a message into the FBI in New York and gave them a garbled message about a bomb, Bakaar and how he could help save tens of thousands of lives. All he wanted was $1 million and immunity. I think that's what got the Americans going. And once they get the bit between their teeth they want everything done yesterday. Maybe you could have a look next week while you're out there and give us a call."

"What was that about a phoned message?" Peter was back in full defensive mode.

"I don't know any more. It was just said in passing. It was probably all a misunderstanding and has nothing to do with Bakaar. For all we know whoever called was talking about Baccarat and winning a million dollars. Not Bakaar and wanting a million."

Brian Turner gave Peter a phone number and made sure that he had Peter's number in Bakaar. All three left the hotel together and Peter took a cab back to Sarah's. On the one hand Peter thought he was now in a position to know what the other side was up to, on the other was someone really making calls to the FBI?

Chapter 22

Doug and Tim arrived in Bakaar in the afternoon of Sunday, June 7. They were met by Julius' security men and were taken to the apartment they had complained of on their previous trip. In spite of their distaste for the place, they welcomed the chance to sleep and did not awake until a little before nine on Monday morning. Peter arrived at ten.

"I thought we'd gotten through to you," Tim blasted Peter as he entered the apartment, "We're not staying in this rat hole this visit!"

"Shut up Tim!" Peter responded with a degree of humor. Tim backed off and the two men shook hands.

Doug wandered into the kitchen, "Hi, boss, everything OK?"

"I hope you're not going to start bitching," Peter replied aggressively.

"Who, me bitch? Never!" Doug gave an impression of looking sheepish, "I'm just gonna take in all the night life this trip. I gotta couple of girls lined up for tonight, I'm gonna have a ball, man…"

They sat down at the kitchen table, which had become their customary meeting place in the cramped and dismal apartment and Peter passed on the good news. "In answer to your prayers I've found new accommodations for you. You'll only be here a couple of nights."

"That's a relief!" Doug responded gleefully.

Peter continued, "I've organized rooms out at the plant. You can stay there while you're working."

"What about the girls?" Doug asked plaintively.

Peter raised his eyebrows, "We have to test the bomb. By the time we leave we've got to be ready to finish the job in the States."

"So, what's the program?" Tim asked more seriously, satisfied that the time he would have to spend in the apartment was limited.

"The cradle that holds all the components together is back at my apartment. The VX gas is at the plant and Frederick should be there tomorrow. I'll pick you up early in the morning and we'll head out to the lab."

"How long we gonna be out there? For what I'm getting paid I can't stay out here forever." Doug seemed belligerent.

"As long as it takes. We've got three weeks to make sure we've got it right. Does it matter?" Peter was irritated, sometimes Doug displayed a bloody minded attitude that made Peter wonder if he would be able to stay the course.

"No, just wondered." Doug responded, backing off.

"You're free today. Pick up anything you'll need out at the plant," Peter turned to Doug. "And that doesn't mean girls! Assume we'll be there a couple of weeks."

"At least we get out of this fucking place!" Tim said with obvious and heartfelt relief.

"It'll be great to get out of here but sounds if we're gonna be imprisoned at the plant," Doug added becoming agitated. "I can't be locked up out there. No one told me I was gonna be locked up. I can't do that."

"OK, OK calm down. We'll talk about it."

Peter pointed at the lamp and the radio, reminding them of the possibility of bugs and put his finger to his lips. "Let's go and have lunch, you must be hungry."

Tim got up from the table and faked a response suitable for the bugs and their masters, he did not act well, "That's the best idea you've had all day. The weather's great! Let's enjoy it. We'll pack up after we've eaten."

It was twelve thirty and the temperature had risen to just over one hundred Fahrenheit, but it was dry and relatively comfortable. For Tim it was better than the smog that accompanied high temperatures in the summer in Los Angeles. They traipsed out of the house and climbed into Peter's Landrover. As soon as they were out of the compound, Peter began to talk.

"We've got some planning to do out of earshot of those bloody bugs. Let's go out to the hotel, we should be able to talk there."

They drove to the hotel and selected a table on the porch. The food was nothing to write home about, but the tables were well spaced and no one outside was likely to overhear them. They all ordered beer and the Bakaaran version of steak. They knew it would bear little resemblance to anything they might have received under the same name in the States, but it was probably the best bet.

"So, what are we doing?" Tim asked the question again.

Peter pulled his chair closer to the table, circled his hands around the cold beer and spoke softly. "We have to make sure we've got our act together. We have to practice assembling the bomb. We've got to test the detonators and develop a method of safely handling the gas. At the end we've got to detonate one bomb. So far the Bakaarans have left us alone. We've had no interference, but now that we have a supply of the gas I'm damned sure we'll be watched more closely." He turned to Doug. "You're not going to be imprisoned at the plant. There's even a car for you to use, but I expect security'll get tighter."

"Good. I may be the hired help, but this place is getting to me!"

"Are the detonators here?" Tim asked.

"Yep, we've got everything," Peter answered. "The problem's going to be the quantities and the numbers. As far as the Bakaarans are concerned we need enough gas to practice. We need a supply for New York, a backup and that's all. In fact, we've got four cradles stored at Kennedy. We've got plenty of detonators and the electronics are no problem. They're already in the States. We have to make sure we ship out enough gas for more than just the New York bomb without them getting suspicious. We have to be careful."

"How's the gas gonna be shipped?" Tim asked.

"In groundnut oil cans. Each chemical component in a separate shipment," Peter replied. "It won't be shipped as VX gas. The chemicals are sealed in plastic bags inside the oil cans. Each bag takes up about half the can. The oil's poured in around the bag. The specific gravity of the chemicals plus the weight of the bag is near enough to the oil so that the weight of the can is still within limits. Customs can open a can and pour out the oil to test it. So long as they don't completely empty the can we're OK. You have to cut the top off the can to get the bag out. In any event our cans are only a small part of each shipment. The chance of anyone finding one is very small. Don't forget the ground nut oil is going to the States every day." Peter continued, "We need more gas than we can justify for just one unit. So we've designed the unit we'll use here for practice to include a larger amount of gas. This unit is a hybrid, but the Bakaarans don't know that.

"How do we get our hands on the chemicals in the States?" Tim asked.

"Hang on Tim! Let me finish off the Bakaaran end of the operation," Peter answered taking a sip of his beer. "The Bakaarans think we've got just one practice unit here. In fact we've got two, the practice unit and a real one. We have a little job to do here before leaving."

It did not take Tim long to guess what had to be done, a wicked look began to creep across his face. "So, we're gonna leave the Bakaarans a little problem…"

"More like a guarantee that we get paid,. But there are difficulties. The phones are unreliable. They still operate by pulses not tones. You know how long it can take to make a connection into Bakaar and the line's often cut during a call. We may have difficulty detonating the bomb if it comes to it. But we think it's worth setting it up. We also don't have access to many places where we could install it. I guess the best place is in the apartment in Rapanda." Peter thought for a moment warming to the idea, "It's in the center of the city. For God's sake it's in the police barracks. That ought to cause some confusion if we had to detonate it. On the other hand we couldn't afford to threaten, they'd soon find it, but that's where you earn your keep lads. Hide it!"

"Sounds to me like we need an anti-tamper device. They find the bomb and it blows if they touch it and it blows if they don't." Tim was getting into the right mood.

"Exactly. The phone line in the apartment is intercepted by the SP. I checked out the line after it was installed. The SP can't answer it, all they can do is listen." Peter paused.

"All they'd hear is the data transmission, I doubt if they'd know what it was. They'd just think it was a wrong number or a fax," Tim offered some of his new found knowledge.

Peter was impressed, "Does it matter if they stay on the line?"

"No, if they have no capacity to transmit, it won't matter what they do, except cut the line. But there's no reason for 'em to do that and they probably wouldn't have time. The only problem is our box of tricks will answer the phone and they'll know no one's in the apartment. That might make 'em wonder what the hell's going on."

"But they couldn't do anything, it takes less than a minute to get through to the switch and trigger it. By the time they got curious it'd be too late." Peter convinced himself that it could be done. "We'll put it in the roof and use the cable and components from the practice unit. We'll pack explosives around the roof to make sure the sucker blows itself away and the gas would blow in the wind. We just need to get the components out of the plant and back to the apartment. I doubt that anyone'll come looking after we've finished." Peter stopped talking as the steaks arrived and all three started to eat.

"Not bad!" Doug was the first to comment. For all they knew it was zebra, but it was edible.

"So we head out to the plant tomorrow." Peter began to sum up the activity for the next few days. "Let's say it takes two weeks. We'll make excuses for a bit of R & R back in the city before we leave and give ourselves time to set up the bomb in the apartment."

"We should have a party then I get the girls anyway," Doug joked.

"Hey, that might be a good idea. It gives us access to the apartment for a day or two." Peter thought that would work well. "You should be able to set up in a few hours during the party, Tim?"

"Oh, sure. I'll get the wiring done the day before, it's no problem. Just make sure all the components are in place. I'll need a few extras for the anti-tamper device, but I can get them at almost any hardware store, even in Bakaar. I'll go shopping over the next couple of weeks."

Peter took them back to the center of the city and dropped them off. He then headed out to his apartment. As he drove through the city it seemed that Rapanda had grown accustomed to the presence of troops on the streets. They were still very much in evidence, but the atmosphere was more relaxed than when he was last in town. The troops tended to stand in groups at road blocks and barricades talking and laughing. Few carried their rifles. They were left leaning against the truck or the barricade itself—sloppy, but it suggested they were not expecting trouble.

Peter arrived at the apartment, parked and climbed the stairs. He walked over to the desk and shuffled through a pile of paper. He pressed the play button on the answering machine. He was surprised to see it was still working. There must have been no power cuts while he was away. Julius wanted to meet with him and Mr. Gordon had called. For a few seconds he considered the name.

"Damn!" he whispered as it dawned who Gordon was.

"I wonder when Mr. Gordon called ?" he asked the machine.

Gordon had to be in England. Peter had assumed that he would be left to report back to his old department in London in his own time and had expected to stretch it out. At least to the end of the week. The call bothered him, Gordon could just be fussing, but there might have been more developments. Peter needed time. He had to know when they would be finished in Bakaar, before he reported back to London. If he was going to use his old colleagues as he and George had agreed the timing was critical. He decided not to return the call.

As Peter continued his examination of the papers on the desk another thought struck him. It could be dangerous if anyone in London knew he was spending time out at the fertilizer plant. Now that the satellite photographs had focussed interest on the plant he had to be much more careful. He smiled to himself as he remembered the definition of the photographs. You could bet those he had seen weren't the best that could be produced. Maybe the Americans already had a snapshot of him at the plant. He must remember not to look up.

Peter called Julius, "Hello, my friend," Julius replied as Peter greeted him, "nice to have you back. What are your plans this week?"

"I'm going out to the plant tomorrow and I'll probably be backward and forward daily for the next couple of weeks."

"Could you meet with Robert and myself on Thursday, in the morning at ten?" Julius asked.

Peter could tell from the tone that he was not expected to refuse.

"Yes, of course I can. At the Ministry?"

"No, at Robert's house. Where shall we pick you up—at the apartment?"

"Yes, that sounds fine." Peter replied feeling far from fine.

He put the phone down with growing apprehension. He was losing control of events. Mr. Gordon in London was making him cover his tracks and now Robert Berruda wanted to meet away from the Presidential offices. Peter suddenly felt very lonely.

Chapter 23

Next morning Peter collected Tim, Doug and their possessions and drove out to the plant. He had assembled the component parts of the practice bomb and they were lying in the back of the Landrover together with a large soft bag. Tim had not seen the cradle or the canisters.

"Interesting," Tim said as he leaned over the back of the seat and picked the larger of the canisters out of the bag.

"Yeah, that's the big one. That's the one the Bakaarans get to see...to justify the amount of gas we need." Peter explained, "The other one, the smaller one, that's the real size that we'll attach to the bombs".

As Peter spoke, they turned off the paved road onto the dusty dirt of the road leading to the plant. The Landrover lurched and rolled and the red dust began to blow in thorough the open windows. There was no point closing them, the olive green of the vehicle soaked up the heat from the sun and with the windows closed, the heat was unbearable. The choice was simple, dust or heat. Today they suffered the dust and unless they wanted to eat it as well as breath it, conversation was over until they reached the plant.

The guard at the gate flagged them down and the barrier remained closed. When Peter had last been at the plant he was waved through without stopping. He hoped this was just a new and over zealous individual rather than an increase in security. Peter stopped at the barrier and the guard approached in an unhurried casual manner. Peter did not recognize him.

"Passes?" He almost stuck his head through the window in an effort to see into the back of the truck as they fumbled for ID cards. The guard examined each card closely.

"Stay in the truck!" he ordered and retreated to the gatehouse taking the ID's with him. Peter grew more uncomfortable as he saw him pick up the phone inside the gatehouse. The guard spoke and waited, the minutes ticked by. Then he put the phone down and returned to the truck.

"O.K. Mr. West, thank you, sir." He returned the ID cards and waved to his colleague in the gatehouse. The barrier swung open and Peter breathed a sigh of relief.

"I hope this isn't shades of things to come!" Peter said as they drove on into the plant. The telephone call from Mr. Gordon and the upcoming meeting with Robert Berruda had rattled him. He felt pleased he had an old unidentifiable Landrover, one of hundreds in Bakaar, he just hoped the damned satellite could not read the number plate.

Peter drove up to one of the recently erected buildings. It was a single storey structure, looking like a small, cheap motel. The front of the building had four doors evenly spaced along its length, one door to each room. Adjacent to the door there was a window, covered by a venetian blind the bottom of which rested on an air conditioning unit balanced precariously on the sill and taking up about a third of the window. The building was graced by a covered porch, running the entire length. If the building had been raised on piles, as its designers had intended, the porch would have been accessed by four or five steps at each end. However, it had been erected quickly and placed directly on the leveled ground. It looked legless and out of proportion. Peter had arranged for

Tim and Doug to have a room each. Officers commanding the troops at the plant occupied the remaining two rooms. Peter pulled to a halt in front of the building and waited for the comments. There were none.

"Your new home," He announced nervously. Still no comments were forthcoming. Tim and Doug climbed out of the vehicle and collected their belongings without a word.

"Which are ours?" Tim asked as he lugged his baggage toward the porch.

"The two at the right end", Peter responded relieved that was the only question. It obviously suited Tim and Doug better than the apartment. Maybe it was the venetian blinds. Perhaps it was the air conditioner, whatever it was did not matter.

"Leave the unpacking until later," Peter requested, "let's go over to the workshop and see if Frederick's arrived."

The workshop was at the end of the line of new buildings, closest to the plant and just a walk from the living quarters. Apart from a heavy workbench along one wall, there was a cleared, bare wooden table in the center of the room and Nirina and Frederick were sitting on wooden benches, one on either side of the table. The benches reminded Peter of the wooden forms he sat on to eat his lunch at school when he was about six. The workbench was littered with tools and looked well used. There was a large American refrigerator in the corner and a coffee machine hissed and spluttered as it finished brewing a fresh pot. The coffee smelled good.

Peter carried the cradle into the building and Tim followed with the large canister. Frederick stood up as Tim approached, "Hello Tim, how you doing?" he greeted as Tim put the canister down on the table and then shook hands.

Nirina remained seated at the bench clasping his coffee cup that rested on the table. He looked up and glowered at Peter as he entered the room but said nothing as Tim and Frederick shook hands. Peter put the cradle on the table and sat down opposite Nirina. Tim and Doug walked away from the table and helped themselves to the fresh coffee.

"So, how are you?" Peter asked Nirina.

"As well as can be expected." Nirina responded curtly, with suppressed but obvious resentment.

"I'm pleased you've succeeded…"

"There was never any doubt I would succeed. I'm a professional. I said it would be done on time and it has been!" Nirina cut across Peter in his usual arrogant manner. If all went well, Nirina would not be needed in a week or so. Other than to supervise the loading of the gas into the oilcans, Nirina had finished.

"Well, we should've known that", Peter added cynically. "All we need you to do is load the gas into the oil cans and you're all done! You can go home in a few days."

"It's about time! As you are aware I have not been comfortable here and I've been treated like a common…"

"Just finish the damned job. Don't get in my way this week. The sooner we get you out of here the better for all of us." Peter did not like his attitude and did not let him finish his sentence. "Get sensible, you're no longer much use to us. Just try being pleasant…" Peter hesitated and then let his frustration get the better of him, "It might get you paid and home in one piece!"

Peter bit his lip as soon as he said it. He did not want to fight with the man at this stage of the project, but he was unbearable. Nirina did not respond, but Peter thought there was a change in his demeanor as he was forced to face his fragile situation. Nirina got up and left the room without saying a word. Peter followed him and brought in the remainder of his gear and the soft bag from the Landrover.

"O.K. gentlemen," Peter called the others who seemed not to have noticed Nirina's sullen departure, "Let's get on with it!"

Frederick and Tim walked over and sat down at the bench. Julius had asked that Frederick be included in the planning discussions as he was now one of the team. Frederick was undoubtedly Berruda's eyes and ears and had probably known about the project from the first day Peter met with him in the apartment. Doug joined them.

Sounding like a British sergeant major addressing a class of new recruits, Peter began, "Gentlemen, you've all been involved in bits of this project, but this is the first time we're going to put it all together. Here…" Peter gestured towards the cradle and components on the table, "we have our equivalent of an atomic bomb. It may not look like one, but its effect is about the same."

The cradle was designed to hold all of the components; it was a strong, rigid but lightweight basket. It was the largest of the components and would have to be carried into the buildings openly. It was a latticework of metal straps, each about an eighth of an inch thick and an inch wide all joined to a solid sheet metal base. It looked like a large, metal version of the plastic crates in which students transport and store their possessions at college. It was three feet six inches long, two feet wide and eighteen inches deep. More metal straps welded to the base and to each other divided it into compartments

A circular clamp was mounted on bearings at one end to hold the gas canister in place and permit it to spin when the electric motor started. A few inches from the opposite end a substantial triangular support rose eight inches from the bottom of the cradle and attached to it was another clamp, intended to hold the electric motor in place.

Peter picked up the electric motor and bolted it onto the triangular support. When in position the motor was offset, the drive shaft pointed upwards towards the clamp at the other end of the cradle, it was also angled across the sheet metal base. The short cable hanging from the motor remained unconnected. Peter placed the arming switch, which Frederick had designed, in the bottom of the cradle underneath the motor and secured it with small self-tapping screws. He added the electronic timer to be used only on this prototype. He reached for the cylindrical gas canister. It looked like a very large thermos flask, two feet six inches long and eight inches in diameter. One half was red, the other blue. Until Peter began to carefully, unscrew the two halves it looked like a single unit.

"We stole the concept of the canisters from nerve gas artillery shells. You can see it's two canisters and in between, separating them, there's a collar." Peter removed the collar. It was the same diameter as the canisters and about an inch wide. There were two wires trailing from it. He held it up for all to see.

"In the center there's a diaphragm which separates the contents. It's electrically ruptured during the arming process; a couple of seconds later the motor starts and spins the canister to mix the two chemical agents. Then the detonator is triggered. This is the first time in this process that we have VX gas. Just seconds before it explodes." Peter reassembled the two halves into the collar and laid the complete canister in its supports in the cradle.

"How do we fill the canister?" Tim asked.

"Each half is filled separately with one of the inert chemicals and we have caps that screw on to allow the canister to be transported when it's full." Peter picked up one of the caps from the table and handed it to Tim. "The only time there's any danger to us is when we fit the two gas canisters together at the point of installing the bomb and even then there's not much chance of them mixing accidentally. Each agent alone is harmless. The canisters are designed to shatter in the explosion and I guess they could break if they received a heavy blow during transportation, but it's unlikely."

Tim examined the cap and put it back on the table.

"This week," Peter continued, "we have to perfect the assembly of the unit and filling and connecting the canisters. The batteries slide into this compartment and the plastic explosive is packed into the space down each side." Peter demonstrated where each component fitted as he spoke. "Then we have the wiring harness." He pulled a bundle of cables out of the bag, untangling it and laying it out on the table. "This connects all of the components through the junction box…the cables are color coded for the appropriate terminals. Any questions?"

"How does the arming process work?" Doug asked.

"There's a computer chip in the arming switch that receives the signal from the telephone and then transmits signals to destroy the diaphragm, start the electric motor and detonate the plastic explosive. The whole process including the telephone call takes about two minutes."

"What if someone answers the phone when we make the call to detonate the bomb?" Tim asked, "Can we still arm it?"

"Yes." Peter answered. "As soon as we send the code it'll open the circuit to the switch and we can arm it."

"It seems simple enough," Doug commented.

"Yep, it really is. Now, what about the timetable." Peter took out his calendar. "Today's Tuesday, Nirina's going to finish loading the cans by Friday and they'll be packed into two separate shipments leaving the plant on Monday. That's Monday the thirteenth, then on to the States."

Tim leaned forward, "That brings up my question again, Peter. How do we pick up the cans in the States?"

"Each shipment will be broken up on arrival. The shipment addressed to us, with our cans in it, must be collected from the airport. It'll still contain cans with just oil, but there's a small red spot on the cans with one of the VX components, a blue spot on the others. You and Doug separate the cans and the chemicals and take each chemical to a different storage location. We've got to be certain we can load these things with our eyes shut by the end of the week, and you two," Peter looked at Tim and Doug, "have got to be able to assemble the unit in any possible position, on its side, on end, in a tight space, you name it."

"Are we gonna have any protective clothing in the States?" Doug asked.

"Yes, face masks and gloves. At least that'll protect you from a minor spill. You'll also have antidote kits."

"Nice to know there is one," Tim mumbled. He already knew there was and that it was more or less useless.

"Yeah, we've got some of the British kits." Peter picked one up out of his bag. "It's a container with a needle in it. You inject yourself, straight through clothing, into a muscle, preferably your thigh. However, don't rely on it, it's a last ditch chance. You've got to inject yourself immediately after contamination and even then, it's less than an even chance you'll survive. You can't afford to get contaminated."

Peter paused for a moment and then addressed Doug; "You'll work with Tim this week and make sure you can load the canisters and set up the bombs. If Tim's out of commission, you'll have to do it. Assuming no accidents, your primary role is transport and protection. You've got to get everything in the right place at the right time and secure the location while Tim sets up the bomb. If anyone gets in the way you'll have to deal with them."

"O.K", Doug replied.

"Have you got a silencer for that cannon of yours?" Peter asked.

"Yeah, I had it threaded years ago, don't worry I know what I'm about!"

Peter did not comment. "What about you Tim?"

"No, I haven't got one, but I don't expect to use it. Doug won't let anyone get that close."

Peter knew Tim well enough to know that although he was being flippant, he meant what he said. There would be no shoot-outs. From almost any viewpoint, if Tim had to start shooting the project was over. They could not risk causing that sort of disturbance in any of the target buildings.

"Nirina can leave anytime at the weekend. Let's plan our goodbye party in the apartment for Thursday. We'll leave here on the following Monday."

"No problem," Tim drawled. There was no explanation provided for the party in front of Frederick.

• • •

Having established the timetable Peter wanted to test the security at the fertilizer plant. The soldier at the gate had not searched the Landrover when he entered, but Peter needed to know if they would when he left and whether they might have been briefed on what to look for. As he left the plant he picked up a couple of empty groundnut oil cans and placed them in full view on the front seat of the Landrover. He drove up to the barrier and stopped. It remained closed and one of the soldiers walked over to the vehicle. He got to within about five feet, bent a little to see in through the open window and squinted at Peter.

"Hello, Mr. West, how are you?" He asked with a broad grin spreading across his face. "Haven't seen you for a while. Where you bin?"

Peter recognized him from his previous visits to the plant. He had once told him his name, which Peter had found impossible to pronounce and had christened him 'Andy'. Much to Andy's amusement. He was proud of his English. He had learned more than the school taught version during the tourist boom when he had earned a living as a guide.

"Hi, Andy", Peter waved his arm out the window. Andy stood up straight again and signaled to his colleague in the gatehouse to raise the barrier. Peter was relieved.

"See you! Are you on duty tomorrow, Andy?" Peter asked hopefully.

"Oh, yes sir. I'm here all night tomorrow."

Peter knew he could get the gas out.

Chapter 24

Peter had a restless night. The events of the past few days tumbled through his mind as he drifted in and out of sleep. He must phone Mr. Gordon in London and provide some sort of a report. He guessed that Gordon had not told him everything and during his fitful sleep, dreams mixed with reality. What the hell was the story behind that phone call to the FBI. Maybe Gordon had photographs with better definition, perhaps he could read the number plate on the Landrover. As he dreamed, a snapshot of himself, taken from above drifted across the scene. He was standing outside Tim's room at the plant with one foot resting on the bomb, arms folded, looking upward smiling triumphantly at the satellite. It looked like an old photograph of a white hunter with his trophy.

He awoke exhausted at seven o'clock wet with perspiration. He decided that his phone call to Gordon and his upcoming meeting with Berruda needed a second opinion. He did not want to make this call from his own phone. He drove into Rapanda, found a working payphone and at eight o'clock placed a collect call to George in London.

"Yes, yes, I'll accept the charge," he heard George respond to the operator. Even at six o'clock London time George was awake.

"George, good morning. You got a minute?" Peter asked.

"At this time in the morning I've got a couple of hours. Where are you? How are you getting on?" George fired questions without waiting for an answer.

"I'm well. Everything's O.K. Maybe it's all moving a little quicker than expected. But we've got a couple of problems. I've got to call Gordon today and wanted to go over what I'm going to tell him. When I met him in London he said the FBI had received a phone call about a bomb and that Bakaar was mentioned. Can you think of anyone who would benefit from shopping us. Whoever he is, I'm assuming it's a he, wants a $1 million to spill the beans."

"Beats me. Only half a dozen people know. It's probably a red herring."

"I've also been asked, well summoned would be a better word, to a meeting with Robert Berruda."

Peter and George discussed the report to Gordon and Thursday's meeting with Berruda. George agreed, Peter had no choice. He had to call Gordon and provide just enough information to stop him pursuing any other line of inquiry. Peter had to make sure that Gordon and his chums made no progress for at least a week.

Knowing he was unlikely to find anyone working in a British Ministry before nine o'clock Peter had two and a half hours to kill before he had any chance of getting hold of Gordon. He climbed back in the Landrover and drove a few miles out of Rapanda, took a turn down a dirt road he knew passed through several small villages before petering out in the bush. He parked short of a bridge over a small, fast flowing river that rushed down from the hills and crossed a rocky ledge below the bridge. The noise from the cascading water drowned the sound of his approach. The half dozen women already washing clothes on the rocks, still partially in deep shadow, on the far bank of the river, were unaware of his presence. They continued working. Shouting to each other over the roar of the water. As he watched, the sun crept across more of the far bank. In an hour or so it would begin to warm the rocks and dry the washing spread across the ledge.

He had an overwhelming feeling of nostalgia. What had happened to Africa? It seemed hardly any time at all since the place teemed with wildlife. But now, even on a good day, you were lucky to see a few monkeys. The traditional huts and villages had all but disappeared as people crowded into the ugly concrete and corrugated iron towns attracted by electricity and piped water. Down below, under the bridge, twentieth century junk stuck out of the shallow water, rusting engines, broken furniture and ironically only a few feet from where the women were working, a battered washing machine. So much for electricity and the twentieth century.

Beyond the far bank about fifteen miles away, on the horizon, Peter could see the mountains and on the plain in between, the thick trunked baobab trees were casting long, deep red shadows. Bakaar was still beautiful, but only beyond the corrugated roofs. The village had become a frontier, just like the frontier towns of the American West at the end of the nineteenth century. Western civilization was forcing its way through Africa and the stark contrasts were ugly and easy to see.

What would this country be like in twenty years if George and Peter were successful and a billion dollars poured in. Would it mean better education, medical care, enough food for everyone? If the politicians had their way, he doubted if the benefits would be too widespread. At best the money would be squandered on pet projects with hefty commissions taken at every turn. At worst it would buy a few jet fighters or missiles and enable old tribal differences to be settled in a more modern manner. On the other hand what right had he to impose his standards on the Bakaarans.

Would the women down on the riverbank be any happier, would their lives be easier? Did they want the progress forced upon them? He doubted it. The broken washing machine and the clothes on the rocks seemed to say it all. But he had no right to expect them to live in thatched huts and cook over a fire.

The raucous noise of a truck approaching the bridge snapped him out of his melancholy. The women on the river bank looked up and saw him and the moment was gone. He drove back to the city, returned to the payphone, fed it with coins and dialed the Ministry in London.

The phone rang for half a minute, "Good morning, can I help you?"

"Is Mr. Gordon available?" Peter asked.

"Just a moment." The operator was gone almost before she finished speaking.

Peter waited and waited, "Can I help you?" another female voice answered. The payphone beeped for more money.

"Is Mr. Gordon there?"

"I'll check, who's calling him?"

"I'm at a payphone. I don't have any more coins, take down this number," Peter gave her the number of the payphone. "It's in Bakaar, that's in Africa, tell Mr. Gordon that Peter Williamson wishes to speak with him, I'll wait by the phone for ten minutes." The phone went dead as he finished speaking. He wondered what chance there was that an international call could even be received on the phone. Peter placed his elbow on the hook, cutting off the connection, but keeping the handset to his ear. There were few working payphones in Rapanda and he could not risk losing this one to any of the people who were now gathering on the sidewalk. He pretended to be speaking. It must have been five minutes before it rang, Peter answered before the sound of the first ring had died.

"Hello, is this Mr. Williamson? Sorry to take so long to get back. The call wouldn't go through." Mr. Gordon stuttered on. "Thank you for calling us, how's the weather out there today?"

"Dry!" Peter answered irritably, "I'm trying to help you. What on earth do you think you're doing calling my apartment? Half the world listens to my phone calls! Are you trying to get me killed?" Peter asked aggressively.

"I'm sorry, I didn't realize." Peter did not respond and Mr. Gordon continued, "We've had another call from the Americans, for some reason they seem to be in more of a hurry. They've had another call from their informant and they seem to be giving him some credibility. Apparently the call came from Bakaar. He repeated the same information, there's a plan to place a bomb in a U.S. city. He wants $1 million to provide the date and place."

"Have they agreed to pay?" Peter asked fearing the response

"No, they're playing hardball at the moment. They want some facts before they agree to a deal. They're being very polite and pleasant but we owe them a favor or two. Have you got any news for us yet?"

"Yes, I have."

"What have you got?" Mr. Gordon inquired eagerly.

Peter pitched into his story, "I've been out to the plant. It's surrounded by a wire fence and there are barriers across the road. Troops are living in temporary buildings, there must be fifty of them." Peter was only telling him what he already knew from the photographs. "I talked to one of the soldiers and there's definitely something going on out there. He was prepared to be indiscreet for a few pounds and said there was a Pakistani," Peter deliberately provided the wrong nationality, "living and working at the plant, he seemed to be important. He's been there for weeks."

"Do you have a name for this Pakistani?" Gordon asked hopefully.

"Something like Nerrin or Nurin," Peter wanted Mr. Gordon to have just enough information to keep his interest and to keep faith with the Americans. Just enough to get their teeth into and allow Peter a couple of days while they worked trying to identify the 'Pakistani'.

"Anything else?" Mr. Gordon asked.

"No, but I've got another source and I'm meeting with him on Friday. I'll call on Friday or Monday if I learn anything of interest."

"Good, thank you very much. I'll pass it all on to the Americans. I'll expect to hear from you at the end of the week." Mr. Gordon rang off.

Peter was more than concerned. Who in Bakaar would benefit from telling the FBI what they were up to. Who in Bakaar knew. It could be Julius, but he was sure to be making more than $1 million. Maybe it was one of the guys in the ministry who knew a little and was trying to bluff his way into a fortune. If Nirina was not locked up and out of communication Peter could easily believe that he was the culprit. If there was any good news, and if it was true, it looked as if the U.S. would not do a deal until they were certain there really was a threat. Peter took the view that he knew Tim well enough, it was not him. Peter would share the problem with Tim and maybe between them they could figure out who it was.

There was no reason to change their plans at this stage. It was a gamble, but given that Bakaar was receiving more attention than Peter would have wished, he and George had decided to use it to their advantage. They would try to control the timing of the revelations. Once the Americans had the information it would take only an hour or two for the CIA's computer at Langley to identify Nirina and then they would put two and two together. But by the time the bureaucrats had decided who should take the credit and the information had been passed along the line, it would be more like three or four days. Even a couple of days would mean that Peter's team could finish at the plant before anyone in the U.S. realized what was going on. By then it would be too late. Peter's intention was to ensure that the Americans could provide confirmation that Bakaar had produced the VX gas. It would create credibility when Bakaar made its demands.

Peter made a call to Rudi Van Haute, whom he had summoned to Nairobi a week previously and then set off for the fertilizer plant. He went via the apartment at the police compound in the city. Since Tim and Doug moved out to the plant the apartment had not been guarded and Peter intended to visit each morning taking one component of the bomb each time. If he was stopped no one would be able to identify what he carried or even question it, but by the end of the week, the bomb would be waiting to be assembled.

Peter went on to the plant and spent the day with Tim and Doug. The chemical agents were loaded into the cans. No one, except Peter's crew, was counting cans and the supply was well in excess of what was needed. Just to be on the safe side Peter punctured a few and asked one of the Bakaarans to put them in the garbage trailer. He could now excuse the loss of a few cans if anyone had a tally and wanted an audit.

At the end of the day he and Tim carried four cans, packed in a cardboard shipping box, out of the plant to his Landrover. Two of each agent.

As they carefully placed the cans in the vehicle Peter looked inquiringly at Tim.

"We've got a problem. How I heard is a long story so don't ask, but some guy is calling the FBI in New York and has offered to tip them off to a bomb being placed in…"

"You've got to be joking. You're pulling my leg."

"No I'm not."

"Christ almighty Pete. There are only about six or seven people know about it. You're one, I'm another. It's not going to be George, is it?"

"No, course it's not!"

Then that only leaves Nirina, Julius, and Doug. It's got to be Nirina, somehow he's getting to a phone."

"They tracked one of the calls to Bakaar. It could be. Whoever it is wants a million dollars for the information."

"What are we going to do?"

"For the time being keep your eyes and ears open and don't share it with anyone. We're not going to change anything just yet. I'm told the FBI is playing hard to get. They're not going to do a deal."

"How the fuck do you know what the FBI are doing?" Tim looked taken aback and suspicious. He grabbed Peter by the neck "Sounds like it's got to be you. How else…"

"Let go of me!" Peter shouted through almost crushed vocal cords as Tim loosened his grip. Tim let go and ruffled Peter's hair, "Just kidding boss! But how do you know?"

"I told you. It's a long story but it makes our task a little easier to know what they're doing."

Peter left the plant without a problem and the Landrover started bucking and rolling along the well-worn and familiar dirt road. He was feeling good, they had nearly accomplished their goal in Bakaar and he allowed his mind to run over the meeting with Robert Berruda next morning.

He was so engrossed in his thoughts that he did not see the truck approaching in the center of the road until it loomed out of its dust cloud just a few yards ahead. He swerved violently and everything in the back of the Landrover flew across the vehicle. Bang! Bang! Bang! He hit three deep ruts at the edge of the road. As he hit the first, the cans were thrown out of the flimsy protection of their cardboard box. The second sent them falling clumsily on top of each other on the floor and finally they jumped sideways and forward coming to rest piled up on the floor behind the seats. It was not until the Landrover stopped that he realized.

"Oh my God!" he shouted into the air as he scrambled out of the cab as if it were on fire. He slammed the door shut and slapped his hand against his thigh in anger and frustration as he looked down the road. No one had seen the incident, the truck continued on its journey, the driver probably oblivious to the near miss. He decided that it was unlikely that the contents of the cans had leaked and even less likely that one of each agent had leaked and then mixed. However, he gingerly opened the driver's door. He had an urge to shield his eyes with his hand, like a child watching a horror movie. He had to look but he did not want to see.

The cans were lying awkwardly piled one on another. The bare metal floor was covered in red dust which years of vibration had shaken into the cracks and humidity had encrusted around the framework of the seat. It acted like a litmus paper, any spill from the cans would have dampened and darkened the red dust. He could see a darkened area near the neck of one can. He knew how little it needed. "How stupid!" he repeated to himself aloud over and over again.

He examined the floor and the seat. Using the jack handle, pulled free from under the passenger seat, he gently moved the cans to see if there was any leakage around the caps. One can was wet and oily. It was probably groundnut oil and he knew that the VX agents would not react in any way with the oil. This had been confirmed when they first decided to use the oil cans. The torn cardboard of the box showed no signs of any liquid. The other cans were all intact. He gradually calmed down and after ten minutes of careful inspection decided there had been no other leakage. An awful but comforting thought crossed his mind, if he were contaminated he would be dead by now.

He left the cans where they were. He was not going to touch them until he could find a pair of gloves. He still had to make sure the plastic bags containing the agents had not ruptured inside the cans. It would be dangerous to go back to the plant to deal with it. He had no choice, he would go to his apartment and hope he could get Tim on the phone. Peter would get him to bring a suit, mask and gloves out to the apartment. He already had an antidote kit. He would then wait until dark. He could not risk anyone seeing him dressed in the protective suit, fishing cans out of the Landrover.

"What a mess!" He hissed through clenched teeth as he climbed back in the vehicle. They were finished. Most of the risk in Bakaar was over and now he would have to remove protective clothing from the plant and raise questions he might not be able to answer. As he started the engine, he recalled a film he had seen as a kid about truck drivers transporting nitroglycerine over rough roads to a plant where it was converted to dynamite. As he gently maneuvered the Landrover back onto the road he knew how they felt. They earned their pay!

Peter carefully steered around the ruts and bumps at the edge of the road. Finally and very slowly he eased the vehicle back onto the road and breathed a sigh of relief. He drove back to his apartment more carefully than he had driven on his driving test.

When he arrived he called the plant, whoever answered went to fetch Tim. He had never asked Julius if his own phone was tapped. He had always assumed it was. In any event there was little point using a public phone to call the plant because the plant's phone system was now wired through the SP. He had no real problem if anyone knew he took the protective clothing home, but he would prefer not to have any awkward questions or the answers recorded for posterity. He waited several tense minutes.

"Hi there, Pete. What's the problem?" Tim's relaxed drawl had never been more welcome. Peter hoped Tim would catch on. Tim had to do exactly as he was asked and not dream up any intelligent questions. When Tim had worked with him in the Special Services years ago, they used a simple signal, if Peter used Tim's full name it meant, 'Do exactly as I say and no questions'. Would Tim remember?

"Hello, Timothy," Peter emphasized Timothy. "Sorry to bother you, but I have to do some testing with the mask and gloves and I forgot to bring them home with me. Could you bring them over to the apartment tonight when you pack up?"

There was a pause, "Mr. Williamson, sir, you need some time off. You're overdoing it! You'll leave your fucking head behind one day!"

That was it, Tim would respond with 'Mr. Williamson, sir.' He had remembered.

"I'll bring them over, do you need them right away?"

"No, when you leave'll be fine. Thanks, Tim."

Peter put the phone down and walked into the kitchen. The fridge was working and he had ice. He took a handful, filled a glass with it, poured himself a large whisky and sat down at the table still cursing his own stupidity.

The door bell rang, Peter opened the door. He could see no one. He stepped out onto the landing, Tim was standing flattened against the wall, one hand behind his back resting on the grip of the Smith & Wesson hidden under the tail of his khaki bush shirt. All Peter noticed was that he was not carrying the protective clothing.

"You OK?" Tim asked cautiously remaining flat against the wall.

"Yeah, it's just the clothing."

"It's in the car," Tim said as he relaxed and started back down the stairs to fetch it.

"Haven't used the ole, Timothy, Mr. Williamson, sir, routine for a while," Tim shouted over his shoulder as he descended the stairs.

Peter smiled, "No, am I glad you remembered!"

Tim returned with the clothing, they both entered the apartment and Peter began to quietly relate his tale as Tim helped himself to a whisky and slumped down into a chair. "Fuck!" he exclaimed as the pistol tucked into the rear waistband of his jeans jabbed into his back. He leaned forward, removed the old Smith & Wesson and laid it on the table. "Didn't know what the problem was when I left the plant. Didn't know what you needed. Came prepared!"

They waited until dark consuming more of Peter's whisky than was wise. Peter donned the hood and gloves and then fumbled in a kitchen drawer. Hampered by the gloves and the alcohol it was difficult to get a grip on the flashlight. Peter caught sight of himself in a mirror as they walked through the hallway and burst out laughing. He thought he looked like he was going to a Halloween party. By the time they reached the landing neither of them was taking the task seriously and both were giggling like schoolboys.

"What about the light?" Tim rasped in a loud whisper, his mouth pressed against the hood where he thought Peter's ear should be.

"What light?" Peter said turning his head quickly to see Tim behind him, but only succeeding in turning his head within the hood, his view obscured by the fabric. Tim laughed loudly and Peter raised his clumsy gloved forefinger to where his mouth should be on the outside of the hood. "Shhh!"

"What light?"

"The light on that goddamned pole!" Tim answered in his loud whisper as he pointed to the mercury vapor lamp, that lit up the front of the apartment building.

"Oh, that one," Peter answered feebly. "It's on a time clock, there's a little door in the wall under the staircase, but it's locked. Get a screwdriver from the kitchen."

Tim went back into the kitchen and grabbed a sturdy screwdriver from the still open drawer. They both held onto the rail as they unsteadily descended the stairs, Tim saw the door to the time clock and attacked it with the screwdriver as if it were a bank vault. The door popped open to reveal the clock and a fuse box. Tim could not think too clearly and simply unhinged the clock cover and turned the clock until the lights went out.

"Now I can't see anything!" Peter said, not knowing whether the eye glasses in the hood were in place and it was dark, or whether he was still trying to see through the fabric of the hood.

They waited a couple of minutes to see if extinguishing the lights had created any interest. It should not, there were power cuts and bulbs blew daily. No one stirred.

Peter picked up the cans out of the Landrover and after a further examination carried each one into the apartment while Tim kept an eye on the other apartments. As he worked he sobered up and by the time the task was completed they had both regained their equilibrium. Peter marked the cans as to which agent was in each and removed the groundnut oil labels. He unscrewed the cap on the can that showed signs of leakage and poured the oil out into a bowl, checking that the plastic bag containing the harmless agent was intact. It was. He then separated the cans and stored the two agents at different ends of the apartment.

Chapter 25

The car arrived to collect Peter at nine in the morning. It was unmarked but the driver was accompanied by a uniformed, armed guard. They arrived at the village where Berruda lived with ten minutes to spare. They passed through the center and turned into a paved drive that curled around through a grove of trees. At the end of the drive they were confronted by a substantial metal gate set in an eight foot wall that encircled the house. A television camera stared blankly down from the top of the wall. The driver and guard got out and spoke to the uniformed men at the gate.

Peter was requested to step out of the car. He was expertly frisked and the car was thoroughly searched. A guard came out of a small building, behind the now partly open gate, accompanied by a dog that leapt through the open passenger door and sniffed under the seats. The driver opened the trunk and hood and the dog sniffed its way around every orifice in the vehicle. It seemed respectful of the exhaust pipe and the hot engine, Peter guessed it might have burned its nose on a previous occasion. When it had finished, Peter was ushered back into the car, the gate was fully opened and they drove on.

Inside the gate was a green oasis. The grounds were manicured and planted like a Bel Air mansion. The driveway continued for about two hundred yards and ended in a large circle in front of a sprawling, white stucco single-story home. There was a uniformed guard at the front door who stepped forward and opened the car door. Peter could hear laughter, children playing somewhere beyond the house. As he looked for them, a miniature jeep driven by a boy of about nine appeared on the service road alongside the house, chased by a girl who may have been a little younger. It had never occurred to Peter that Berruda had a family. Being at Berruda's home reminded him of that first meeting with George in Sarah's apartment in London. It seemed to remove the aura of President, but Peter was determined not to allow the informality to lower his guard.

A man dressed in black uniform trousers, a short fitted white jacket with red epaulets and a black bow tie ushered Peter into the house. He looked like a cross between a waiter and a military cadet in dress uniform. Peter followed him into a large opulent sitting room. Peter could see through the glass doors along the far side of the room, Robert Berruda and Julius were sitting on the flagstone terrace at a table laid for breakfast. Julius wore a shirt and tie, his jacket hanging on the back of his chair. Robert Berruda was casual in a short sleeve white shirt and khaki, light weight trousers. As Peter walked through the glass doors Julius stood up and greeted him.

"Hello, my friend it's nice to see you. Please join us. I hope you haven't had breakfast yet."

"No, I haven't." Peter replied.

As he approached the table Robert Berruda pointed, without standing up, to the chair opposite him.

Peter had worn a dark suit and felt overdressed. It was as if Berruda read his mind, "Feel free to take your jacket off. We're very informal at the house. It's already warm."

Peter thankfully removed his jacket and sat down.

Julius seemed a little tense as he opened the conversation. "We wish to discuss the progress of our project and tie up some loose ends. You may speak freely in front of the staff. But first, let's have some breakfast."

Breakfast was served and the discussion remained bland. There was mention of the kids, who were now driving across the manicured lawn, and the origins of the trees and shrubs in the grounds. As Peter finished eating the conversation quickly changed direction and became serious. "Is it going to work, Mr. Williamson?" Berruda asked, looking Peter straight n the eyes.

"Yes, sir!" Peter replied.

"Good! I like your confidence. Have we provided all that you need? Is there anything else we can do to assist you?"

Peter felt apprehensive. Berruda had not summoned him out here to ask if he could provide any more help. He knew they were virtually finished.

"No, sir. We've received cooperation from everyone and I have no doubt we'll be finished on Monday...and subject to New York going as planned we'll be ready on time."

"Good. When is your Indian scientist leaving us?"

"He'll be finished on Friday and I'm suggesting he leaves on Monday. That gives him a couple of days to pack up." Peter felt increasingly uncomfortable.

"Do you have any further plans for him, Peter?" Julius asked.

"No, he's served his purpose." Peter replied.

"Good!" Berruda said still looking into Peter's eyes.

"We had a number of items on the agenda for this morning," Julius explained, "but we are unsure whether an incident which occurred yesterday has anything to do with you. Perhaps we should address that first." Julius looked at Berruda as he spoke seeking approval to open the subject. Berruda gave an almost imperceptible nod.

Peter tried to retain his outward composure whilst his mind did its usual trick of presenting every conceivable possibility of what may have gone wrong. It must be the damned chemicals. Someone must have seen them removing the cans from the plant. Or perhaps Tim was followed to the apartment last night.

Julius continued, cutting across Peter's silent search for a defense against whatever…"We refused entry to a Mr. Rudi Van Haute at the airport yesterday. He came in on the flight from Nairobi and indicated that he would be staying a week or so, on vacation. However, we know Mr. Van Haute and thought it better if he did not spend his vacation with us."

Peter could not think of a reason. Rudi was visiting following Peter's phone call. Why the hell would they turn Rudi away?

"Do you know him?" Berruda asked Peter.

"Yes, sir, I do. He occasionally works for us."

"Was he working for you yesterday?" Julius inquired.

"Yes, he was. Well, he would have been if you'd let him in. Where is he?" Peter was suddenly concerned at what they might have done with him.

"He returned to Nairobi." Julius answered.

"What was he going to do for you?" Berruda asked.

"He was going to dispose of Nirina Ghose. He can't be trusted and we don't see any way of letting him loose."

Robert Berruda gave nothing away. Julius shuffled a little in his chair and seemed relieved.

"That's probably a good decision, but you should have told me." Julius admonished Peter.

"I didn't think you needed to be involved. We brought Nirina in and we felt it was our problem. We had to deal with him. We felt it was better that you in particular and Bakaar in general should know nothing of it." Peter defended himself.

"Well, now you don't have to. We'll deal with him!" Julius said with finality. He looked more at ease and Peter assumed that as far as they were concerned the problem was solved. Julius continued, "OK! That seems to clear up both our concerns. The second was going to be, what are you going to do with Nirina? We could not see any way that we could let him leave the Country." He paused, but no comments were forthcoming, "So, we seem to be in agreement. You need not concern yourself with him. We'll send a driver to collect him on Monday."

Peter did not like what he heard, but could see that discussion was not required. Julius wanted to deal with it. But Peter could not allow that to happen. Nirina could not be set free and if he had made the calls to the FBI, Peter had to remove him from the scene.

"Now that we have clarified Mr. Van Haute's position, I think the remainder of our discussion becomes a little easier." Berruda added. "The other reason for this meeting is to discuss the question of reward." Robert Berruda sat back in his chair and gestured towards Julius. This was going to be Julius' pitch.

"Reward for all concerned." Julius picked up where Robert had stopped. "When we first discussed and agreed this project we indicated that the money would be paid directly into a Bakaaran Government account."

"Yes, you did." Peter agreed.

He had not expected the subject to be raised now. He hoped George would deal with the question of their fee after the bomb was in place in Rapanda. Everyone concerned had accepted the fee, but how they would receive it had not been agreed. This was the reason for the bomb left in Rapanda. It was to ensure payment should President Berruda become reluctant after the event. George and Peter expected the division of the cash received from the United States to become very complicated. Peter expected that both Julius and Berruda would want a commission paid somewhere for the benefit of their old age and he did not want to get into the details. George had already accepted that the payment from the U.S. would have to go to the Bank of Bakaar. This was the weakest link in the entire operation. At this point the Bakaarans had all the money."

"We had expected to discuss the payment of our fee once we'd finished in New York. But now is as good a time as any." Peter continued, lying. "We also expected there might be some commissions to pay, possibly to third parties of your choosing."

"Possibly," Julius confirmed.

"As we said when we first discussed the idea, we'd like the Barnard Company to be appointed as a consultant and buying agent for Bakaar. It would receive fees and commission for its work. George Barnard expects to receive $100 million as a fee." Peter found it quite difficult to say, 'one hundred million dollars'. It was not part of his normal vocabulary, but he was damned if he would accept any reduction in fees or changes to the deal.

"Ten percent," Julius calculated.

"Yes! As we've already discussed." Peter had originally accepted that the question of fees was George's territory, but he guessed that was why they were discussing it with him. They thought he would be easier to deal with than George. What they had not appreciated was that this was to be Peter's route to riches and he was probably more determined than George to receive that hundred million dollars.

"As you know it's very difficult to handle large sums of money without half the world knowing where it comes from and where it goes. How do you intend to handle your $100 million?" Julius asked.

"We presume that transfers made by the Bank of Bakaar can be dealt with so that they cannot be traced?"

"Yes, we can do that within our Bank."

"With your agreement, one of us is planning to be at the Bakaaran Embassy in London at the time of the transfer from the U.S. One of your people, a Bakaaran, will speak with the U.S. and they'll think he has his finger on the trigger. He'll disclose the location of the bomb when the Bank of Bakaar receives the cash. However, George or I will pull the trigger if needed…and we will detonate the bomb if we don't get confirmation that our commission has reached our banks."

"It sounds as if you do not trust us," Julius said as he looked at Berruda for guidance.

"So, I understand that if the money does not reach your bank you will detonate the bomb anyway, even if the U.S. has made the payment into the Bank of Bakaar." Berruda looked a little angry, but sounded resigned.

"Exactly!" Peter replied. "I don't think it's a question of trust, it's just a guarantee. George and I have no way of knowing what may happen over the next few weeks. For all we know we could be dealing with a different government. We felt this arrangement provided the best guarantees for all of us." Peter then added, "In any event I'm sure that neither of you would want to have to detonate it if this goes wrong and who else other than George or I could you trust?"

"But it will take additional time for the transfers to be made into your accounts. We will have to release the location of the bomb to the U.S. Government when the cash is received at the Bank of Bakaar." Julius replied.

"It doesn't matter. We'll confirm the arrival of the cash in London and the Americans will know the location of the bomb. They'll think they're off the hook. Our transfer instructions will be lodged with the Bank of Bakaar in advance and our cash will be transferred for immediate value and we should know that we've received it at our banks within fifteen minutes or so."

"But what if the worst happens and for some reason your money does not arrive in your accounts within the time you have calculated. Do you detonate the bomb? What will the Americans do then?"

"Probably take retaliatory action against Bakaar," Peter stated simply and without emotion. "We just have to make sure that our money does arrive. We've done a lot of work on the timing. We know how quickly the U.S. can respond and get people to the bomb location. Believe me, it's long enough to transfer the cash. That won't be a problem."

What Peter was not about to admit was that there would be more than one bomb. This and the bomb that would be left in Bakaar were the reasons they had to produce more VX gas than might seem necessary for one bomb. Even if the Americans found and disabled one, or if the cash transfer went wrong, Peter could still explode the second one. This would bring down the wrath of the U.S. on Bakaar and should provide the incentive for Bakaar to pay up if there was any hesitation at the last minute.

Neither Julius nor Berruda made a comment. This was the first time Peter had openly presented the plan. He could see no flaws. Berruda could still decide to ditch the entire operation, but given the state of the country and Berruda's fate if he did, Peter doubted that would happen.

Julius finally commented while looking at Robert Berruda to see if he wanted to add anything, "You seem to have thought of everything, my friend." There was nothing else to say.

For the first time since he had finished breakfast, Peter became aware of his surroundings again. The laughter from the kids became audible and drifted back into his consciousness as did the smell of the grass. His shirt was damp and his right leg had gone numb from sitting tense on the hard chair. He shifted his position to relieve the leg and his movement seemed to signal the end of the meeting. Robert Berruda stood up, "Thank you for coming out here today, I feel we've clarified a great deal." He turned to go back into the house. "Julius will be in touch to finalize the arrangements."

"I'll walk you back to the car." Julius said as they made their way around the outside of the house.

Chapter 26

It was Friday and Nirina was alone in the laboratory. The Bakaaran chemists had filled the last can and left. Peter went over to the laboratory as he often did at the end of the afternoon.

"Our plans have changed a little," Peter said as he entered.

Nirina was edgy, "What do you mean?"

"The Bakaarans are going to look after you. They're sending a car out from Rapanda to take you to the airport. Then you'll be on your way home."

"What about my money?" Nirina asked aggressively.

"Your money'll be delivered to your home sometime in the next few days." Peter responded testily.

"You'd better not send the same messenger as last time." Nirina threatened, "If I see him again I shall call the police." Then he added as an afterthought, "And don't expect a receipt this time!"

Peter was no longer surprised at Nirina's stupidity. He was only surprised that the man had survived so long.

"Has the contaminated side of the lab been cleaned up?" Peter asked as he took a clean protective suit off a hanger and began to dress.

"Yes, it has. But the samples of the gas used on the animals are still in the cabinet. I was told to leave them there." Nirina replied as he continued to clear up.

Peter attached the hood, pulled on the gloves and reached up above the first of the double doors, which led into the contaminated side of the laboratory, and turned off the alarm. As far as he knew there had been no accidents and the contaminated description was simply to differentiate the two rooms. It described the room in which VX gas had been present in its final form when it was tested. The alarm was intended to be heard every time one of the doors was opened and it automatically locked the second door until the first was closed. In the event of a spillage it was meant to prevent the spread of the gas outside the contaminated side of the laboratory. Peter stepped into the air lock between the doors, opened the second door and walked over to the heavy steel cabinet in which the samples were stored. Nirina, Peter and the senior Bakaaran chemist were the only people who had keys to the cabinet. The gloves made it difficult but he unlocked the door and checked the dates and numbers on the samples against a written log. The samples were, 'Ready to use VX gas', some had been used on animals to test its effectiveness. Each sample was about two fluid ounces and was sealed in its container.

Nirina watched him, his eyes narrowing, "What are you doing?" Nirina's voice vibrated through the loudspeaker.

"It's none of your damn business," Peter replied without turning round, his muffled voice picked up and relayed to Nirina by the microphone over the bench.

"They're all there! You're wasting your time. I want to close up and get out of here. I've finished!" Nirina shouted.

Peter convinced himself that all of the samples were accounted for. He returned to Nirina's side of the laboratory, climbed out of the suit without decontaminating it and they both left together. At Peter's insistence security had been tight. Everyone was searched each time they entered or left, but the guards had become accustomed to Peter's visit's and knowing he was the boss, rarely searched him. As they left the building Nirina approached the guard and waited for the customary search.

"It's OK, Nirina, it's all over tonight, you needn't go through that." Peter waived the guard away, "Don't worry about it. He can leave!"

The guard sensing the relaxed atmosphere and knowing he would be going back to his normal duties in a couple of days, smiled and stepped back. Nirina walked away towards his house without saying a word and Peter opened the door to the Landrover.

"Goodbye, Nirina, I guess we won't be seeing each other again!" Peter called after him. Nirina continued to walk away towards his house and did not respond.

Peter met briefly with Tim and Doug, both were confident and were looking forward to getting back to the States. The practice bomb had gone together as planned and it would be detonated on Monday. Assuming it went as expected they would depart. All that was left was to assemble the bomb in the apartment in the city.

Doug was staying at the plant but Tim joined Peter and they left to discuss the plans for their last few days.

• • •

Nirina received a call on Friday evening from someone at the Ministry of the Interior. As Peter said, they had changed his travel plans. He was now to fly out to Nairobi on Monday. He assumed he would be in Paris sometime Monday evening and depending on the flights would be in Marseilles late that night. Perhaps it was a result of reaching the end of his task, knowing he would be home in a couple of days, but he felt exhausted. He went to bed early and quickly fell deeply asleep.

Half way through the night Nirina was awakened by barking dogs and vaguely thought he heard a door close somewhere in the house. Still half asleep he listened for a moment. There was no sound except the dogs. The dogs were often disturbed by some remnant of African wildlife that occasionally strayed under the wire, the nights had never been peaceful.

He awoke early next morning feeling refreshed, looking forward to the weekend, to getting packed up and leaving. He just wished it was sooner. He now knew what a prisoner feels like the day before his release.

It was another warm, dry morning. He walked into the bathroom, cleaned his teeth and turned on the shower. The temporary buildings were not designed for Bakaar. The designer had assumed there would be adequate water pressure in the mains to which the plumbing system was connected to ensure the shower worked. There was no pump. Unfortunately, in Bakaar the water supply was limited and the pressure was poor.

The water dribbled out of the shower pathetically. Nirina let it run for several minutes while he shaved, he knew it would take a while to warm up. The demand for water from the plant was far less on Saturday and he usually got a decent shower. He glanced across at the slowly increasing dribble and sniffed. He thought perhaps he had a cold. His chest felt a little constricted. He coughed and his nose began to run. The water was now running as fast as it was going to and he stepped into the shower cubicle. He picked up the soap and began to perform the contortions required to direct the feeble spray on to each part of his body. He began to wash his face and dropped the soap. He reached down to retrieve it, keeping his eyes closed to prevent the soap getting in. As he blindly felt around the shower for the soap he lost his balance, slipped and fell against the side of the cubicle. He tried to get up but slipped again. He could not stop his nose running and his eyes were irritating. He knew it was not the soap. He began to cough uncontrollably.

Shakily he pushed himself up the side of the cubicle, supporting himself by hanging on to the shower curtain. He felt nauseous. Without warning he gagged and vomited. He began to shake and involuntarily began to urinate. He could no longer focus his eyes and could not think clearly. He now knew what it was. Somehow, he had come into contact with VX. He tried to think how or when. It must have been within the past few minutes. It was the shower water. No it could not be. The symptoms had started before he got into the shower. The toothbrush? Yes, it must have been the toothbrush or the toothpaste. There was an antidote kit in the laboratory. He knew he could not get to it. His chest tightened and he gasped for breath. As he struggled to hold himself upright he began to defecate, terrible diarrhea. The shower curtain was unable to support his weight and tore away from the track. He fell into the filthy mess in the shower, coughing and convulsing. After ten agonizing, choking minutes he died of suffocation as he lay gasping for breath with his face buried in the foul liquid in the bottom of the cubicle.

The shower continued to run with its unusual Saturday pressure.

• • •

Peter's phone rang early on Sunday morning. It was Julius. "Hello my friend, how are you?"

"Good," Peter responded, "To what do I owe the pleasure of a call on Sunday?"

"I am confirming our arrangement made out at Robert's house last week. We will go along with you. That's the official response. I am personally disappointed that you feel you cannot trust us to pay your share. But I suppose that is the way of the world."

"Julius, there are two statements I was always taught to regard with some suspicion, 'The check's in the mail', and 'Trust me'. Nothing personal. Just common sense. A hundred things could go wrong and I have to know I did everything to make sure it all goes smoothly."

"Well, you may be right." Julius replied, "Oh, by the way, we found Nirina this morning."

"Found him…where? Did he get out of the plant?" Peter asked conveying concern that he might have escaped.

"Found him dead in his shower!"

"Dead?" Peter repeated the word as a question, "How did he die?"

Julius did not answer the question, "One of the maintenance men found him and we are very concerned. There is usually good water pressure on Saturday but on this Saturday there was very little. No one could use the showers. An engineer went looking for leaks. He found Nirina in his shower with the water still running." Julius paused. Peter said nothing.

"Apart from the shower curtain being torn off, there does not appear to be any sign of a struggle."

"Has anyone searched the house or checked out the body?" Peter asked.

"No, the man who found him just turned him over. We need to examine the house. Perhaps you could come over and help us. A Doctor from the Ministry is on his way out there now."

"Yes, I'll go. Are you going?"

"I am already here," Julius replied.

Peter picked up the small plastic bag containing a toothbrush and toothpaste and left the apartment for the plant. He drove straight to the workshop, unlocked the closet and put two NBC suits, gloves, hoods and a couple of antidote kits into the vehicle. Julius had supplied a dozen of the British detector papers from the Bakaaran Army's supply and he took a couple. They were just strips of coated paper with adhesive backing which could be attached to the suit or anything else and changed color if they came into contact with the nerve agent. He then drove to Nirina's house. Peter knew what had killed him.

Peter met Julius at the plant and warned him that Nirina's death could be the action of VX. If it was, any part of the house might be contaminated and no one should go in without protection.

"Has everything been left as it was?" Peter asked.

"Yes, as far as I can tell. Except the shower was turned off. If it was VX there has been no evidence of it. The shower was still running when the maintenance man went in. Depending on when it happened, any evidence would have been washed away."

"How's the maintenance man?" Peter inquired.

"He's OK. He'd have been dead long ago if he had been contaminated."

Peter took one of the suits from the Landrover, put it on and attached a detector strip. "I'll go and have a look."

As he entered the house he stopped, partially opened the suit and took the plastic bag out of his pocket. There was no guarantee that he would have the opportunity to swap the toothpaste and brush. But when they first arrived he made sure that no one except Tim, Doug and he had access to the NBC suits at the plant. That at least provided a good chance that one of them would be the first one on the scene of any accident. He had not envisaged this scenario, but it was working to his advantage.

The NBC suit was a standard NATO issue. Not heavy, weighing only about four pounds and although the fabric breathes, in high temperatures it can quickly cause heat stress. Peter was grateful that it was not the middle of the afternoon. As he had experienced when he was unloading the VX agents from the Landrover at his apartment, the field of vision through the separate eye-pieces was restricted. He had to turn his shoulders from side to side to point the eye-pieces in the hood in the correct direction and make up for the loss of peripheral vision. Breathing through the filter was laborious. It made him feel he was under water.

He went straight into the bathroom, reached to the back of the cabinet under the sink and found the container of VX. The seal was broken, but the top was securely fastened. He returned it to its hiding place to be discovered later. He then swapped the toothbrush and toothpaste he had brought in the bag with those in the bathroom, taking great care to ensure the bag was well and truly sealed.

Nirina's body was still lying in the shower and in spite of the effect of the steady stream of cooling water it had begun to bloat. Totally against the man's character, Nirina could not have been more obliging. By dying in the shower it was almost certain that any traces of VX around his mouth or on his body would have been washed away. The body could be moved with little risk to anyone and it was unlikely that an examination would reveal how the VX had been administered.

Peter left the house and once outside checked the detector strip before removing the hood. He walked towards Julius who was talking with a man he had not met before. Julius moved back a pace or so as Peter approached, not wanting the possibility of any accidental contact with Peter.

"It's hard to tell, but I can see nothing to suggest how he died. Let's get the other suit and a couple of us should try and bring the body out." Peter suggested.

Julius introduced Peter to the doctor from the Ministry. The doctor donned a suit and he and Peter returned to the house. The doctor made a cursory examination as best he could wearing the suit and with some difficulty they succeeded in half carrying half dragging the body out of the house.

"I cannot tell for certain what caused death until I perform an autopsy, but I would say he died early on Saturday.

Peter looked as if something had just occurred to him, "Has anyone checked the lab to see if any of the gas is missing?"

"No, not yet, but I think we should." Julius placed heavy emphasis on 'we' indicating that he wanted his men to carry out the search rather than Peter.

The laboratory was checked and one of the test samples was missing. Julius insisted that Nirina's house must be checked and a couple of the soldiers donned the suits, searched the house and the sample was found at the back of the bathroom cabinet.

"How on earth did he get the sample past security? Why would he take it?" Julius asked Peter later in the day when they had finished.

"Perhaps he intended to contaminate the house hoping that some of us might be killed. I never trusted the man. But I think I may have provided the opportunity." Peter answered. "When we left the laboratory yesterday, I walked out with Nirina and told the guard not to bother with the search. It didn't occur to me that he might actually be trying to get a sample out."

Julius gave Peter a long hard look, "I suppose it doesn't matter much in the scheme of things."

"No, it probably saves you the task."

"Yes. Perhaps it's better this way, none of us had to do it." Julius again gave Peter an old fashioned look. Peter thought that Julius had a very strong suspicion that the situation was not exactly as it appeared. But the chance of the matter being taken any further was slim. It had served their purpose. At the meeting at Robert's house, Peter had gained the strong impression that Nirina would not have been eliminated—just locked away. Later on, if anything went wrong Julius could have produced him and with little persuasion he would implicate George and Peter. The fact that Nirina was dead tipped the balance back in Peter's favor.

• • •

The final shipment of chemicals would be on their way on Tuesday. Peter felt that he was regaining control. On Monday morning he had a leisurely breakfast, drove to the city and found a pay phone.

"Mr. Gordon, good morning," he said as they were connected, "I have good news and bad news."

"Hello, Mr. Williamson. I think I'd better have the bad news first."

"It looks as if the Bakaarans have been using the plant to make some type of chemical for military use."

"Yes, I think you'll find it's nerve gas," Mr. Gordon interrupted. "We made some sort of sense of your name, the Pakistani, we think it's Nirina, Nirina Ghose. And by the way he's Indian."

"That could be right, my contact here confirmed the name was Nirina, but how does that suggest nerve gas? Is that poison gas?" Peter asked, surprising himself with his own naivete and sincerity.

"Yes! Mr. Ghose is an expert on certain types of nerve gas. He's sold his services a number of times in recent years." Mr. Gordon paused for a second, "What's the good news?"

"They don't appear to have got very far. I'm not an expert, but apparently they're working out of a small building inside the fertilizer plant. My contact said it looked like a laboratory. If they're up to no good I think we might have nipped it in the bud."

"Yes, maybe. Anything else you can tell me?" Mr. Gordon asked. Peter thought there was just a hint that perhaps Mr. Gordon knew more than he was letting on.

"No, I don't think so. Any more phone calls?

"Phone calls?"

"The phantom informant from Bakaar!"

"Oh, no I haven't heard any more."

"Is there anything more you want me to do?"

"No, you've done enough. Many thanks. When are you coming back to London?"

"I'm leaving here on Friday." Peter answered, "I'll give you a call when I get back if you wish."

"Yes, do that. Bye, bye." Mr. Gordon rang off.

Within a matter of hours, the CIA received the report from London.

• • •

The final test of the bomb on Monday went well. The operation was declared a success and Tim and Doug completed the wiring of the fertilizer plant, placing explosive charges around the foundation.

Late in the afternoon Julius arrived and found Peter in the laboratory.

"Hello, my friend. Are you finished?"

"Yes, I think we're all packed up."

"So, when's the big bang?"

"We're about to remove the samples of gas and as soon as that's done we're ready. It'll be at six o'clock."

"Most of our men have gone, they should all be out of here in the next hour or so. Are you staying?

"Yes, I'll stay with Tim and Doug until it's finished. You're all set with the press release for tomorrow?"

"Yes, it may cause us some problems but we will release it." Julius confirmed.

"Good! By the way Tim and Doug want to have a party on Thursday in the apartment in the city. Just to say thanks to the chaps they've been working with. I know it's within the barracks, but can we arrange it?"

"Yes, I'll authorize it, but I'll need a list of those you're inviting and I'll make sure the guards on the gate know. Am I invited?" Julius asked.

"Of course you are, you'll be welcome." Peter answered.

Julius did not reply, but it was obvious he would not go.

Trucks had been ploughing backwards and forwards along the dirt road all day. The final contingent of the Bakaaran army left at five o'clock, confirming to Julius, who was sitting in his car at the entrance with his bodyguard and driver, that the plant was clear. Peter, Tim and Doug drove out in the Landrover and stopped as they came alongside Julius' car. They spoke through the open windows.

"Well, my friend, once you press the button we are going to need a new plant. I trust we receive the cash to rebuild it! We'll meet in my office on Thursday, Peter. Just to make sure we all know what we are going to do." Julius wound up the window, in a vain attempt to keep the red dust out on the journey back to the city.

Peter looked at Tim and Doug, "Ready?"

"Yep, I'd like us to be at least half a mile away," Tim drawled. "Just in case you left one of those fucking samples lying around somewhere!"

"Don't worry, I didn't. The only idiot to leave one around seems to have been Nirina." Peter looked at Doug, who smiled. "Nice job, Doug. I don't think there'll be any repercussions."

"Thanks boss." Doug answered appearing embarrassed by Peter's praise.

Peter turned to Tim with a knowing smile, "I bet that's the end of the phone calls."

"Yeah it's got to be."

Doug looked at Tim as if for explanation. None was forthcoming.

"By morning the NRO's little spy in the sky will just have a big hole to look at. That should start them scurrying around," Peter added. "I'd love to be a fly on the wall in Langley when the CIA gets the pictures."

They took a last look at the plant. Peter started the engine and they drove down the road towards Rapanda. After a couple of minutes he stopped and looked at his watch. "It's five fifty-five." He glanced over at Tim who had been carefully cuddling the radio transmitter since they left the plant. Tim uncovered the push button and turned on the power.

"OK at exactly six o'clock," Peter waited and then began to count. Just Peter at, "Ten, nine, eight," then Doug joined in, "seven, six, five, four," and finally Tim, "three, two, one…" Tim pressed the button. For a split second nothing happened, then they saw a huge red dust cloud erupt and then the blast and pressure wave from the explosion rocked the Landrover. As the noise and dust subsided all they could hear was the squawking of hundreds of birds frightened out of the trees by the blast.

"Fantastic! Aren't explosions great!" Tim was enjoying himself.

They waited five minutes and drove back to admire their handiwork. The dust had not settled, but through the red haze, they could see their task had been accomplished. There was nothing left except the remains of the chimney, even as they reached the gate there was nothing more to see. The old building had gone. The chimney now stood about twenty feet high looking like the broken mast on a sailing ship. The only clue as to what had been there just minutes before. Even the laboratory, built to withstand an earthquake, had gone.

"Well done, Tim," Peter complimented him, "No one'll find anything in there without a microscope."

They turned around and drove back into the city.

Wednesday, July 8. New York:

Doug drove carefully through the New York afternoon traffic. The last thing he needed was a traffic violation or, even worse, an accident. He and Tim were on their way to the first selected building.

Earlier in the year they had worked from a list of one hundred and twenty customers that George's company had provided, to find just four suitable locations. Each customer had responded to an offer to fit an updated computer board to their phone system, free of charge, in July. The offer was restricted to systems which could be used for Peter's purposes and installation of the board gave access to the building. To be of any use to Tim and Doug the buildings had to conform to a rigid set of parameters.

They did not want to apply to the City for on-street parking permits and therefore the buildings had to have off-street garage parking. If their truck was parked in the garage it would make it easier to move their equipment into the building and would ensure that a parking permit could not be used to trace them after the event.

It had to be a large building. There must be enough tenants to ensure that telephone installations and maintenance were happening daily. And there had to be at least two additional customers on the list apart from the primary one chosen to have the new computer board fitted. They did not intend to fit the detonation device in the system of the customer who received the updated computer board. That privilege was reserved for one of the other customers in the building, for whom there would be no record of any work being done. They wanted miles of old wiring from long gone tenants snaking through the ducts and it had to be an older rather than a new building. The ideal location of the customer to receive the bomb was on a floor adjacent to a mechanical floor. It had to be above the tenth floor to ensure the gas spread widely as it descended to the ground. It was a laborious task. After they had eliminated those that did not fit the bill, there were six that seemed suitable. They selected two.

After the event, the FBI or the police would dismantle the bomb, looking for clues as to its creators. The Government would know that Bakaar planned and set the bomb, but the FBI would still try to discover who had been involved and whether there were connections to any other country or organization. By building the detonation switch into a phone system which would have no record of having been altered, there was little chance that George's company would be implicated.

Doug swung the truck into the parking garage entrance, flashed the security guard a sight of the pass and parked. By the time they carted their equipment up to Hope and Nagle on the fifteenth floor it was two o'clock. They had to disconnect the telephone to fit the board and they would not do that until the office closed. In the meantime, having got access to the building, they began to install the wiring on the mechanical floor squeezed between the twelfth and fourteenth. All of the heating, air conditioning and utilities and services were installed on this floor. It should have been the thirteenth, if mechanical floors were numbered—but normally they were not and in any event thirteen was rarely used. The passenger elevators glided past the mechanical floors with no access and most visitors never realized they exist. The customer designated to receive the switch was located on the fourteenth floor. Tim checked to find a vent where the bomb could be located ensuring it could rip a hole through the outside wall to allow the gas to drift into the street and also be sucked in through the air conditioning system to contaminate the interior of the building. By seven o'clock the building was almost empty. Tim had finished the legitimate installation of the computer board on the fifteenth floor and was assembling the bomb.

Doug brought up the plastic explosive from the truck and carefully packed it into the cradle to be hidden behind the ducting alongside the external wall. All that was left was to make the connection and adapt the phone system of the innocent tenant on the fourteenth floor. Doug checked out the offices, they were empty. He dealt with the lock, Tim entered and began the task of wiring the device into the system. The lights in the corridor provided illumination in the office through the glass partition separating the offices from the corridor and with the aid of a flashlight Tim could see well enough to do the job without the need for the office lights.

Doug pressed the transmit button on the radio to test it. Tim responded—all was quiet. They knew from their research that the occupants of this office were normally gone by six o'clock and the cleaners did not start work until early morning. The risk was that some workaholic might return to the offices or a security guard would visit the floor. They had a pass to the building but they had no right to be in these offices.

The low hum of the elevator broke the silence. Doug walked over and looked at the indicator. It was coming up from the lobby. He raised the radio to his mouth ready to warn Tim. It stopped at the tenth floor. He relaxed but remained watching. Five minutes passed, the hum began again, the elevator continued up, past the twelfth and stopped on the fourteenth. "Kill the light! Company." Doug transmitted to Tim. Tim's flashlight went out. The doors clanked open. There was little Doug could do. From where he was standing, to one side of the doors he could not see who was inside. He quietly approached the elevator. A uniformed security guard stepped out tunelessly whistling to himself. He was about fifty, overweight to the point of obesity and had a radio attached to his belt, pulled up beneath his grotesque and sagging stomach, but as far as Doug could see he was not armed. The guard took a couple of small shuffling steps into the corridor to ensure his backside was not blocking the elevator doors. Sensing Doug's presence his head snapped round to face him, "Can I help you?" He asked aggressively.

"No, I'm just finishing off, I'll be out of here in ten minutes." Doug replied walking nonchalantly towards the elevator, the doors of which had remained open.

"Can't use that one! I'm making my rounds." The guard was belligerent and began to pant as he spoke, the exertion of moving his massive bulk to point in the same direction as his head seeming to exhaust him.

"Where you working?" The guard made the assumption Doug was working. It was after hours and he had a note of about fifteen work crews in the building during the night this week.

"I'm finishing work on the phone system for Hope and Nagle." Doug answered remaining relaxed.

"Did you getta pass?" the guard asked relishing his authority.

"Yeah, I've got it somewhere," Doug walked towards the guard, searching in the top pocket of his denim jacket. He pulled out the crumpled yellow paper and handed it over. The guard unfolded it.

"Says. Tim Schwartz and Doug Barnes. Hope and Nagle, telephone installation, July 8."

"Yep, that's what it says," Doug responded condescendingly.

"Which are you?

"Doug…" Doug began to respond, but he was cut off.

"This is the fourteenth floor, they're on the fifteenth. What you doing here?"

As he spoke the guard took out a notebook from the inside pocket of his ill-fitting uniform jacket and began to thumb through the pages. The act of reaching into the pocket and now reading the content of the notebook seemed to cut off any expectation or perhaps ability to deal with answers to his questions.

Doug remained silent. Just my luck, he thought as he watched the guard puff and pant his way through the pages, 'Nine out of ten guys might have asked a question or two but would have cared less.'

"I don't know about a pass for you, where's your buddy?" He asked the question again, "Which one are you, Schwartz or Barnes?"

Doug answered only in part, "He's up on the fifteenth."

"You'd better come with me, we'll go and find your buddy and get this straightened out."

There was no point arguing, Doug could see the guy was going to make him his reason for being on duty. He was going to make a meal of it and Doug could not allow that.

The guard entered the elevator first. Doug followed. The guard released the 'open door' key, but Doug quickly leaned across and pushed seventeen. The elevator responded and began to climb.

"What the hell you do that for?" The guard bellowed in Doug's face. "We gotta go and pick up your buddy, then we're gonna get some answers!"

The guard did not attempt to select the fifteenth, apparently resigned to wait until they got to seventeen. As the elevator stopped, he reached for the floor selector button, Doug blocked him.

"Hey, we need to get down to the fifteenth!" The guard responded still trying to reach around Doug for the button.

The doors opened and Doug blocking the guard's view with his body, reached across and turned the 'open door' key, which was still in the lock. He stepped backwards until he could lean out and see the area to both sides of the elevator. The floor was deserted.

"What the hell d'you think your doing?" The guard shouted as he reached down toward his belt and the radio, his face was now the color of cooked beet root and his panting was getting out of control.

Doug moved back into the stationary elevator and smoothly drew the Browning pistol from inside the rear waistband of his pants. The guard's hand had reached the radio and he pressed and locked the transmit button. The radio was hidden from Doug's view by the guard's excessive stomach but seeing his hand move out of sight Doug hooked the barrel of the pistol under the guard's forearm and roughly pulled his hand back into view. The guard looked down checking that the transmit light was on. He saw the pistol now pointing at the lower reaches of his stomach. His belligerence turned to fear. He knew the radio was on. He was congratulating himself on how clever he was to think of it. But now as he looked at the pistol he wondered if he had done the right thing. Would his colleague, on his rounds elsewhere in the building, hearing what was broadcast, try and contact him. This would tip off his assailant and might be disastrous. No, that could not happen, his radio was locked on 'transmit' and would not receive. He felt clever again.

"Leave the radio alone!" Doug warned, his manner leaving the guard no room for doubt. Doug took hold of the guard's shoulder and firmly but gently pushed him out of the elevator. All the bathrooms were located in the same position on each floor and Doug pushed the guard ahead of him toward the nearest.

"Head along to the bathroom," Doug ordered calmly, his mind made up and now looking to carry out the task as quickly as possible. Doug walked behind the guard and out of his sight he took out the silencer and screwed it onto the Browning. As they neared the bathroom door, Doug ordered the guard to open it. He did so using a key on the bunch attached to his belt.

"So, what's your problem? We can work something out," the guard said, half turning his head as he opened the door, his voice showing signs of fear. Doug placed his left hand on the back of the guard's neck and without answering, pushed him steadily through the door and towards the far wall. The door closed behind them. The guard's stomach met the white tiled wall, his head still six inches from it. Doug maintained his grip on the guard's neck, forcing his face closer to the wall. There was now little doubt in the guard's mind that Doug intended him harm. The realization of his imminent fate bolstered his courage and in an attempt to warn and get help from his colleague via the open radio, he began to curse.

"You asshole! What the fuck are you doing? "

Doug raised the heavy pistol and aimed at the base of the guard's skull.

Out of the corner of his eye the guard saw the pistol as Doug maintained his grip with his left hand and was forced to bend his right wrist at almost ninety degrees. He placed the end of the silencer on the guard's collar to be sure of hitting the spot where the spine supports the skull.

"Asshole, what's the point of this? We can…"

Doug released his grip on the guard's neck and squeezed the trigger simultaneously. The recoil flicked the barrel upwards and sideways twisting Doug's wrist, "Fuck!" He cursed more from being forced to kill the man, than from the pain of the awkward recoil. His curse almost drowned the dull thud of the silenced pistol. The guard's head hit the wall and blood spattered back over Doug's hand and wrist. The guard died instantly. A.45 fired at point blank range breaking the spine does not require death to be confirmed by checking a pulse, it makes a mess. Doug wished he could have done it more tidily. He washed his hands and the pistol, drying it on a paper towel. He checked his clothing and made sure there were no tell tale stains. "The problem's solved, you can carry on," Doug transmitted to Tim, "but we still need to finish off ASAP."

Doug reached down to remove the radio from the guard's belt and he saw the little red light. He pressed the release and immediately the voice of the dead guard's colleague was loud and clear.

"Dan, what's going on? Dan can you hear me, where are you?"

Doug took the elevator back down to the twelfth floor, just in case the other security guard who had overheard the events of the past few minutes might be watching the progress of the elevator from somewhere else in the building. From his radio call he did not know where Dan had been. That meant that Doug and Tim probably still had time to finish the installation, but they had no idea what had been overheard. Doug walked back up the stairs to the fourteenth floor to resume his watch and listen out for any other transmissions on the security guard's radio.

The radio remained silent and fifteen minutes later Tim called, "Finished".

Doug summoned the elevator as Tim appeared out of the office, "What happened?" Tim asked.

"Security guard appeared out of nowhere. Wouldn't leave it alone, insisted on a checking us out. Would you believe he couldn't find our pass in his notebook. It was legit wasn't it?"

"Yeah! What did you do with him?"

Doug drew his finger across his throat, "Finito! But the bastard had his radio on and his buddy may have heard the whole thing. I don't know what we're going to find when we get down to the garage. They've had fifteen minutes to get some help in here."

"Shit! Where d'ya leave him?"

"In a bathroom on the seventeenth, it'll keep anyone away from our work on the fourteenth."

They climbed into the elevator and headed for the garage. Tim's mind was racing. They could not just stand in the elevator and wait to see what was waiting in the garage. Tim reached out and punched the button for the second floor.

"Let's get out at the second floor and try and suss out what's going on here."

Unexpectedly the elevator stopped at the fifth. Doug cursed again and made another quick examination of his clothes for blood-stains placing his hand behind his back on the butt of the pistol and waited for the door to open. Tim pressed himself into the side of the elevator trying to reduce his exposure when the doors opened. His pistol was in his hand hidden from view by his tool box.

A young attractive woman got in and smiled. "Evening." She looked at the floor selector and seeing the garage lit stood back from the door, "You're going to the garage?" She asked rhetorically.

"No," Tim drawled pressing the second floor button again, "We still got work on the second floor?"

Their new companion shrugged her shoulders but made no comment. The elevator stopped at the second floor. Tim and Doug got out.

"OK," Tim had worked through the possibilities, "Even if the other guard heard it all, what did he hear? What was said?"

"He just called me an asshole and asked what I was doing," Doug replied. "No, wait a minute. He read our names off the pass. I don't know how long that goddamned radio was on. I told you Tim this job's worth a hell of a lot more than $100,000. Christ the security guard's worth that."

"I can't pay you any more Doug."

"Then you better start negotiating with our friend Peter. Between us we gotta get a couple of million."

"Yeah, but just for now we got to get out of this building in one piece. C'mon Doug remember. What happened? We don't wanna go off at half cock when we get to the garage. We may still be able to walk out of this place."

"I can't be sure, but I bet he turned that radio on when we were in the elevator. I noticed he slid his hand down to his belt and I knocked it away. Yeah, I bet that's when he did it."

"So what would have been heard?"

"Just him calling me an asshole. Then I shot him. But the silencer's good, unless you knew, no one would hear that noise as a gun shot. The last thing you'd think of…"

"Alright, let's assume the other guy heard a couple of stupid questions…"

"And he didn't even know where we were. When I turned off the transmit there he was, asking for Dan. Where he was and what's going on."

"I don't think the other guy would do much. I reckon he heard some of it then the transmission stops as you turn it off and he asks, 'What's going on.' He has no clue! There's nothing more than an argument between this Dan and some guy working late."

"Yeah, we're getting skittish."

"OK. Let's walk down to the garage. If we meet any trouble follow me. I'm prepared to shoot our way out, leave the truck and break up and disappear on foot. We'll meet back at the apartment."

"Let's go!"

They walked down the stairs and emerged in the lobby. The stairway to the garage was a separate door at the back of the lobby.

"Hey, you guys see Dan anywhere?" A security guard called out as they walked across the lobby. He was standing at the reception desk. He did not look concerned.

"Dan who?" Tim responded.

"My colleague. He's not talking to me. I heard him having an argument with someone."

"No, we've been working. Haven't seen anyone except a chick you'd swap for you're old lady."

"Didn't see her. Guess I'd remember. I expect he's gone back to sleep."

"Yeah, night!" Tim replied as they walked towards the door, opened it and started down the stairs to the garage.

"That was him!"

"The guy on the radio?" Tim asked.

"Yeah, he had no idea, we're O.K."

There was no one in the garage. No one in the kiosk, the exit was guarded only by two rows of steel spikes set into the top of the ramp facing the street. They folded down as they drove across them, springing back into position ready to tear the tires off any vehicle entering uninvited.

Thursday, July 9. New York:

The police car's siren tried in vain to cut a path through the solid wall of morning traffic on Fifth Avenue. Patrolman Keefe and his partner were responding to a call to investigate a body in the bathroom on the seventeenth floor of an office building on East 46th Street.

The radio dispatcher from the 17th Precinct called again, "One twenty eight, are you responding?"

"One twenty eight affirmative, yeah, we're responding, in traffic on Fifth!"

"How long to destination?" the dispatcher inquired.

"You tell me, maybe ten!"

"Is Homicide on the way?"

"Yep, Lieutenant Anderson."

Eventually the crew in One Twenty Eight'confirmed they were at the building. The police car bounced over the sidewalk and down into the parking garage. The security guard waved it into a space by the kiosk.

The two officers got out of the car, straightening their hats and adjusting their belts with a studied unhurried attitude that belied their wailing, flashing arrival. Patrolman Keefe pushed his nightstick through the carrier on his belt and walked over to Todd Reardon, the security guard who had been called to the bathroom when the body had been found. Todd was waiting in the garage. A colleague was now guarding the bathroom and his boss, the Chief Security Officer for the building, was in the security office on the ground floor with the poor guy who found the body.

"Can you take us up to the floor first?" Keefe asked.

"Yeah, I'll take you up. The body's in the bathroom about three doors down the corridor from the elevator. He's awful smashed up," he said as he recalled responding to the call from the unfortunate man who first tried to use the bathroom nearly half an hour before.

"What's your name?" Keefe asked the security guard as they traveled up in the elevator.

"Todd Reardon," Keefe's partner wrote it down and asked for Reardon's home phone number and address, and for the phone number of the security office in the building.

"Did you know the guy?" Keefe asked.

The radio dispatcher from the 17th Precinct called again, "One twenty eight, are you responding?"

"One twenty eight affirmative, yeah, we're responding, in traffic on Fifth!"

"How long to destination?" the dispatcher inquired.

"You tell me, maybe ten!"

"Is Homicide on the way?"

"Yep, Lieutenant Anderson."

Eventually the crew in One Twenty Eight' confirmed they were at the building. The police car bounced over the sidewalk and down into the parking garage. The security guard waved it into a space by the kiosk.

The two officers got out of the car, straightening their hats and adjusting their belts with a studied unhurried attitude that belied their wailing, flashing arrival. Patrolman Keefe pushed his nightstick through the carrier on his belt and walked over to Todd Reardon, the security guard who had been called to the bathroom when the body had been found. Todd was waiting in the garage. A colleague was now guarding the bathroom and his boss, the Chief Security Officer for the building, was in the security office on the ground floor with the poor guy who found the body.

"Can you take us up to the floor first?" Keefe asked.

"Yeah, I'll take you up. The body's in the bathroom about three doors down the corridor from the elevator. He's awful smashed up," he said as he recalled responding to the call from the unfortunate man who first tried to use the bathroom nearly half an hour before.

"What's your name?" Keefe asked the security guard as they traveled up in the elevator.

"Todd Reardon," Keefe's partner wrote it down and asked for Reardon's home phone number and address, and for the phone number of the security office in the building.

"Did you know the guy?" Keefe asked.

"Oh, yes! It's Dan Thurber, I worked with him every other week. His ID's still pinned to his shirt. Anyway I know the guy, even without a face."

"Has his family been told?"

"No, other than call you, we just locked the bathroom. My boss kept the guy who found him in our office."

"How many of your staff on duty in the building last night?"

"Two…Dan and a new guy."

"What happened to the new guy? Why didn't he report Dan missing last night?"

"Well…Dan's a bastard. We all know he sneaks off duty early and he's been caught asleep before now. The new guy was told what he's like and he just assumed that Dan had sloped off."

"Wonderful security operation!" Keefe added cynically. "Does the whole building know what happened?"

"No, I told you…other than call you guys, no one knows."

"Good, at least we haven't got a crowd to deal with."

"How is he smashed up, Todd?" Keefe's partner asked Reardon. "We were told it was a gunshot."

"Half his face is spread all over the wall. It's not very pretty." Reardon answered, obviously having a hard time with the experience.

"It never is!" Keefe answered as they walked out of the elevator and saw Todd's colleague standing guard at the bathroom door. Todd took out a bunch of keys and unlocked the door. The sickly smell from the small closed room hit them. It stank like a slaughter house in spite of the air conditioning. Todd leaned in and switched on the lights.

Keefe entered the room first and carefully approached the body now frozen by rigor mortis into the grotesque position it had assumed after it slid down the wall. "There's not much doubt he's dead," Keefe observed to his colleague as he checked and noted down the time. "So, who's been in here since he was discovered?"

"The guy who found him, my boss, me and my partner,"

"OK, let's go and see your boss, we'll need some names, addresses and times. I assume no one touched or removed anything."

"No, sir!" Todd Reardon replied positively.

Keefe's partner stayed on guard at the bathroom and Keefe and Reardon descended to the ground floor and headed for the security office.

Ten minutes later Lieutenant Anderson and Sergeant Tucker from the Homicide Unit arrived at the security office and were briefed by Keefe. Over the next fifteen minutes the team began to assemble and the Medical Examiner arrived.

"Lieutenant, there's something not quite right about this one." Tucker told Anderson after they had looked at the body and interviewed the security staff and the still distraught man who had found the body.

"Yeah, it looks like a professional hit," Lt. Anderson agreed. "But why, and more to the point, if it was a planned hit, why the cannon? I bet we'll find that bullet in the wall is a.45. No one would choose to use a.45 if it was planned at that range."

"The only other alternative is that he stumbled across someone who shouldn't have been there, but we've got no reports of anything suspicious, no break-in's nothing."

"Why wasn't he found last night and what about the cleaners this morning?"

"I guess the cleaners don't clean everywhere every night."

"Yeah, but a bathroom. Surely, they clean the bathrooms every night. We've got some work to do." Anderson sighed. He knew the odds of unraveling this one were about the same as winning the lottery, but they had to go through the motions.

By mid morning the bathroom was dusted for fingerprints and the photographers had recorded the event. The Medical Examiner had examined the body. The body was removed at a little after 1.00 p.m. It was just another, probably insoluble murder in New York, but the inconsistencies disturbed Lt. Anderson. By the end of the day, all the offices on the seventeenth floor were checked. Nothing was missing.

None had been broken into. There was no motive that could be quickly established.

The Medical Examiner confirmed that Dan Thurber was shot at point blank range with a.45. The large caliber bullet had caused massive damage to the lower part of Dan's face. However, there was little doubt that the bullet's entry point was exactly where it should have been to kill instantly. It had smashed the first three cervical vertebrae and severed Dan's spinal cord. The bullet had been dug out of the wall, but it was so deformed that ballistics could do little with it. Whoever had wielded the gun knew what he was doing.

Lt. Anderson arranged for a team to visit every office in the building and ask the same question that was asked on the seventeenth floor. The other line of inquiry was to see if they could establish anything in Dan Thurber's life that could result in his untimely end. If the dead guy was such a bastard to work with maybe he had enemies. Perhaps he gambled.

Whatever the outcome, it would take time and time was the enemy. As each day passed and no motive or lead was established the likelihood of solving the crime diminished. If they had to get to the 'Who was in the building that night' stage, Anderson knew it would end up on the unsolved pile.

Friday, July 10. New York:

Peter arrived in New York on a Friday afternoon using his now familiar American passport.

He checked into the hotel and received the message that Tim Schwartz had called and would call back later that night. Peter knew Doug and Tim would be out during the day and evening. They were busy installing replacement computer boards for legitimate customers most days and today, if they were on schedule, they would be installing the second bomb.

It was agreed they would call him at the hotel on Friday night to confirm they had been successful. The message was too early, something must have gone wrong. Peter had little to do this trip. He was there to confirm that the installations had been completed and to troubleshoot if needed. It was a long wait. He stayed in his room and slept for a while. It was a quarter after ten and he was watching the news when the call came in.

"Hi!" Tim said as Peter answered the phone.

"What's the problem?"

"Both devices are in place, but we did have a problem. It's solved but we need to talk about it." Tim was very concise.

"Where shall we meet?" Peter asked.

Tim mentioned a bar just off Times Square on Broadway, which he knew to be open most of the night. Peter grabbed a cab and was at the bar twenty minutes later.

Tim was already there, sitting alone at a table near the door, "What would you like to drink?"

"I'll have a gin and tonic," Peter answered as Tim hailed a passing waiter.

"So, what's the problem?" Peter asked, concerned and wanting to get it out in the open quickly.

"We were disturbed on Wednesday night, on East 46th. A goddamned security guard wouldn't go away and Doug had to shoot him."

"Damn!" Peter responded as if he had just spilt his drink. He helped himself to a handful of nuts. "Is there anything to connect you to the incident?" he asked after a minute or so of chewing.

Tim breathed a sigh of relief. He had expected Peter to grill him on the necessity to take such drastic action. "No, nothing! Doug took the guy up to the seventeenth floor. We were working on the fourteenth. I've not seen any publicity about it."

"Was there anyone around in the building when you were working? Were you seen by anyone?"

"Yeah, we went down in the elevator about twenty minutes later and a girl got in at the fifth floor and rode with us to the second. We walked down through the lobby and the other security guard spoke to us. But they won't be able to determine the time he was killed that accurately."

"You wait and see!" Peter commented, "I think you have to assume they'll do just that. Why didn't you wait to leave later?"

"We couldn't do that. If anyone found the body they'd have sealed the place. We had to get out as soon as we could. Anyway, the dead guard left his radio on. We didn't know how much he heard."

"Christ, it just gets worse! This thing's got to happen Tim." Peter's voice got louder as he spoke, "We can't fuck up now! Is that it? Is that everything? Or are you saving the best till last, uh? Maybe they arrested Doug and you don't want to tell me till I've had another drink!"

"Take it easy." Tim looked around the bar as if he expected everyone to be listening.

"So do we know what this other guard heard?"

"The guy in the lobby? He heard nothing. He just thought his buddy was having a row with someone. Seems, the guy Doug wasted was a real bastard and he took no notice."

Peter acknowledged the sense of Tim's reasoning. They probably had to do what they did. It was not the need to kill the guard that was worrying Peter. It was the thought that the project would fail and he would never see what he had already considered to be his fortune. He was not going to miss out this time, for anything.

"Well there is one more problem but it's really mine." Tim almost whispered.

Peter shook his head and waited for more bad news.

"Doug's bleating on about more money. I can't pay him any more I've already told him, but after he killed the guard he's started whining again."

"You said it, he's your problem. You deal with him. Shoot him for all I care and keep it all!"

"You've really got a bug up your ass tonight, Peter!"

"Yeah! We're this close," Peter put his thumb and forefinger together and virtually pushed his hand into Tim's face. "You've got some of your money already, but I don't get paid until it's all over. I'm going to get paid Tim!" Peter paused and took a gulp of his drink, "We may well have to detonate that bomb in August and you can bet that girl will remember the incident when the Feds start crawling over everyone in the building for the second time in a couple of months." Peter warned.

"We had no choice, Peter!" Tim added, "I know it's gonna complicate the issue, but it's done, there's nothing we can do about it. We did everything we could."

Tim was right. There was nothing to be done now. But, down the road, the woman could confirm that a couple of engineers were in the building on the night of an unexplained murder a little after the time of death. The security guard would confirm when Tim and Doug left. The Feds would check out everyone who had access to the building that day, even if they had not already done so and they would find the pass issued to Electronic Communications.

"Have you got the pass with you?" Peter asked just to confirm his fears.

"No, Doug's got it. What do you want if for?"

"How did you apply for it. Was the company name on it?" Peter asked.

"Hope and Nagle just asked us for our names, I don't think it was issued by security. The damned guard couldn't find it in his list–that was the problem! It was provided by Hope and Nagle. I don't think the company name was on it. I don't think a legit pass existed."

"Well, we might be lucky." Peter said resignedly as he sipped his drink. "Has anything else gone wrong?"

"No, everything else is good. We're gonna be busy for the first few days next week, but we should be finished by Wednesday. Everything will be cleared out of the lock-ups and dumped. Then we get paid!" Tim felt he should remind Peter that it was soon to be pay-off time.

"We've made the arrangements and we'll pay you as soon as the Americans cough up their cash." Peter responded. There was nothing else to add and Tim accepted it.

Wednesday, July 15. New York:

By Wednesday, July 15, they had finished. Peter called George and discussed the possibility of a connection being made back to him through the pass. They agreed that it might still be traced, but that the information was far from incriminating. They had fitted a computer board to a customer's phone system that day. They had done the same to many others during the preceding weeks, using a variety of company employees. George was not too concerned. By the time any investigations began, Tim and Doug would have left the company, as would a number of other employees. They always laid people off at the end of the summer.

Regardless of George's lack of concern, Peter saw no reason to let Tim and Doug off the hook that easily. It might help keep them on their toes if they thought there was a chance of being caught. On Thursday, Peter, Tim and Doug went out on the town to celebrate. Tim would be on his way back to California on Friday. Doug was staying in New York for the rest of the summer. The evening ended back at Peter's hotel room at about 2:30 a.m. They were all drunk.

"It's been a pleasure working you…for you, with you, Peter. I'll mish it, but I'm gonna fucking well retire you know. I'm all finished." Tim had one arm round Peter's shoulder and was whispering hoarsely in his ear as they stood at the door saying goodbye. Doug was still lying on the bed, almost out for the count. "But, Peter don't forget, don't fucking well forget. If we don't get paid, me and my buddy Doug, then we'll find you and your little friend Sarah and we'll blow you away a little bit at a time." As he spoke, the Smith and Wesson appeared in his hand and Tim wiped the cold tip of the barrel across the end of Peter's nose.

Peter roughly pushed the pistol away, "How the hell do you know about Sarah?" Peter was not in a much better state than Tim, but the cold steel of the pistol on his nose sobered him up. He had no idea they knew about Sarah.

"Just a little inshurance. We know all about lil ole Sarah and her daddy, so you make sure they pay up!"

"Tim, you're drunk, go home!" Peter decided to ignore it all, the job was almost over. Tim put the gun away, dragged Doug off the crumpled bed and supporting each other, they staggered down the corridor.

"See you!" Peter called after them as he closed the door.

Monday, July 20. London:

Peter arrived back in England and if all went as planned he would be based at Sarah's apartment until the end of the project.

Peter and George had done everything required of them. The bombs were ready in New York and the work in Bakaar was over. It was now in Robert Berruda's hands to advise the U.S. President of the bad news and ensure the U.S. was convinced that Bakaar's threat was real. The next few weeks were going to be the most difficult part of the entire project...waiting.

The plan was for President Berruda to send Hassan Maalin, his private secretary and James Bwanjini, the Bakaaran Ambassador to the United Kingdom, to Washington to present the ultimatum. Not having an Embassy in the United States, the Ambassador to Britain was the next best choice.

The diplomatic privileges afforded the Ambassador would allow both he and Maalin to enter the country without any risk of a customs search and they would be able to carry a small sample of VX gas with them. They had to be able to prove they had a supply of the gas. The container was designed to ensure there was no risk, even if the aircraft crashed, the container would survive intact.

The attempt to set up a meeting with the U.S. President had started back in June and finally, with the help of the British Government and at the request of Ambassador Bwanjini, the date had been set for August 10. It was intended that the U.S. would be given one week to make payment of the $1 billion and the deadline for detonating the bomb was set for August 17.

Peter knew it was going to be four weeks of nail biting. The bombs might be discovered by chance. The buildings could burn down. The bomb in Bakaar might be found. Anything could happen and almost all of it was beyond Peter's control.

Peter was relieved that the operation had almost reached the point of no return. In recent conversations with George there had been an uncharacteristic and Peter thought, increasing ambivalence. Peter had not told George that Doug had killed Nirina. George had never asked and seemed content to believe that Nirina had met his end in the explosion and that the cover story, that it was an accident, was real.

It was as if George was trying to convince himself that his project was nothing more than a hostile boardroom takeover It began to dawn on Peter that his boss was a tough enough son-of-a-bitch when the stakes were financial. But when it came to physical, face to face conflict in which only one party remains standing, it was a whole different matter. It was obvious that George had not foreseen that in the process to extract a billion dollars people were going to get hurt. George sounded as if he had doubts. In the business world George never had doubts.

In the past few weeks as they moved into high gear, Peter had found himself driving the project. More often than not George was asking for reassurance. It was almost as if he had become soft. Peter was not quitting and he re-assured George with a passion. $33 million dollars worth. The deadline was only weeks away and Peter could smell and taste the money. There was no way he was going to miss this one. It was probably his only chance at wealth and a life of ease and luxury. George would have to live with the fact that even if he did not have to pull the trigger, he was in it up to his armpits whether he liked it or not.

Monday, August 10. 9.30 a.m. Washington:

After several communications between the Bakaaran Government and the State Department, the President's Aides had agreed to a meeting between Ambassador Bwanjini, Hassan Maalin and the President on August 10. The purpose of the meeting seemed somewhat vague. On the one hand, the President did not want to appear uninterested in the problems of this third world country, but on the other he did not want to be caught off-guard. The British had lobbied for the meeting and removed any risk that the U.S. would be stepping on their toes. The meeting was placed on the President's schedule provisionally for three o'clock. But the two Bakaarans were to attend a pre-meeting at 10.00 a.m. with Louise Hennessy, Deputy Assistant to the President, to clarify the content of the afternoon meeting and to agree to the wording of a Press Release.

A limousine collected the Ambassador and Maalin from their hotel and whisked them to their appointment in the Old Executive Building alongside the White House. The driver opened the door and directed them to the security desk inside the outer doors where passes were waiting for them.

They passed through security and wandered down the somber marble hallway looking for Louise Hennesy's office. They found it, knocked and entered. They were greeted and offered refreshments by a young intern.

As the two men sat waiting for their ten o'clock appointment in the small, busy reception area they said nothing. Both shared a wish to be somewhere else.

Another young aide emerged from the inner office and stood holding the door open, "Ms. Hennessy will see you now."

Ambassador Bwanjini looked in his worn, soft leather briefcase to ensure that the sealed letter from President Berruda was available and easily identified among the other papers. Satisfied, he rose to his feet and followed by Maalin he walked past the young aide into the inner office.

Louise Hennessy provided them with little more reassurance that they were being heard by those in power than did the youngsters in the outer office. She was standing in front of her desk, a slight, smart woman who looked about thirty. They shook hands and she invited them to sit on the couch. She took the easy chair. The Ambassador rested his briefcase on the table and awkwardly shuffled himself back in the deep seat.

"I would like to prepare for your meeting with the President this afternoon." Louise Hennessy advised them efficiently.

"During the communications to set up this meeting, few details of what you wanted to present were offered. It has been simply described as a discussion on the plight of the Third World and a recommendation as to how it might be improved. The President is well versed on this topic and is very concerned, but we would like to make your meeting as productive as possible. I would ask that you be specific as to your suggestions now, then we can ensure the President is briefed and ready to help."

Maalin and the Ambassador had already discussed the fact that they really had nothing to talk about as far as the meeting was concerned. As soon as the content of their meeting arose they had agreed that the Ambassador would hand over the letter from President Berruda and they would then respond to whatever transpired. That is if they were not arrested and thrown in jail.

Ambassador Bwanjini extracted the letter from his briefcase. Louise leaned forward and took it from him. She broke the seal and began to read the two pages. She made no comment for about half a minute, but the slight smile on her face as she opened the letter intended to reassure her visitors that interaction with the White House was a pleasant affair, turned to concern and then to almost panic. The two men sat stone faced and watched.

"Have you read this letter?' She asked, in a high pitched whisper, hardly able to finish the question, her face now completely drained and gray.

"Yes, I've seen it." The Ambassador replied.

"Do you have anything to add to it? I'm. I'm at a…loss for words. I…I must ask you to wait here. I..er have to contact the President." She stood up and rushed out of the office, pulling the door closed behind her.

The next half-hour was like nothing Louise Hennessy had ever experienced before. She made a call to the President's office, but unable to speak with him, she had no alternative but to advise his personal secretary of the contents of the letter. She was immediately transferred to the President's senior Aide and on and on it went. For just over thirty minutes Louise hung on the end of the phone in her outer office. She responded to a battery of questions and requests to hold on for a minute, as more and more people were patched into the call. By the time the Vice President joined the discussion, he had a copy of the letter which Louise had faxed to the President's secretary at her request.

Four Secret Service Agents arrived about thirty-five minutes after she placed the call and the two Bakaarans were politely escorted out of her office. Once she was off the phone, still distraught, she collapsed into the easy chair, clutching the letter which she had been told to retain at all costs. Her staff plied her with coffee, aspirins and questions. Ten minutes passed and another phalanx of Secret Service Agents arrived and gently escorted her away still gripping the folded letter in her left hand. Refusing vehemently to give it to anyone except the President.

By midday she had been debriefed and sworn to secrecy by more Presidential aides and attorneys than she could count. The letter had been gently pried from her hand by a man she finally accepted was the senior Secret Service Agent at the White House and the matter was taken out of her hands.

Tuesday, August 11. The President's Private Study 3.50 a.m.

The Agent walked towards the desk and handed the envelope to the President.

The President put on his glasses and picking up the letter opener he had been given as a memento on his first election to public office, which at this moment seemed light years ago. He slit open the envelope. The rustle as he unfolded the report was the only sound in the small room.

He read and for just a fleeting moment his face showed a mixture of frustration and despair. He looked up over his glasses at the Africans and almost musing to himself he addressed Ambassador Bwanjini, "We now know you have VX gas. I had to be certain." The President hesitated for a moment and added, "It's not really appropriate but as President Reagan used to say, 'trust but verify'…we also know how easily you got it into the U.S." He let out an audible sigh, "So what do we do now…?"

Pat Palmer, the Secretary of State, spoke, "Mr. President can I suggest that we take these two gentlemen back to their hotel and ensure they remain secure until they leave the U.S."

The President was not in the frame of mind to get involved with it, "Yes, Pat. Good idea, deal with it!" He addressed the Africans, "Thank you gentlemen. We will of course continue to treat you with the respect your diplomatic status requires and I'll contact your President as necessary."

The Secret Service Agent walked forward and escorted the two Africans out of the office.

Tuesday August 11. The White House:

The President got up from the table in the Situation Room and walked to the coffee pot, "Well, ladies and gentlemen, it had to happen sooner or later," he said addressing the room as he filled his cup. "We've got until the seventeenth to defuse the situation. Just a week. What can we do?" he asked rhetorically.

All of those present had received copies of the Bakaaran letter and the President's briefing earlier in the day.

The President continued, "The CIA and the NRO have been suspicious over the past weeks and now we've confirmed that Bakaar has VX gas. You'all have read the report and know what it is and what it can do. I'm telling you, we've got a real problem if it's released in a city. It could kill thousands."

"Have we ruled out military action at the present time?" The Vice President asked.

Most heads, including the Chairman of the Joint Chiefs, nodded.

"But I presume we have the capability if we need it." The President inquired.

"Yes, we have, Mr. President. The John F. Kennedy will be off Rapanda in three days. We could obliterate Bakaar in about an hour, but there's little point, it wouldn't remove the threat. I don't think Berruda would back down if we threatened military action."

"Everything we've checked about Berruda suggests he's in it to the end…" The Director of the CIA added.

The President was sitting in his familiar posture, elbows on the table, both hands supporting his coffee cup in front of his face. He put the cup down and interrupted, "We're going to try damned hard to stop them, but we can't afford to let the cat out of the bag on this one. We can't even whisper nerve gas! If word gets out, Iraq, Libya, India or Pakistan—any of 'em could see the threat against us as a reason to try their luck and join in. We could end up in the middle of World War III!" The President absentmindedly picked up his coffee again and sipped it, then almost as if trying to convince himself, continued, "We're between a rock and a hard place. If we play for time and push the deadline they don't even have to detonate it, they just go to the media…and if we can't reassure the people, we risk panic."

"Mr. President, the Bakaarans have already scheduled a Press Conference for August 17," one of the Aides, sitting away from the table with his back against the wall, interjected.

The President continued with his preoccupation of leaks, "Can you imagine what will happen in New York if word gets out there's a bomb full of nerve gas somewhere in the city. After the World Trade Center it'll be taken seriously, there'll be panic. We have to solve this one quietly. Pray to God nothing leaks out. If it does become public knowledge there'll be a hundred copy cats within a week." The President unlike some around him was a realist.

"But, Mr. President, we can't just sit here and do nothing. For God's sake, we're threatened by some tin pot country no one's ever heard of and we're powerless?" the Vice President phrased the statement like a question and voiced the frustrations felt by many sitting around the table.

"We've discussed this scenario, or at least something like it, many times. We knew it was going to happen, it was just a matter of time," the President was almost philosophical. "The problem is we can't put the anti-terrorist plans into effect without letting everyone know what's going on. I personally don't have any answers. Let's hope we learn from this one. We should thank God for small mercies, at least we seem to be dealing with a man who may well be desperate but he is probably sane." He ended his musing and looked around the table, "So, we have a week to try and find the device or to find a way of stopping them without making it public. If we can't, we pay!"

In the letter Ambassador Bwanjini had delivered, the Bakaarans had stated that their bomb was in New York City and that it would be detonated at 10.00 a.m. Eastern Standard Time on Monday, August 17 unless their demands were met. They said it contained sufficient VX nerve gas to wipe out a city block and their demand to stop the horror was simple. They wanted $1 billion.

"Does anyone have any bright ideas?" the President asked as he looked in turn at each of those present. He nodded to Colonel Ferreira, an anti-terrorism expert from the Pentagon, who acknowledged that he wanted to contribute.

"Well, Mr. President, the best, or maybe it's the worst example we have is the IRA. They proved that they could assemble large quantities of explosives at targets in highly populated cities in the United Kingdom. They did it, in spite of England being an island which was virtually on a war footing. I see no way of preventing anyone who wants to place a bomb in a city from doing it." He hesitated for a moment. Those gathered around the table were waiting for more, "The Bakaaran device doesn't have to be very big. It can be placed in the subway, as they did in Japan. It could be on top of a building. It could be in a vehicle— a car bomb. It can be detonated remotely by radio and it could be kept on site for months before it's used." The Colonel's news was enlightening but it was all bad.

"You're depressing me Colonel," the President commented. "Does anyone have any good news?"

The Director of the FBI offered his report. It was not good news. "You know we've had some phone calls telling us there's a bomb. All he told us in the first call was that a bomb would be placed in New York City by a terrorist group. He wanted $1 million to tell us where and when. We get them every week. We gave the guy a code word to use in future calls and told him to give us something concrete to work with. The second call came from Bakaar and he told us it would contain nerve gas and he specifically said it was VX. We started taking notice. We guessed he was one of the terrorist team trying to make his fortune. But it went cold. We haven't heard anything for over a month. So, we're calling every Police Precinct in New York City under the pretext of a bomb threat. No mention of VX gas," he added to reassure the President. "And we're asking for information on any incident which entailed illegal access to a building. We think they've already set up the bomb and a building is their best bet. Apart from that and checking out our local informants, there's not much more we can do."

"I have to repeat, be very careful that no word leaks out about VX gas. If that gets out people will be killed in the rush to leave New York, let alone as a result of the bomb!" The President wrapped up the meeting, asking for a full update at 9.00 a.m. each morning from the Vice President who was appointed to liaise with those present. Everyone filed out of the room except the Vice President.

Once they were alone the President commented, "You know it's a real possibility we're going to have to pay and announce to the media that we're giving them the money as aid. I suggest we put a story together to cover that." The President seemed resigned to the fact that they would not find the bomb in time. "That way we may keep what they've done quiet for a while and hold back the avalanche. We can't afford to take a public stand and say we won't be blackmailed. I don't think we're gonna win this one."

"I agree. It makes me mad that some half baked goddamned country has the gall to do it, but you're right," the Vice President commented.

"Now that the Soviet threat has gone the balance of power has changed. We know the rules have changed but we don't know what the new ones are gonna be. We've lost the stability of the Cold War and between you and me, that could be more dangerous than the Cold War itself. For just peanuts any little country or even a lone fanatic can hold us to ransom. It's gonna be a very bumpy ride."

"You're not quite right, Mr. President, the Bakaarans call 'em groundnuts, not peanuts."

The President looked puzzled for a moment and then smiled.

Wednesday, August 12. New York:

Like all police precincts in New York City, the 17th received the inquiry from the FBI on the morning of Wednesday, August 12.

"This is Special Agent Newell, there's been a bomb threat in New York City and we're looking for any help we can get."

Mike Reilly, the desk officer, sighed. Help for the Feds always meant work. "Yeah, so what can I do for you?"

Agent Newell had already made several of the calls assigned to him and he knew he was going to get a hard time. "I need to know if you've got any unsolved break-ins, illegal entry's, intrusions, any unsolved incidents in a substantial office building."

"Christ Almighty, I'm not sure we even record unsolved murders let alone break-ins. You've gotta be joking," Officer Reilly replied in his thick Irish brogue, "Go on tell me you're David Letterman and this is a joke." Officer Reilly shouted across the open office to Patrolman Keefe, "Hey, Keefey, pick up your phone and be my witness, I've got a crazy on the phone."

"Now tell me again, Agent Newell, you want to know about break-ins and illegal entries…would you also like lost dog reports. I believe we used to keep them back in the sixties…" Reilly laughed raucously, looking at Patrolman Keefe for his reaction.

"Please…give me a break!" Agent Newell cut across the comments, "I know you're up to your eyes. This may not seem important but I can assure you it is."

"It's a big bomb then, is it?" Reilly asked still close to hysteria at the thought of checking break-ins.

"Yes, it is!" Newell was sick of the ribbing and although he had instructions to provide no details, he needed some cooperation. "We're talking about lots of people dying if our tip-off's right."

"OK, what addresses are you interested in?" Officer Reilly had had his fun.

"I don't have any addresses, it could be anywhere in a substantial building."

"You don't make it easy. How far back do you want me to go?"

"Three months for now," Agent Newell replied.

"And I suppose you want it all a little before yesterday?"

"I need it as soon as you can get it to me," Agent Newell implored.

Reilly took Newell's number and called out towards the back of the office for some help. Patrolman Keefe put his phone down and walked over to the desk. "Hey, Mike you remember that homicide on East 46th., they never got to the bottom of that. I was talking to Lt. Anderson just yesterday. He passed it on to the Task Force, thought it looked like a professional hit, thought there might be some mob connections. Would that fit what the Feds are looking for?"

By three o'clock, Reilly had four incidents that he called in to Agent Newell, the homicide on East 46th was one of them.

All leave had been cancelled at the FBI offices in New York City and every available agent was working the phones. Coats off, desks littered, crumpled paper balls littered the floor. The office looked like a street market at the end of a busy day.

"This is Agent Newell." He answered his phone for the umpteenth time.

"It's Christmas in Bakaar."

Rick Newell had been the Agent who had received the calls from the informant back in the summer. The code was 'Christmas in Bakaar'. It was a recorded line but he signaled to his colleague at the next desk to trace the number calling.

"We thought you were long gone. What do you know?"

"What about my million?'

"We need something positive, how do we know what you've got or who you are?"

"I gave you something positive. I told you this bomb is different, it's full of VX gas. It'll wipe out a couple of city blocks, thousands of people."

"Yeah, we know. We know what it contains and we know when it will be detonated. You're running out of time. All you can tell us now that would be worth anything, is where it is. I doubt if you know."

"I know where it is! And I know how it works." Doug reinstated his credibility.

"So maybe we should talk." Rick Newell did not want to lose him.

"By the way I'll save you some time tracing the call. I'm at a pay-phone in the City but I'll be out of here long before you can find me."

"So where is it?"

"You think I'm nuts. I want a million bucks for that little gem…and immunity," the caller added, as if it was an afterthought. "And I want in on the witness protection program. I'll have fucking governments chasing my tail once I talk."

"We need to meet. If you're in New York we can set it up today."

"Just slow down. I need confirmation that there's a million dollars on the table. How do I know you'll keep your word?"

"There are some powerful people want to know where that bomb is…we'll keep our word."

"I gotta go. You get the O.K. then I'll meet you. You get the O.K. on the money and the witness thing. I'll call back later."

The caller hung up.

Agent Newell had an idea that this guy was for real. He passed the information up the line and decisions began to be made. Late in the afternoon the word came back that subject to a face to face meeting, protective custody for the informant and accurate information on the location of the bomb, the government would pay and 'Christmas in Bakaar' would be entered into the witness protection program.

The incident reports began to come in a little after lunch and by mid afternoon they had a hundred and forty three which fitted their parameters. They still had no reason to believe any of them were connected with the bomb threat. By the end of the day just forty-one remained. The homicide on East 46th was still one of them.

By 8.00 p.m. the informant had not called back. Any call from 'Christmas' as he was now known would be patched through to Rick Newell on the radio wherever he was. The forty-one incidents had been assigned to Agents who were to investigate as soon as the offices were open for business next morning. Special Agent Newell received the homicide on East 46th along with two others. He decided to chase down the homicide first and scheduled a meeting at 7.30 a.m. next morning. Lt. Anderson, Patrolman Keefe, who was the officer who responded to the call the day the body was found, and Sergeant Mike Jones of the Borough Homicide Task Force, who currently had the problem of solving it, would be present.

Thursday, August 13. New York:

At 7.30 a.m. Lt. Anderson arrived at the Precinct and sleepily greeted Agent Newell who had been waiting for half an hour. "What's this all about? It's got to be one hell of a bomb scare to get you guys out on the street at seven thirty in the morning!"

"Yeah, we've got pressure from the top on this one," Agent Newell replied, eager to get down to work.

"Coffee?" Lt. Anderson asked, already half way to the machine. Newell hurried after him, they were obviously going to have coffee. Anderson carefully poured two cups, shook in creamer and taking his time, slowly and deliberately stirred each in turn.

"Hey, come on!" Newell said as he accepted the offered cup, "I don't have any time to fuck with the coffee! Let's get on with it! Where are the other two guys?

We said seven thirty didn't we?"

"OK, OK!" Lt. Anderson replied, "For Christ sake, they'll be here in a minute!" Lt. Anderson quickened his pace, the overfilled cup slurping coffee over his hand as he headed for his office now following Agent Newell.

Once inside the cluttered office, Agent Newell put his cup on the desk, cleared a pile of files off a chair and sat down. He noticed a file in the center of the desk. It was the largest on the surface and the only one that was not in a group or pile. He opened it hoping it was the one they were to look at."

"Make yourself at home!" Lt. Anderson muttered quietly under his breath as he walked around Newell to get to his chair.

It was the file on the homicide on east 46th and Agent Newell began to leaf through, stopping to read anything which caught his eye. He reached the statement made by Christine Kowalski.

"This woman says she left the building within an hour of the estimated time of the shooting and says there were two maintenance guys in the elevator with her. Did you follow up on them? Did you find them?"

Lt. Anderson turned the file around and read part of the statement, "Well, we had some names." As he spoke he thumbed through the pages and then half read and half recited from memory, what had taken place. "We traced them back to an office on the fourteenth floor. Yeah, they were telephone engineers, not maintenance. They put a new phone system or something in the office that day."

"Did you find them?"

"No, but we checked 'em out!" Lt. Anderson leaned over the file again, "Yeah, we checked out Hope and Nagle, that's where they'd been working. They confirmed they had a new system board or something installed that day, the guys were legit..."

"Did you interview them?" Newell asked, insistently.

"No, we got their employment records but they'd been laid off, the company does that at the end of the summer."

"Do you have Social Security Numbers for them?"

"Hey, these guys just happened to be working in the fucking building. So were about four thousand other suspects and according to our records nearly three hundred people visited the building that day. I only have five guys and we have over twenty..."

"Have you tried to find them?"

"No!"

"OK, I'll give you a hand, I'd like to talk to them."

It was eight twenty-five and Patrolman Keefe and Sergeant Mike Jones, had still not turned up. Special Agent Newell signed out the file and returned to his office.

Agent Newell had the Social Security numbers for Tim and Doug checked out. The numbers existed but the owners had died, one two years ago the other five. Whatever else it might mean, the two engineers were far from legitimate and had something to hide. That both were fake was not a coincidence.

The building on East 46th remained at the top of the list. A security guard was killed for no apparent reason and two phony engineers had access to the building after hours.

• • •

"Hi there! How you doing?"

"I'm good. What's up?" Tim replied gripping the portable phone between his neck and his shoulder as he wiped the grease off his hands. It was the beginning of a warm morning in San Luis Obispo. Tim was doing some pre-breakfast work on the old Harley Davidson he was rebuilding.

"When am I getting the rest of my money?"

"Watch what you say, Doug. We agreed no discussions on the phone."

"Yeah, well that's O.K. for you. But I need my money and I told you $100,000 isn't gonna cut it."

"There's nothing I can do. Peter won't budge. We did a deal."

"The Feds are all over the place here. They're searching buildings and they know when the bomb's gonna blow…"

"Watch what you say or I'll hang up. What the fuck did you say…the Feds know what?"

Doug could kick himself. He hesitated, how would he know what the Feds were up to.

"Well, they know. I'm gonna make a million out of this thing whether you like it or not. Either you pay me or I'll…I took all the risks, I shot that fat bastard. I'm the one at risk.."

Tim hung up the phone as realization dawned. Tim would bet his life it was Doug who had made the calls to the Feds. He had been in Bakaar and could have made the call from there.

There was an eight hour time difference between California and London, it was late afternoon for Peter when Tim called.

"We've got a problem. Remember the phone calls to the Feds."

"Oh yeah, I remember!"

"I think it's Doug! He's just called whining about money again. It sounds as if he's falling apart."

Tim explained how Doug was aware of what the Feds knew.

"He also mentioned a million dollars. Wasn't that the price you said the guy wanted?"

"Yes a million."

"We got to do something Peter. If they agree to the million he'll talk."

"Do you know where he is?"

"I know where he's been living. I'll betcha he's still there. Just a minute." Tim recalled the number of the last incoming call.

"Yeah. It's his number in New York. I know where he is. I'll tell you Pete, he's got to be getting soft."

"How long will it take you to get to New York."

"I've got to get to LA I guess there's a commuter out of here this afternoon. At the worst I can be at Kennedy by eight tonight. But you're going to have to come over and make some decisions if we get to him."

"There's a Concord out of here early this evening. I think it's at seven. Gets into JFK at six Eastern. Stay put for half an hour. If I don't call I'll be on my way and I'll see you at the Hertz rental desk by the Concord gate. Call my number and leave your flight details. I've got to run."

Thursday, August 13. Washington:

By the time each of the forty one reports had been checked out it was narrowed down to twenty six. Twenty six incidents where someone had broken into an office building for no apparent reason, or where a crime had been committed which had not been solved or explained. It seemed a futile task at best.

The Director delivered the FBI's report to the Vice President personally. 'We're chasing rainbows!" he said as he handed over the report. "All we've got is twenty-six locations where there may have been a crime or where an incident occurred that the police can't explain."

"What else can we do?" the Vice President replied, "Even if it's only a chance in a million we have to try. If this thing goes wrong and one of these locations turns out to have the bomb, the Chief will be looking for our resignations."

"There may not be a bomb at all. It could all be bluff."

"Yep, could be."

The Vice President looked down the list of the twenty-six buildings, "Are you following up on these buildings?"

"Yes, we're doing our best. But if we don't get 'em done by the end of tomorrow chances are, most of the buildings will be unoccupied Saturday.

"What about the informant? Any more calls?"

"We offered him a deal and we're trying to meet with him. But he hasn't called back."

"I guess there's not much more we can do today. Keep me posted!"

Thursday, August 13. New York:

Peter arrived at the Concord gate at JFK on time at 6.00 p.m. He went immediately to the Hertz desk and rented a car. Then he called his home number and checked for Tim's message. As promised Tim would arrive on a Northwest flight at a little after 8.00 p.m. He decided to take it easy for the two hour wait and went to the British Airways Lounge.

At eight he went back to the Hertz desk. Tim was already there. He had arrived a few minutes early courtesy of a higher than forecast wind.

'What a mess!" Peter greeted Tim. "You said you'd deal with this when he first started asking for more money."

"Hey, Pete, I told you what he wanted. You didn't offer any more cash and I'm not going to share any more of mine…"

"Yeah, O.K. there's nothing we can do about it now. We're just going to have to put it right. I got a car, let's go see if he's at home. You know where we're going?"

"Yeah, he's got a place over in Queens. It'll only take about twenty minutes at this time."

Peter drove and they left Kennedy on the Van Wyck Expressway, took Queens Boulevard and were parked outside of the apartment building at eight forty-five. During the drive they agreed they had to try and find out if Doug had called and given the Feds the location. Tim was convinced that if Doug was still at the apartment it was more likely that he had not. Peter agreed, once Doug had given the location, he would be whisked away out of sight.

Tim drew his old Smith & Wesson from the holster on his belt, racked the slide and chambered a round.. He was prepared for anything. "He's in four twenty-five. I've been there. We can't just press the bell, he may not let us in. He could panic and make the call. We'll have to wait until someone leaves or opens the door."

"Christ Tim, we could sit out here all night and someone's bound to see us."

"I can't just break the fucking door down and it'll look worse if I spend five minutes trying to crack the lock."

As they discussed the problem, a man appeared and climbed the steps to the door. Tim and Peter jumped out of the car and timed their arrival at the door to coincide with the unwitting accomplice.

"Thanks," Tim murmured as he took the offered open door. All three entered the elevator. Tim and Doug left on the fourth floor.

Peter suggested that he would announce himself at the door. It was unlikely that Doug would connect his earlier call to Tim with the arrival of Peter just a few hours later and probably the surprise would take him off-guard.

Tim stood away to one side to avoid the peephole and Peter knocked on the door. If Doug was not home they had a bigger problem than they could deal with and the entire venture was in serious trouble. Peter was mad. There was no way he was going to lose a fortune at this stage of the game.

"Who's there?" Doug asked through the door as he looked through the one way lens.

Peter looked into the peehol. "Hi there Doug, it's Peter Williams."

Before Peter had finished saying 'Williams' he could hear Doug unlocking the door.

"I didn't expect to see you again!" Doug exclaimed as he opened the door and Peter took a step inside.

"Well, I didn't expect to be here. It's a surprise for both of us."

As Peter spoke Tim moved quickly towards the door, stepped in and catching Doug by surprise pushed him back towards the wall.

"Tim! What the fuck's going on!" Doug managed to blurt out before the breath was knocked out of him as he was slammed back against the wall.

"We need to talk," Peter said in a calm matter of fact way which belied their violent arrival. He walked into the apartment and looked around for any signs of life other than Doug.

"Hey, guys, what the hell's going on here?" Doug asked as Tim frisked him and finding nothing slowly backed away. "I spoke to you in California this morning. You didn't say you were…How the hell did you get here?"

Doug was totally confused and it seemed could not yet even apply the simple logic that his threats to Tim played any part in their presence.

"Peter, you were in London."

"I was, but it seems we might have a problem and I wanted to deal with it."

"What problem?" Doug was regaining his composure and Tim not wishing to be aggressive at this stage just kept close to him, steering him towards a couch where they both sat down.

"Do you want a drink? I've got some beer…"

"Maybe later." Peter replied, remaining standing. Tim said nothing.

"So what's it all about?" Doug asked, his manner changing from confused to concerned.

"I hear that you want more money for your part in our venture." Peter looked straight into his eyes. Doug shot a glance at Tim, half asking if he had passed it on, half suggesting Tim had let him down. But not knowing.

"Well yeah, I told Tim. I'm not getting a fair deal. I had to kill that…"

"Yeah, yeah, I know. You knew why you were on board. It's just the luck of the draw."

"How much do you think you should get?"

"Hey, you guys are getting a billion. Ha, ha, I don't even know how many zero's that is." Doug made an attempt at humor but his voice was hollow and he got no response.

"How much do you want, Doug?" Tim asked, his face only a foot away from Doug's. "Didn't you suggest a million might be right?"

"That's the amount you asked the Feds for." Peter decided he would push now, while Doug was still confused.

"What do you mean?" Doug started to lean forward, Tim pulled him back in the seat.

"I heard from a friend of mine that the Feds have had a few calls from some guy wanting a million bucks to tell them where a bomb full of VX gas is. Can you believe that one of the calls was made from Bakaar."

Doug looked at each in turn his concern becoming fear. He could deal with physical situations, he was good at what he did. He could work well when he knew what he had to do, but he was not good at this stuff. He could not remember exactly what he had said to the Feds or even to Tim this morning. He had been upset and he needed more money.

"I'm supposed to believe the Feds tell you what's going down?" Doug scoffed.

"You called them from Bakaar. You said you wanted a million bucks! You tell me if that's what you told 'em."

"Fuck you, Peter! The Feds don't know who called."

"Uh, Uh. But someone did."

"If they tell you so, I guess someone did."

"What did you tell 'em Doug. How much do they know."

"They don't know nothing.' He paused. He knew these guys he could talk to them. "If I'd wanted to tell them what they wanted, I'd be gone. I'd be in the witness program. I'd be running a strip joint—all the girls I wanted. I'm still here, it's obvious I haven't told 'em anything."

Peter had heard enough. When was anything for sure, but this time he was sure. Doug was the caller. But if Doug had done a deal and had told them where it was, he would either be dead or would have disappeared with a million dollars.

"O.K. Doug. So you told 'em nothing. Just checking out what they knew."

"Yeah, that's right."

Peter looked at Tim. "Well if the Feds don't know where it is and if our friend Doug needs some more money I guess we'd better talk about it."

Tim acknowledged by just raising his eyebrows.

"Let's go out and have something to eat. Have you eaten Doug?"

"No, well I had some lunch." Doug looked across to the sink where the emptied McDonald's packages sat waiting to be thrown out.

"Come on Tim, let's go."

Doug was still unsure, but stood up and turned towards the bathroom.

"Hey, Doug, it's getting late you can pee at the restaurant." Tim said, blocking his path to the bathroom. "Come on, let's get out of here."

"I need some money."

"No, you don't. It's on us tonight."

"What about my keys?"

"These they?" Peter asked picking a bunch of keys off the dresser by the door.

"Yeah, thanks.' Doug took them reluctantly and put them in his pocket.

Tim put a friendly arm around Doug's shoulder. Peter led the way and they left the apartment.

Peter got into the drivers seat, Doug sat in front and Tim in back.

"I know a good place if you want steak." Doug offered as Peter pulled away from the curb.

"We know where we're going," Peter said. "Tim knows a great place down by the piers in Red Hook. Over in Brooklyn."

"That's a Godforsaken place. There's a good place to eat out there?"

Peter got on to the Brooklyn Queens Expressway and turned south. Little was said during the twenty five minute drive. They passed through Brooklyn Heights and as they entered Red Hook Peter turned off the expressway and made his way out to the piers overlooking Upper New York Bay and facing out onto Buttermilk Channel,

It was a warm cloudy night. There was no moon, the only light came from the distant yellow street lights of the city reflecting off the low cloud. Peter turned into a deserted street running down towards a pier.

"Where the fuck are we going?" Doug spoke for the first time in ten minutes.

"Just sit quietly." Tim said as he placed the barrel of the old Smith and Wesson against the back of Doug's neck.

"You bastards!" Doug shouted and began to turn.

Tim put his left arm around Doug's neck and tightened it across his throat. "Keep still Doug and shut up!"

Peter braked and parked by the side of a disused warehouse. Peter got out of the car, taking the keys. Tim dragged Doug out and pushed him down towards the water.

"I told 'em nothing. I don't even want the money now. Hey it's all over in a couple of days. I can't do you guys any harm!"

Tim moved around to place Doug between himself and Peter, "Hey!"

He beckoned Peter towards him with his head. Still hanging on to Doug with his left hand, the pistol in his right.

Peter walked across to Tim an inquiring look on his face, "Yeah, what's the matter?"

As Peter got within arms length Tim was careful to take a tighter hold on Doug and handed Peter the pistol.

"Your turn. You're making the big bucks. I think I'd sleep easier if you finished the job."

As if to leave Peter with no option, Tim released Doug and stepped back all in one movement. Peter looked at the old pistol and looked at Tim. Doug now free, saw his chance and began to run towards the water.

Saturday, August 15. New York:

The President, Vice President, Director of the FBI, Chairman of the Joint Chiefs and half a dozen aides and advisors were seated in the Situation Room at the White House waiting for the call from London.

An aide was quietly talking on a telephone at the end of the table and another phone was in front of the President. The aide signaled to the President who picked it up.

"Good morning, Mr. President, this is Ambassador Bwanjini in London."

"Good morning, Mr. Ambassador", the President replied.

Everyone around the table in the Bakaaran Embassy in London shifted in their chairs as they heard the President's familiar voice. The Ambassador was using a hand held phone, but a speaker unit was relaying the call to those assembled around the table. The call had been set up a couple of days previously in order to ensure there could be no misunderstandings that the Bakaarans intentions had not changed and to provide detailed instruction on the cash transfer. The Bakaarans were assuming the payment would be made.

"Mr. President I have a prepared statement I have been asked to read by our President."

"Go ahead!" the President replied.

Ambassador Bwanjini began reading, "You have forty-eight hours to deliver the $1 billion," the Ambassador spoke slowly and deliberately like a child aware that its voice is being recorded, he sounded stilted and nervous. "The money is to be deposited in the Bakaaran Government's account, already identified at the Bank of Bakaar in London. The cash must be in London on the seventeenth and the transfer must be made within the British clearing system, the funds must not come in from overseas. The deposit must be made before three o'clock, London time on Monday, August 17." The Ambassador paused and glanced at George. George was staring blankly at the table, outwardly he showed no sign of tension. George could feel the hesitance in the Ambassador's voice and could believe that he might just refuse to continue at any minute.

The Ambassador continued, "At the same time, three o'clock London time, you will advise the media that the payment has been made to open a new era of cooperation between the United States and the Third World. Will you please confirm that you have the statement we provided."

"Yes, we have the statement. We're not prepared to make any comment at this time, but we'll communicate with you again before the deadline."

The President signaled to the aide, who picked up his handset, "Thank you Mr. Ambassador, please ensure that you remain available. We will call back in an hour or so to arrange contact numbers twenty four hours a day until the deadline."

The President looked at the psychologist at the end of the table, "What do you make of him?"

"I need to listen to the tape carefully, Mr. President, but obviously the man's under a great deal of pressure."

"Yes, but is he bluffing?"

"Off the cuff sir, I'd say he was genuine, but I'll give you a more informed answer in an hour or so when I've listened to the tape."

"How are the checks on the buildings going?" the President asked the Director of the FBI.

"We started again at seven this morning, Mr. President, but it's Saturday and many buildings are unoccupied."

The President addressed those present, "Ladies and gentlemen, thank you for your help." He then turned to the Vice President, "Are the funds available?"

"Yes, the cash is in London ready to be transferred."

"Is the John F. Kennedy off Bakaar yet?"

"By dawn tomorrow," the Chairman of the Joint Chiefs answered, "We covered up its change of schedule with a press release two days ago. We used the 'secret satellite' story. We said we're placing ships in strategic positions around the world along the orbit of a failing satellite to recover it if it re-enters and the Kennedy will be off Bakaar on Friday."

"One of the problems on Monday is that if we have to pay them, we have to do it before they give us the location of the bomb. They could just take the money and run and then try and squeeze us again. If they do that I've conveyed to President Berruda–that we will retaliate. We have no choice, but at least he knows what he's risking. In the meantime, I want no hostile action or even suggestions of it. There are to be no intrusions into Bakaaran airspace."

"There won't be!"

"I don't want any imaginative journalist coming up with a story that the U.S is about to invade Bakaar. But, if the bomb is detonated I want my options open. What happens if we locate the bomb? Have we got a team ready to go in and dismantle it? Will there be any problems disarming it?"

"We've got a team in New York already. We've also got decontamination units moving in under cover of the bomb threat and we've got the National Guard geared up to assist with evacuation if needed. If it's what we believe, it's a simple device, just a bag of explosives wrapped round a container full of nerve gas. We'd just disconnect the battery and remove the detonator."

"What about the media? Have we organized a press conference?"

"Yes, it's all set for Monday afternoon. I'm not sure what we'll be telling 'em, but they're coming!"

"Good! We don't want any leaks, keep it simple. We'll meet again tomorrow."

The Director of the FBI returned to his office and checked the progress of the reports coming back from the twenty-six buildings. FBI Agents were in every building having called building managers and security companies to provide access and to be present to assist. By the end of the day nothing of any significance had been found. The media had got wind of the searches and seemed satisfied that it was precautionary action following a bomb threat, and on most TV Channels, Saturday's Six O'clock News carried footage of the FBI and Security Guards rummaging through closets.

Saturday, August 15. London:

Ambassador Bwanjini replaced the phone and sat back uncomfortably on his chair, there was no going back now. His eyes wandered around the table, it was as if everyone was frozen. No one moved or spoke as the conversation with the President ended. All of the Bakaarans were smoking in spite of the signs prohibiting such behavior scattered all over the Embassy. The ash from the cigarettes was variously balanced on top of notebooks, on scraps of paper or caught by hand and retained for later disposal. The heavy frame of the window at the far end of the room cut the low August sun into narrow brilliant beams forcing their way through the smoke. Like spotlights on a set they drained the color from the room, it looked like a scene in a black and white movie.

Peter and George both looked relaxed. Peter had his hands thrust deep into his trouser pockets gazing across at the far wall his simple wooden chair pushed dangerously back on its rear legs. George was leaning forward, emotionless, elbows on the table, hands supporting his chin.

The moment was broken, as Mr. Embola, the President of the Bank of Bakaar, scraped his chair back on the hardwood floor and got up from the table. He walked down to where two of his colleagues were sitting and crouched between them and began speaking quietly but earnestly.

Ambassador Bwanjini was unsure what to do next. The sense of anti climax was overwhelming. 'What do you do after you've directly and personally threatened the President of the United States'. This was beyond his experience and in his discomfort he found himself stupidly wondering whether advice could be found in any guide for international etiquette. He was being instrumental in providing Bakaar with more aid than he could ever have dreamed of. He was a player on the world stage. If the bomb had to be detonated he felt it undermined his entire career in the Diplomatic Service of his country. Even as the thought surfaced, he could see the contradictions. His thoughts were suddenly interrupted by George, "Well, Mr. Ambassador, I suppose there isn't much more to do today, I suppose you'll hang on here and let the Americans have the phone numbers they want."

"No…I'er…think not. No nothing much more to do today." The Ambassador forced his mind to focus and addressed the other Bakaarans. "Is there anything more?" "No, we'll have to wait until we receive agreement from the United States on Monday." The President of the Bank of Bakaar replied, "I'll be at the Bank on Monday and you may contact me there or at home, you have the numbers."

The chairs scraped on the floor as everyone stood up. The Bakaarans walked out, followed by Peter and George.

"You said we'd solved our informant problem." George questioned Peter as they left the room.

"Yes, we dealt with it."

"Who dealt with it?" George insisted.

"I did."

"What did you do?"

"What do you think?" Peter replied becoming irritated at what he saw as false naiveté

"Who was it?"

"It doesn't matter. It's better you don't know."

George looked behind him as they approached the street door and half whispered, "Did you kill him?"

"Yes!"

Monday August 17. New York:

The vibration from the loose duct had been driving the women on the fourteenth floor crazy. It started a week ago and sounded like the theater sound effect for thunder. Few people know how buildings are constructed and most of those working on the fourteenth and fifteenth floors had no idea that there was an unoccupied mechanical floor between them. The passenger elevator does not stop at the floor—and who uses the service elevator or the stairs! It had taken three days to track down where the noise came from, but finally someone who knew the floor existed thought it could be a loose air conditioning duct on that floor.

The maintenance engineers were called on Friday, but August was one of the busiest months for the air conditioning business. A heavy schedule and the bomb scare had prevented them getting to the building until today, Monday.

It was the first job on the schedule. The two guys arrived at the building on East 46th at 7.00 a.m. and headed up to the mechanical floor in the service elevator.

It took less than a minute to see the problem. A duct along the outside wall had broken away from its anchor bolts. To see it was one thing, to get at it was another. The younger of the two engineers finally managed to get into the restricted space and began to assess how best to fix it.

"Hey, Scotty, what the fuck's this? You gotta come and look." The young guy shouted back to his colleague.

Scotty was sixty years of age and fifty pounds overweight, "Christ, I'll never get over there! You fix it!"

"Hey, I don't want to look like an asshole. There was a bomb threat or something here, wasn't there?"

"Yeah, that's why we didn't come on Friday."

"Come on! You're a Vet, you'd know a bomb if you saw one. You gotta come and look at this. I don't know what it is!"

Scotty reluctantly labored his way into the small space and lying on his side, looked at the object.

"Christ almighty! That looks like plastic explosive," Scott said knowledgeably, attempting to impress his young colleague and trying hard to remember if he'd ever seen any during his tour in Vietnam.

"There's a couple of wires disappearing under the duct," the young engineer observed, beginning to trace them with his finger.

"Leave it alone! Don't touch it! Come on we gotta get outta here!" Scotty shouted with difficulty as he began to desperately struggle his way back to the footway. "Whatever it is ain't part of the system. We'd better report it! Scotty panted.

Scotty found the security office on the ground floor and at a quarter of eight reported what he had found. The security guard on duty had been involved in the bomb escapade earlier in the week and called the FBI at the number Special Agent Newell had left with him as soon as Scotty reported it.

Within fifteen minutes of the call, two Special Agents were on their way to check out the suspicious object and by 9.00 a.m. the fact that it was a bomb had been confirmed to Washington, and New York's finest—the Bomb Squad, the Office of Emergency Management and the EMS.

The White House, 9.00 a.m.

Because of the five-hour time difference between London and Washington, the billion dollars was already in a U.S. Government bank account in London. If the payment had to be made, this would allow the transfer during the normal London working day. All it needed was a wire from the White House and the funds would be transferred immediately to the Bank of Bakaar in Lombard Street.

The device on East 46th in New York was the first break in the search, but no one was optimistic, time was tight. If he did not receive the cash, Berruda was going to detonate the bomb at 10.00 a.m. Washington and New York time, 3.00 p.m. in London. There was no way they could evacuate the building, get a disposal team to the site and defuse the bomb by 10.00 a.m. But that was not going to stop them trying. The fire alarms in the building began to wail at ten minutes after nine.

A call was made to the Bakaaran Embassy in London.

London, 2.10 p.m.

Ambassador Bwanjini, had reluctantly made the late night trip to the White House on August 11, to take the sample of VX gas. Now he was sitting in his spartan office at the Bakaaran Embassy in Portland Place in London, waiting for the call to confirm that the funds had been transferred. The phone rang it was an aide to the U.S. President calling from the White House.

"Mr. Ambassador, we've had a problem with the funds. The money is in London ready to be transferred, but we're having a technical problem.

We need a delay on the deadline, we should be able to make the transfer just before four o'clock London time."

Ambassador Bwanjini knew little of the technicalities of banking and certainly not as far as the transfer of $1 billion was concerned. "I'll have to speak with President Berruda", he replied.

George and Peter were also at the Bakaaran Embassy in Portland Place for the conclusion of their mission. The plan was for Mr. Embola at the Bank of Bakaar to call the Embassy when he received the cash. Special arrangements had been made for the after hours transfer to be cleared into the Bakaaran Government account. The cash would be instant value the moment the London bank wired it. A pre-arranged transfer out of the Bank of Bakaar would deal with Peter and George's share of the cash. As soon as they had confirmation from their banks in the Cayman Islands that their money was safely deposited, Peter would make the call to disarm the bomb and Ambassador Bwanjini would advise the Americans of the location.

The Ambassador's call came through to Hassan Maalin, President Berruda's private secretary, who was sitting in the room with Peter and George at the Embassy.

"What's the problem?" Peter asked, as Hassan put the phone down.

"Our Ambassador says the American's cannot transfer the funds across London in time. They want a delay until four o'clock, London time. From three to four o'clock". Hassan was concerned.

Peter looked at the clock, it was two fifteen. He glanced at George who looked back over his glasses, which had slipped down his nose, and slowly shook his head.

"Tell Ambassador Bwanjini to advise the Americans that he'll need time to consult, he'll have an answer for them at two fifty-five London time." George instructed Hassan and turning to Peter whispered, "They've either located one of the bombs and want time to disarm it or they've got some other trick up their sleeve."

"Yeah, problem is, we don't know which one. My guess is it's the one on East 46th, where the security guard was killed, and that's the one we have to detonate first." Peter replied.

New York, 9.35 a.m.

The Bomb Squad arrived at the building on East 46th by helicopter. The Office of Emergency Management integrated fire, police and ambulance services. Emergency vehicles were dispatched under the plan for a terrorist attack on New York set up after the World Trade Center bombing.

The roof of the building was cluttered with antennas and old chimneys and was not large enough for a chopper to land. The Bomb Squad officers were lowered one by one as the helicopter hovered above the roof. The fire alarm was wailing and people were pouring out of the building. There were still a couple of thousand increasingly impatient people inside waiting to file out through the doors on the ground floor. The cover story was a serious gas leak, but already the media was second-guessing it. Among the occupants the story was mutating as it passed from mouth to mouth and the impatience of those furthest from the doors was beginning to border on panic. The streets for two blocks around the building had been cleared and the neighboring buildings were now being evacuated. Police on the outer fringes of the no-go area wore battle fatigues and National Guard units in full chemical warfare gear, patrolled inside the cordon, shepherding the terrified workers out of harms way. The entire area was lit by urgent, flashing, red, blue and white lights. Sirens and fire alarms substituted for the normal roar of the traffic which was now at a standstill.

One of the dilemmas facing the White House, the Department of Defense and the Mayor of New York, had been how to respond publicly to the bomb if and when the time came. If the emergency services had gone in dressed in normal everyday uniforms to try to prevent panic, the personnel could be at risk. The public had become so familiar with the

NBC suits and equipment used to protect allied troops from chemical attack during the Gulf War that the very sight of these safety measures could in themselves cause panic. In the end, there was no choice, the personnel of the emergency services had to know the risks and be protected. If Bakaar had someone watching the building their compatriots in London would know of the attempt to defuse it as it happened.

It was old hat and hackneyed, but once the operation was under way, it would be described in an immediate press release, as an exercise. The Mayor of New York would have to deal with whatever the reality became after the event.

The bomb squad had been advised it could be a chemical or biological hazard and they too were wearing NBC suits as well as their heavy, protective body armor. They looked and moved like a cross between the Michelin man and something from space as they were lowered from the helicopter and clambered down the narrow stairway from the roof to the twenty fifth floor.

The crew was finally assembled. They waited at the only operating service elevator, ready to take them to the fourteenth floor at 9.40 a.m. Assuming they got the time extension, they would have just over an hour to disarm the bomb. At 9.43 a.m. they entered the elevator, and descended to the fourteenth floor.

The team scrambled down the stairs to the mechanical floor and the two members designated to have a first look at the bomb began the struggle to get their increased bulk across the floor and near enough to examine the bomb.

"Hey Matt, I'm never gonna get close enough in this get-up." The first officer transmitted over the personal radio fitted into his helmet.

"Do you want me to have a go?…Told you. You need to lose weight." his colleague offered the advice in an attempt at humor.

"Nah! Believe me, you wouldn't get in here. If it blows we're history anyway, suits or no suits. Stay where you are. I'm gonna lighten the load." He clamped his battery operated spotlight to a support for the floor above and began to awkwardly remove his protective body armor and pass it back to his colleague. Finally he squeezed into place alongside the bomb, still encapsulated in his NBC suit. The effort required to remove the armor had caused the temperature inside the suit to rise dramatically. He knew he would not be able to work for long before heat exhaustion would dim his concentration. If he was going to have any chance he would have to remove the NBC suit. He would never be given permission to remove it. He had already violated the regulations. To hell with it, he stripped it off but left the helmet on so that he could communicate with his colleagues on the radio. Whatever he found, it was vital that he advise the team of his progress in disarming the bomb or God forbid, try to let them know what his mistake had been.

He focussed the spotlight on the bomb and carefully examined the cradle and its contents.

"Simple enough at first sight," he transmitted. "Looks like a charge of cemtex surrounding a canister. Can't see if there's a battery or whether they're using mains power. No they wouldn't do that…"

London, 2.53 p.m.

At exactly two fifty-three, Hassan Maalin called Ambassador Bwanjini and advised him to inform the Americans that with great regret President Berruda could not allow the time extension.

New York, 9.59 a.m.

Captain McGill gave the order to the Bomb Squad, "Go immediately to the ground floor, and wait until you are given positive instructions to resume. We have not secured a delay on detonation. I repeat we have not secured a delay on detonation. Get out now—MOVE!"

Matt's blood ran a little hotter and he noticed his adrenaline surge. "C'mon Art. We gotta get out of here!"

"Yeah, I heard. It's only gonna take a minute to get an idea of how this thing works. Just hang on."

Matt was not comfortable, they had been told to get out. The rest of the team would not evacuate and take the elevator without them. That put them all at risk and they had no say in it.

"C'mon Art, we can't do anything in a minute or two let's get the hell out of here!"

"I tell you, it looks simple." Art was squeezing himself alongside the cradle and trying, without touching it, to see where the battery was mounted. There had to be a battery. This little devil needed power. He could see what he thought was an electric motor.

"There's an electric motor at one end, the canister's attached to it. Looks like it spins."

"Sargent Staples. Thanks for the commentary, but I ordered you out of there! Art we don't want any heroics, we've got to go! This thing's due to blow." Captain McGill was impatient.

"Yeah I know, Cap, but I tell you, there's only a few pounds of cemtex. I don't reckon it'd do that much structural damage. Make sure the other guys know…we're not talking about the building going down. It'll blow a hole in the wall and it'll wreck this floor. But I can't see any shaped charges, it's just a bundle of cemtex. Looks like it's designed to splatter the canister. I guess that's full of the agent. What did they say it was? VX? Oh, yeah, I see there's an air conditioning duct above it, it'll pump the gas into the AC system."

"Yes, it's VX. Now, come on you've done enough. Out of there!"

"You know something, Cap. I reckon I can take this baby apart in about five minutes. I can't see any problems…no booby's"

"I'm ordering you out of there Art, and that goes for the rest of you. I want the Team off this floor, NOW!" Captain McGill left no room for uncertainty and the rest of the Team hurried back into the elevator.

London, 3.02 p.m.

At two minutes past three o'clock, Peter dialed the number for the East 46th Street bomb. Twenty seconds later the telephone rang in the emptying building in Manhattan. It seemed like a lifetime, but on the tenth ring he made the connection to the bomb, Peter handed the phone to George.

New York, 10.02 a.m.

"Matt, get outta here…go on. I'm not gonna let these bastards kill half New York with this stuff. I'm staying and gonna disarm the little beauty."

Matt still restricted by his full quota of body armor began to move away. There was no point arguing with Art Staples once his mind was made up but there was little point leaving. It was past the deadline and he would never make the elevator if they triggered the bomb. He moved back up behind Art. "I'm still here Art. What can we do?"

Captain McGill saw Matt move back towards the bomb in the constricted space,

"I can't endanger the whole team. I'll deal with you guys later. We're on our way. Hey! Off the record. Good Luck!" Captain McGill and the team headed out of the door at the trot.

London, 3.03 p.m.

At the first 'Beep' George dialed in his code and passed the phone back, 'Beep, beep.' Peter dialed in the second code then waited, listening to the phone as if he expected to hear the explosion.

Hassan Maalin looked despondent. He never believed it would come to this. He had expected the U.S. to pay.

Maalin noticed that Peter and George were not sharing his disappointment. What would they gain from the pointless, agonizing deaths of hundreds or even thousands of innocent people? Peter replaced the phone, smiled reassuringly at Maalin and asked him to call Ambassador Bwanjini to pass on an urgent message to the Americans.

New York, 10.03 a.m.

Sergeant Art Staples reached out slowly and carefully, wire clippers at the ready. His hand just caught the edge of the cradle as he reached inside for the battery wires, tucked almost out of sight behind the cemtex. The canister began to spin rapidly but in his heightened state of anxiety he saw it turning as if in slow motion. A haze of blue smoke, the remains of the burned out diaphragm which separated the inert components of the VX gas, drifted into the beam of his spotlight and painfully slowly whirled away from the turning canister in complicated vortices. The metallic canister glinted in the light as it turned. He knew he had to be quick, but his hand moved as if in molasses. As in a dream he seemed unable to hurry. He reached for the wires, they were almost between the blades of his clippers, "Close your eyes and hope for the best, Matt." He squeezed the clippers closed over the wires. "I've got…"

The explosion had the effect of a starting gun at a horse race. Many of those who were leaving the building had reached the ground floor via the stairs. They were following instructions, trying to remain calm, and quietly walking away from the building. The sight that greeted them as they came into the open was not what they expected. Troops dressed in full chemical gear did what the President feared. It suggested the danger was greater than was being made public and increased the fear and concern. The soldiers worked the best they could to keep order while getting the increasingly frightened crowd as far away from the building as possible. The sound of the explosion was the catalyst. Panic erupted instantly and one or two started to run. Within seconds, thousands of people were running aimlessly, trampling each other.

The explosion ripped a hole in the outside wall and tore gaping holes in the air conditioning ducts, ensuring that the gas would be sucked into the system and spread throughout the building. Chunks of concrete and glass from the breaking windows began to rain into the street.

As soon as the noise died away and rubble stopped falling into the street the panic subsided. People stopped running. Few realized that within minutes every horizontal surface for a block or more could be covered with a thin film of VX gas. Any contact with bare skin would result in a dreadful death. Inside the building VX gas would have been sucked into the broken duct on the mechanical floor and was now being pumped out of the air conditioning system inside the building. The Bomb Squad, who knew the worst, radioed back to their command center that the bomb had exploded.

Washington, 10.10 a.m.

"Oh my God, they've detonated it!" The President's Aide announced to the crowded Situation Room at the White House, as he put down the phone.

Almost immediately, the phone buzzed again. The aide on the extension said it was the Bakaaran Ambassador with an urgent message. The President took the call.

"I hope you're praying Mr. Ambassador, your people have detonated the bomb in a building on East 46th Street, in the middle of Manhattan. You have to expect a serious response from us!"

"Yes, I've just heard, but President Berruda has advised me that there is no gas in that bomb. He wanted you to know that he can and will do it, but there was no gas in the bomb we detonated...." the Ambassador hesitated, before relaying the rest of the message..."But the next one has. There's another bomb in New York! We agree to the cash transfer being made before four o'clock in London, but the second bomb will be detonated at 11.00 a.m. in New York if we haven't received the cash."

The President answered reluctantly, "Advise President Berruda that the transfer will be made as soon as I have confirmation that no gas has been released."

An Aide was already in touch with the Bomb Squad on E. 46th. No gas had been detected. The President gave the order to transfer the cash. The room was subdued. "Gentlemen, I suppose we had better meet the media".

He was handed the text of the appropriate statement, which would now be passed out in the Press Room in the West Wing.

"Someone had better get the Mayor to cover the explosion on East 46th."

. . .

Peter and George were still huddled at the Bakaaran Embassy when they received confirmation that they were $100 million richer. Peter turned to George with a triumphant smile and whispered, "How many have we got left?"

George looked uncomfortable and did not respond. Peter unable to think of anything except his bank statement continued regardless of George's apparent lack of enthusiasm, "So, who shall we help next? You ready for that knighthood?"

George still did not answer, he seemed to be lost in thought and said nothing more as they left the Embassy. Outside Peter began to look for a cab.

"Peter, no! Let's walk...I want to talk." George spoke for the first time in ten minutes.

They began to walk in the direction of Sarah's apartment in the late afternoon sun.

"Peter, can you track down, without Berruda's help, that guy in Bakaar who you placed in Berruda's hands all those years ago–the one who kidnapped us that night in Rapanda?"

"Yes, I think so," Peter answered, puzzled by what seemed to be a strange subject to bring up half an hour after making the U.S.A cough up a billion dollars. "Why do you want to find him?"

"I've been doing a lot of thinking since that episode when we were grabbed in Rapanda. You seemed to cope with it, but I thought we were dead. Those people were starving and as far as they knew, we were ready to provide Berruda with assistance to enable him to wipe them off the face of the earth..."

"Yes, but we told them who we were." Peter interrupted.

"I know, but they believed us. What difference would it have made if they'd killed us then and there–none! Do you remember what that guy…David, that's his name. Do you remember what he said?"

"No, I honestly don't," Peter replied still having no idea where this conversation was leading, but realizing this might be a clue as to why George had lost some of his killer instinct in the past weeks.

"He said something like, 'I hope we don't regret this decision'. Then he said, 'Make sure that Berruda distributes it evenly'. He spoke to you, do you remember? 'Once again, you have our lives in your hands'. He's right! We can't just leave it where it is today. If you track him down, I'm going to give him, well Berruda's opposition, half of what I got out of this. Then he, the Bwanis, whoever, can put up enough candidates in the election to keep Robert's feet to the fire."

"I thought you were in it for a knighthood," Peter responded, trying to come to terms with this new aspect of George's character.

"I'll still have thirty million dollars more than I had yesterday. I've got to make sure that the U.S. money is properly used in Bakaar. If I finance a real opposition party, Robert'll be forced to do what's right with the money. He'll have to win support from both the Bwanis and the Witumbis. Whether he wins the election doesn't matter much. He'll not be in danger personally and the money will be used properly…Yup, that's what I'm going to do. I might even get that damned knighthood for the good deed!" Then, as an afterthought he turned to Peter, "What are you going to do?"

Peter smiled, "I'm going to enjoy my cash and with any luck I'm going to marry your daughter!"

George's face hardened and he looked surprised. It seemed that the idea had never entered his mind.

"I don't think so!" George responded softly. For the first time in weeks that old hard glint was back in his eyes.

"What did you say?" Peter asked incredulously.

"I said, I don't think you're going to marry my daughter."

"She doesn't need your permission."

"Maybe not, but she won't be happy marrying a man who kills for money."

"You hypocrite!" Peter exclaimed, his blood pressure beginning to rise.

"You've made a lot of money Peter. You've done a good job, but I can't allow you join the family."

"We'll see what Sarah thinks."

"Ask her!"

• • •

A few days later, at a ceremony in the White House Rose Garden, the President of the United States handed an oversized check for one billion dollars to President Berruda of Bakaar and made a speech as to the new initiative for the provision of aid to the Third World.

The Mayor of New York, at a ceremony in a church on the Upper East Side, praised the efforts of two courageous Police Officers who lost their lives in an attempt to stop the gas leak on East 46th Street.

The public applauded with no knowledge of the drama and how disaster had been averted–for now!

THE END

About the Author

Tony Lockwood was born in the United Kingdom but now lives in Massachusetts. 'The Reluctant Terrorist' is his first novel. He has written and directed several short films and his first feature screenplay, 'The Senator' is expected to be made in the Fall.

Printed in the United States
88939LV00003B/51/A